# TWEET REVENGE

ELLEN RIGGS

BOUGHT-THE-FARM
MYSTERIES

# Free Fun Story!

A sleuthing sheepdog and his team try to solve a riddle in time to save a missing cat.

**E**dna, Ivy, Gertie team up with Keats and Percy to outwit a wily catnapper in this EXCLUSIVE Bought-the-Farm story.

Purrrfect for animal cozy mystery readers who love face-paced adventure, laugh-out-loud humor and characters who feel like family.

Join Ellen Riggs' author newsletter today to receive *The Cat and the Riddle* FREE at **Ellenriggs.com/opt-in.**

Tweet Revenge

Copyright © 2022 Ellen Riggs

ISBN 978-1-998742-06-6 Paperback - D2D
ISBN 978-1-989303-80-1 eBook
ASIN B08ZL5Q4ZQ Kindle
ASIN 198930379X Paperback

Publisher: Ellen Riggs
www.ellenriggs.com
Cover designer: Lou Harper
Editor: Serena Clarke
25074151152

# CHAPTER ONE

S tepping out onto the porch at Runaway Farm late one morning, I glanced around the property and sighed. The grass had faded and the trees were just starting to turn. My first summer in Clover Grove was coming to an end and while autumn in hill country was glorious, winter was a long, hard slog for this hobby farmer.

"Did you know it's nearly our farmiversary?" I asked, looking down at Keats, my sheepdog. "Sometimes I wondered if we'd survive the year, but we did."

He directed his warm brown eye at me. There had been little need for him to communicate with his eerie blue eye lately. Things had been quiet—*too* quiet for my hardworking, ambitious sheepdog.

His signature mumble deep in his throat sounded like a complaint. He wasn't a dog to waste time on sentiment and nostalgia. We could be looking for problems to solve, or livestock to rustle. Often I moved animals from pen to pen just to give Keats something to do. Many of the animals enjoyed the change of scenery, but Drama Llama and the donkey thugs got a free pass. They liked their pasture and no one was taking their turf.

"Well, I think we should celebrate." I ran my hand along the railing and Percy, my marmalade cat, jumped up so that my fingers could be better employed stroking his fluff. He gave me a single blink of emerald eyes, possibly concurring with Keats. Sentiment wasn't the way of cats, either. "Just think about all we've accomplished, boys. The farm is expanding, our rescue numbers are up and everyone's happy."

A year into hobby farming, this former city girl still felt like a novice, particularly when it came to livestock management. Gradually, I was getting to know my critters as individuals and I'd committed to enriching their lives. Most had been saved from neglectful or abusive situations. Some were slow to trust and others downright testy. Each had a separate playbook and I was diligent about researching their unique needs—preferably online, where no one needed to know the depth of my ignorance.

*Do cows get hairballs?*

*How do you make a pig happy?*

*Can a goat digest a work glove? A small scrub brush? A set of keys?*

As soon as one problem resolved, a new one arose, usually by way of the band of vigilante pet rescuers from our neighboring town of Dorset Hills, AKA Dog Town. One of their leaders, a tiny dynamo of a dog trainer named Cori Hogan, delighted in making unexpected deposits in my farm "bank." These included Elaine, the emu, and a trio of pregnant goats. It was always supposed to be temporary, but rarely worked out that way.

That said, I was never happy to see animals go. Recently, two of my own rescues had moved to a new, happy home and it hurt more than I expected. Clippers, my miniature horse, and Bocelli, the singing donkey, had gone to live with my maternal grandparents. I still hadn't filled their empty stall. Cori said I'd never last as a rescuer if I pined for every animal that found a loving home. My plan was to expand indefinitely and keep them all.

Keats took a little dive at my pant cuff to get me moving. We had

20 minutes before heading off to a meeting in Dorset Hills at noon and he didn't plan to spend it in quiet contemplation.

"Stop that," I said, dodging his teeth. "These are my good jeans. I want to look decent today in case we can drum up a little business for the inn."

It was a challenge to market the farm as a sweet escape when we continued to get ourselves embroiled in mysteries and murder investigations. Our first year had racked up nearly a dozen such situations. The number should have been shocking but it was becoming business as usual.

"That's just wrong," I said, walking to the end of the porch. "Murder should never be business as usual."

Keats stayed where he was and mumbled something that sounded like, "Speak for yourself."

"I am speaking for myself, thank you very much. I need a vacation from trouble and the Rescue Mafia's arts and antiques fundraiser comes at a good time. It'll bring hundreds of animal lovers from all over the region—people who can afford to stay in upscale inns. That's our priority right now."

He gave a blurt of disgust. A dog raspberry.

Ignoring him, I collected a birdcage from the corner of the porch. It was ornate and elegant, dangling from a hook on a tall, arched stand. The antique had fallen into my hands when Finch Pefferlaw, an antisocial homesteader, decided it attracted too much unwanted attention. It had caught the eye of Heddy and Kaye Langman, who ran the Langman Legacy antique store in town. In fact, they'd stolen the cage from his barn, and I'd reclaimed it with help from my octogenarian prepper friends, Edna Evans and Gertie Rhodes. It had been in my basement ever since and I was glad to contribute the piece to the fundraiser. The thought of keeping birds in captivity brought back too many memories of being trapped myself in a soul-sucking HR career. Besides, the Langmans were irrepressible. After being fined heavily for their crimes, they'd gone on to bilk other people, and I had no doubt they'd come after the birdcage again one day. If they wanted it that badly, they could bid on it fair and square at the fundraiser and contribute to a good cause.

I carried the cage down to the barn and set it outside among maple saplings that were already tinged with orange. Then I followed the boys inside and out again through the back door to do what I always did when I had a few minutes to spare: turn manure.

Grabbing the spade, I climbed what my best friend Jilly Blackwood called my stairway to heaven. This work was therapeutic, not only because it burned frustration, but also because it created fertilizer that had become quite popular in our region. The Runaway Farm special blend made me feel like I contributed to our community in a simple, positive way.

Of course, solving murders made a far more significant contribution, but that wasn't simple and people had mixed feelings about it. No one got twisted up about manure, and with a veritable rainbow of squash cheering from roadside stands, I could afford a satisfied smile.

Just as I lifted my boot to drive the spade into the pile, there was a flash of blue in the barn doorway.

"Ivy Galloway, are you kidding me?"

Startled, I lost my balance and sat down hard. Well, it wasn't a hard landing. The manure had a lot of give.

"What?" I said, trying to figure out where to put my hands. Why hadn't I worn work gloves?

"You're sitting in manure, that's what." Jilly put her hands on her hips. "I said I'd be twenty minutes. I figured you couldn't get into a predicament like this in such a short time."

I grinned sheepishly at my best friend, who looked impeccable, with every golden curl in place.

"Oh, come on," I said. "You know full well I can get into a predicament in mere seconds."

Keats circled and brought Jilly closer, against her will. She didn't like getting anywhere near the manure pile in case my obsession with it happened to be contagious.

"You said we could woo new clients at these planning events," she said. "How can we do that if you stink?"

I wrapped my fingers around the spade handle and tested to see if it could support me to stand. "I hate sucking up."

The noise Jilly made was similar to the raspberry Keats had blown earlier. "You love sucking up when it can help you find clues to a mystery."

"That's different." I gestured to a pair of work gloves on a shelf and Jilly tossed them to me. After putting the gloves on, I used one hand to push and the other to pull. I got myself righted and then ran down the manure stairs. The damage to my pants wasn't that bad. I'd been in worse condition dozens of times.

Jilly rolled her eyes as if she could hear my thoughts. She'd known me long enough to make a reasonable guess over what passed through my mind in any given moment. "There's still time to go up and change," she said. "I wanted to be early for once. To mix and mingle."

"Fine. But these are my best jeans, so it's a downgrade from here."

Her curls swished from side to side. "Please tell me you'll avoid manure on my wedding day. It's reasonable to want your maid of honor to be huggable."

"Very reasonable, but I was voted least huggable in high school and my rep stuck like... well, manure. That's partly how I earned the nickname of the grim reaper of HR. I like a wide circle of personal space and now Keats helps me maintain it."

She shooed me through the barn and back out the front door. "Ah, so that's why you're always getting into messes. It's a defense against PDAs. Everything makes sense now."

"You chose better with Edna as bridesmaid," I said. "Totally huggable."

We both laughed. With Edna often carrying concealed weapons, possibly explosives, each hug could be your last.

"Even Janelle is a risk," Jilly said. Her cousin was the other member of the wedding party, and their relationship was still a bit thorny. Janelle Brighton claimed to be a psychic and Jilly was a non-believer. That had divided them for years, but the old wounds were healing. With Janelle living down the range in Wyldwood Springs, they could visit more often and get to know each other as adults. I was still going through the same exercise with my four sisters. They'd felt like strangers to me when I moved home and it seemed like I learned something new about at least one of them every day.

"I'd better put the birdcage in the truck," I said. "I worry the Langmans will sniff it out and come calling before I deliver it safely."

"There will be plenty of other antiques to distract them," Jilly said, stooping to scoop up Percy. Jilly cared about her appearance, but she never hesitated to pick up an animal. In fact, Percy's paws rarely touched the ground when she was around.

The thought stopped me in my tracks. Whether I liked it or not, Percy was gradually becoming more Jilly's pet than mine. What would happen after she married my brother and moved away from the inn? I assumed they'd live across town in Asher's small house, although I hadn't dared ask. I wasn't ready to contemplate the loss of anyone else after Bocelli and Clippers.

"Are you okay?" she asked. "You're a little pale."

"Fine," I said. "Just surprised. Look at that."

I gestured at the birdcage. It had been empty when I went into the barn, and the door was ajar.

Now, the most beautiful bird I had ever seen was sitting inside, rocking back and forth on the little swing.

It was about the size of a sparrow but that's where the resemblance ended. This bird looked like it had fallen onto an artist's paint palette and flapped around. Its head was royal blue, its wings vibrant green and yellow, and its belly a vivid red. There was even a circle of scarlet around the bird's eyes.

Looking in our direction, the bird opened its black beak and let out a sweet musical trill.

"Hello to you, too, handsome," I said. "Welcome to Runaway Farm."

## CHAPTER TWO

K eats circled to herd us closer to the cage but I held back to avoid frightening the bird. What if it panicked when it realized it was confined? The door was open, but a flustered bird might not see the exit and end up beating its wings against the metal bars. It would be horrible to see it injure itself after taking a radically wrong turn.

A slight pinch on my calf forced me forward. Keats clearly thought he knew more about songbirds than I did. It would be hard to know less. Ornithology hadn't made it into my curriculum yet. Wild birds were more hobby than farm, and thus on the "nice to know" side of the ledger.

"This bird looks like the one that visited Imogen Pigeon's bedroom window," Jilly said. "It's very distinctive."

"That's what I was thinking." I had seen the bird several times when I visited Imogen to share updates on my research after her deathbed confession. "Ima called it a painted bunting. She said it was a southern bird that didn't belong in Clover Grove. That's why she believed it was a visitor from beyond."

"Beyond what?" Jilly asked.

"Beyond this earthly plane." I grinned at my friend and

shrugged. "To be specific, Imogen thought it embodied the spirit of Carl, her late husband. She said he came to collect her when it was her time."

"Ah," Jilly said. "We know from Edna that people sometimes have delusions when the end looms. Believing the bird was Carl was probably very comforting."

"She said as much, yeah." I eased closer to the cage but Jilly stayed behind, probably because she had Percy in her arms. He was an unusual cat and I'd never seen him kill a bird or a mouse. Still, he had been feral once and hunting was in his genes. "Ima was incredibly composed in the hour before she passed. I like to think she flitted off with the love of her life."

Jilly murmured her agreement from behind me. "This bunting must have stuck around the area since then. You'd think it would want to fly back to the sunny south where it belongs. The nights are so cool now."

The bird swung harder on its perch and gave another melodious trill. I couldn't help but wonder if he'd come to tell us something. Why else would a wild bird voluntarily fly into a cage when it had the whole world at its wingtips? It didn't make sense.

"Carl?" I said, when I was about a foot away from him. "Is that you?"

A short, strident screech sounded a negative.

"Imogen?" I tried, only to get the same answer.

"That's what you get for asking silly questions," Jilly said. "It's just a pretty bird that's lost its way, Ivy. We need to shoo it out so we can take the cage to the fundraising meeting."

"I'm not banishing this bird if he wants to hang around. Maybe he's in trouble and came for help."

Jilly gave the exasperated sigh that she normally reserved for her cousin. I was getting too close to woo-woo for her comfort. "I'm sure it's just a regular bird, Ivy."

"Maybe. Maybe not. None of my animals are 'just' anything as far as I'm concerned. Each is special in its own way."

"So now this painted bunting is yours, too?" she asked.

"Up to him. It must be a male given the brilliant plumage. Females get the short end of the stick when it comes to color." I glanced at Jilly over my shoulder. "There's room on my ark for a bird this size."

"I suppose, but you promised this birdcage for the auction, and it's going to be a hot item. At least with the Langmans, and their coin is as good as any when it comes to fundraising."

"I know. And we can't just leave the cage out here. The Langmans probably have eyes on us and would lift it again if they could."

The bird took matters into his own claws and hopped onto the metal ledge of the doorway. Then he fluttered up onto the sweeping curve of the stand, and finally a branch overhead.

"I admit I'm relieved," I said. "He doesn't belong in a cage." I waggled my fingertips at the bunting. "Fly away and be happy, little guy. Thank you for the visit."

The bird flapped again, this time coming a little closer. Then it moved back. And then just a little farther away.

When we just stood there, it repeated the move.

"How odd," Jilly said. "It's like he wants us to—"

"Follow him? I thought the same thing."

Keats weighed in with what sounded like a "duh."

"Mind your tone, Keats," I said. "Having a wild songbird invite us to take a walk isn't exactly normal."

His next nip in my calf was hard enough to make me lunge toward the bird. The bunting didn't seem startled, and took another small hop that seemed designed to lure us along.

"It's tempting to see how this plays out," Jilly said. "But we'll need to take a pass, Ivy. You know how these things go."

I grabbed my backpack out of the truck and then walked after the bird. "I never know how these things will go, Jilly. Each mission is a whole new ballgame."

"It's like that, is it?" she called after me. "A mission?"

"Feels like it to me," I called back, watching the dog race ahead. "And to Keats. How can you argue with that?"

"My best boots are arguing with that. I don't want to show up for this meeting bedraggled, and that bird is heading into the swamp, isn't he? No good ever comes from the swamp."

She wasn't wrong. Swampland pocked the county and I'd fallen into silty muck several times. When my grumpy pig Wilma was on the lam, the search party had to drive around this particular area and approach from another direction.

"We should get hip waders like the ones we used down south," I said. "Especially after the pond is finished."

In his spare time, my father was working with Charlie, my farm manager, to clear land and excavate. It would likely be spring before the project came to fruition.

"I don't want to think about that adventure," Jilly said. Our trip to help her grandmother at a gated community called the Briar Estates had been one of our strangest missions yet. "I still have night-mares about the alligator."

Her voice was closer and I knew she was following despite her better judgement. When push came to dunk, Jilly enjoyed an animal escapade nearly as much as I did.

Keats circled back, stared up at me with his eerie blue eye and grumbled loudly. He was letting me know that if things got wet and wild, he was out. Unlike Jilly, he actually meant it. My dog abhorred water of any kind, but particularly a swamp.

"There are no gators here," I told them both. "In case you're wondering."

"Asher said people sometimes release exotic pets out here."

"I'd say he was pulling your leg, but Evie Springdale did help close down an exotic pet ring in Dorset Hills. There were snakes. Big snakes." Jilly gave a choking sound and I added, "Those species aren't meant to survive our winters."

"Like this bird," she said, catching up to me.

"True. Maybe he got a kink in his migratory system and will head back to the sunshine soon. In the meantime, let's see what's on his mind."

Jilly groaned as the ground got soggy. "If this bird did happen to be the spirit of Imogen, surely she'd go easier on us. We helped send her on her way more peacefully."

Ima had woken from a coma and tasked me with solving an old mystery before she passed. It had nearly cost us our lives, but we'd pulled it off.

"You would think," I said. "Ima knew the topography as well as Edna. I can't see why she'd lead us into the swamp when there's another way around."

"I don't suppose we could come back later with Edna?" Jilly said.

I stopped walking and turned to face her. "We could. The bird might be gone, but then we'd know it was a wild goose chase anyway."

Jilly's green eyes widened. "Excuse me? You never choose the path of reason."

I laughed. "My boots are leaking. The way things are going, we're going to need an airboat as well as hip waders. When we win the lottery."

As I expected, Jilly walked forward again. "Guess we'd better start buying tickets."

"So, we're continuing?" I asked, as she came up alongside me.

"Against my better judgment. I get this sense of urgency around the bird."

"Me too. When we get where we're going, we can ask Edna to pick us up on her ATV."

Jilly brightened. "Great idea." She clutched Percy closer, although the cat seemed more comfortable around water than the rest of us. For a time, he'd lived in a feral colony in Huckleberry Marsh and darted around on a floating log highway. "Edna said she wasn't coming to the fundraising meeting. She's been awfully busy lately."

"We've taken a back seat to her seminar planning, I suppose."

Edna had been quietly recruiting students for the online prepper course she was launching with Gertie's help. It had turned out to be such a hot ticket that she was screening people out. Jilly's grandmother Bridie had applied, as had Janelle's friends, Sinda and Renata. The submission process included a complicated questionnaire designed to select the bright and the bold. No doubt it was satisfying for Edna to turn down people who'd been unkind to her over the years. She'd been unkind, too, while working as a nurse for the town's doctor and running the school vaccination program. Now, I understood her eccentricities stemmed from childhood wounds that still motivated her today.

The painted bunting flew back, perhaps sensing my attention wandering. He hovered a yard in front of my face and twittered indignantly.

"Sorry," I said. "I'm all in, but if you could choose the driest route, we'd be grateful."

After that, we fell silent and focused on choosing the best footing. It wasn't easy, and Jilly had to put Percy down so that she could grab shrubs and pull her heels out of sucking mud.

"This is nuts," she muttered, and Keats concurred with a mumble. His white paws had turned a tarry black and he shook them one by one in disgust.

My toes were numb from cold by the time the ground firmed up. The bushes got thicker as we emerged from the swampy area, and we had to fight our way through.

"Good thing I brought my go-kit," I said, stopping to pull clippers out of my backpack. "Edna will be proud I finally remembered it. Maybe we'll make the cut for the next session of her course."

"We do okay even without her," Jilly said. "According to our new feathered friend, we've made it. I'm assuming the swooping is a joyful welcome."

"Welcome where, exactly?" I said, staring around. "I have no idea whose property we're on."

"Everything pretty much runs together for me when there's swamp involved," Jilly said. "I doubt I'll ever be able to find my way home in this county."

"That's Asher's job," I said. "He knows the area inside and out. We hardly ever saw him when he was a kid. Out at dawn and back after dark. Turns out Kellan was doing the same."

I didn't know it at the time, but that's how boys in unhappy homes coped. The good ones grew up to be cops, it seemed. Others became robbers... and worse.

"They were childhood preppers, which is strangely reassuring," Jilly said. "There are more immediate threats than Edna's apocalypse."

"Definitely." I spun on my heels and tried to get my bearings. The property had pretty much reverted to its natural state, although it had been cleared at one time. "Why is this place sitting empty? With land at such a premium in Clover Grove I'm suspicious when that happens. Often, it's because the previous owners were tied up in something nefarious. Even the most enthusiastic homesteaders don't want tainted land."

"Don't get me spooked, Ivy," Jilly said. "We can't get out of here easily, unless that bird has super-powered wings."

"We'll add a helicopter to our lottery wish list," I said, leading her out of the bush and into the open. "Although the Mafia would just borrow it all the time for rescues. I bet Cori has her pilot's license."

Jilly laughed as we followed the bright bunting, who soared, circled and dove at us in what amounted to aerial herding. Keats barked a warning at the bird, as if to say, "that's my job."

In fact, he was herding us now, and Percy had become a bright dot far ahead. Everyone seemed to know where we were going but Jilly and me.

"Aha," I said, when a small, old barn came into view. "That must be our target. Maybe there's a lost cow or goat inside."

"I hope not," Jilly said. "Rescuing livestock will make us miss the meeting entirely."

Keats' posture didn't communicate a livestock 911. Instead, the white tuft of his tail swayed gently as he trotted ahead. With the swamp behind us, the jaunt became enjoyable.

The small barn had never been painted and its rotting boards were a weather-beaten taupe. A cement foundation was in better condition and would be standing long after the rest decayed. We circled at the bird's bidding and found double doors on the other side.

Locked.

There were no lost animals here.

At least, I hoped not.

I tried jiggling the rusty padlock but it held firm. Keats went into a point and I saw that several boards at the far end of the building had fallen away completely.

"Looks like we can just stoop and creep inside," I said.

Jilly caught my arm. "Before we start stooping and creeping, maybe we should call Edna. If something's in there, she'll know what to do."

I was already moving. "Don't underestimate us, Jilly. We've done our share of rescues."

"Yeah, and they usually end with you getting trampled. Whether it's Drama Llama, Wilma or the pregnant goats, something's always taking you down."

I laughed as I pulled out my phone and flicked on the light. "Tell me about it."

Percy had already gone inside and Keats was right behind him.

They showed no trepidation, so I doubted there was an ambush wait-ing. Indeed, the hardest part was squeezing through the jagged boards without banging my head or catching my jacket.

Jilly didn't hurry and I waited for her to make up her mind to join me. Eventually, we stood side by side as I flashed the light around.

The interior was exactly as I'd expect from an old building that was partially exposed to the elements. There were sheets of cobwebs and various mushrooms growing in strange places. It smelled of the wildlife that likely sheltered there.

"Sufficiently spooked," Jilly said. "Can we go now?"

"Apparently not. Picasso hasn't finished with us."

"Picasso?" she said, crowding closer to me.

"The bird." I pointed up at the bunting, who had perched in the rafters. "His plumage looks like a work of art."

"You're not going up there." It was a statement, not a question. "That's a death trap."

"I'm not, don't worry. Even if I wanted to get into the hayloft, there's no ladder." I walked around underneath. "Edna could bring one." Keats mumbled at my feet and I looked down. "Where's Percy? Did he...?"

He did. The fluffy marmalade feline had used his claws to good purpose. His big green eyes gleamed over the edge of the loft at us to make sure we noticed him. Then he followed the fluttering bunting out of sight.

"Don't get any big ideas about that bird, Percy Galloway," I called up to him. "You only hunt humans, got it?"

Percy gave a purr-meow that sounded like a promise. After a few moments of silence, there was a scraping sound and then rowdy twit-tering. I didn't know birds well enough to be able to interpret whether the noise was excitement, fear or something else entirely.

Then came a metallic thunk as something hit the floor above us. More scraping and an exasperated meow brought Percy to the edge of the loft again. He turned with a flick of fluffy tail, hooked something with his paw and then pushed it over.

Luckily Keats saw it coming before we did and literally shoved Jilly and me out of the way. Otherwise one of us likely would have been conked in the head by the tin box that landed at our feet.

Percy leapt off the ledge and landed on my shoulder. The 20-claw touchdown certainly shook any cobwebs off me.

"Glad I could break your fall, pal," I said, as the cat dropped to the floor and started pawing at his find. It was too heavy for him to turn over, but he kept trying. "I got it, I got it. Take it easy, Percy."

Meanwhile, the bird dove at me repeatedly, pulling up short each time.

Bending, I flipped the box. It was about a foot long and eight inches wide and secured with a small, rusty padlock. I hoped the lock would give way when I tugged on it, but it didn't.

"What now?" Jilly said, as we both dropped to our knees to take a closer look.

I ran my fingers along the top of the box. It looked very old but must have been well hidden, because it had stood up well to the rigors of time. "I have pliers in my bag, but I don't suppose it would be right to snap that lock. Someone hid it here for a reason."

"Then I guess we'll need to turn it in to the police," Jilly said.

Picasso had other ideas. I felt a light breeze on my forehead and when I looked up, he was just a foot away with wings beating so fast they became a blur of green.

What dangled from his claws, however, was completely in focus.

A tiny key.

# CHAPTER THREE

"Let's take that as permission," I said. "If we peek inside, we might be able to find the owner."

"Maybe we really should leave it to the police," Jilly said. "What if there's something horrible in there?"

"Like what? A severed hand?"

"That hadn't occurred to me, so thanks," she said. "I was thinking more like a murder weapon. Or a confession." Her green eyes looked eerie in the phone's light, too. "It's a shame we always have to think the worst."

"Maybe this time we'll be pleasantly surprised," I said. "Look at Keats. He isn't worried."

On the contrary, the dog was simmering with excitement, prancing on the spot with dirty paws. Percy was more vocal, urging us on with strident meows to finish his work. And Picasso warbled a short and urgent refrain over and over from the rafters.

"Sounds like we have our orders," Jilly said, taking the phone from me and directing the beam at the lock. "Open it."

My hands shook as I tried to fit the rusty little key in the even rustier lock. It seemed unlikely the mechanism would work, given the corrosion. I twisted and rattled it gently and eventually there was a little click as the lock released. Easing it out of the loop, I set it on the floor.

Both of us sucked in a deep breath as I used both hands to lift the lid. Then we released a relieved sigh in unison.

There was no severed hand or blood-stained knife inside the box.

Instead, we found a stack of yellowed letters tied with string and a blue velvet box. I flipped open the latter and the phone light hit a diamond and sent rainbows all over the cobwebby barn. The stone in the center was about a carat, with smaller red stones on either side. No doubt it had been meant to pledge troth to a woman long ago.

"So beautiful," Jilly said. "And probably comes with a sad story."

I sat back on the damp heels of my boots and tried to loosen the twine on the letters. It disintegrated instantly and released a dozen or so short notes. Even before reading the one on top, I could tell it had been written by a woman's hand. The penmanship was refined, although the words themselves had faded.

My voice sounded rusty, too, as I cleared my throat and began to read aloud.

"My dearest Henny: You asked me to take time to reconsider your offer, and after much thought I am sorry to say my decision remains unchanged. There is nothing I want more than to spend our lives together, but with your parents so vehemently opposed, we cannot proceed. No matter what you think now, I am certain you would later come to regret leaving your family and I might regret leaving mine, too. Hearts would harden against us, and it would be wrong to raise a family in such conditions. Therefore, I return the ring I love so much. I wish the garnets had brought us the luck we expected.

At your request, I kept your other engagement gift. It shows your faith in me, and that means so much more than the wonderful gift itself. It will comfort me greatly in the years ahead and perhaps inspire me as you hoped.

Please don't remain sad for long, dear Henny. One day, happiness will settle on your shoulder like a bird and you must not turn it away. I wish for nothing other than knowing you are in the world sharing your generous spirit. Thank you for all you've given me.

In the truest love,

Your Little Brown Wren."

Two tears dropped onto the letter as I finished—one from me and one from Jilly. I brushed them aside quickly to preserve the ink and dropped the note back into the box.

The beam from the light shot around as Jilly mopped her eyes with her sleeve. "Ivy, the severed hand might have been better than this tragic tale."

Despite my sadness, I laughed. "I know, right? I've surrendered old bones before. But a forbidden love story like Romeo and Juliet? That's going to stick with us."

"I hope no one died." Jilly's voice had a quaver. "This lady was heartbroken and her beau was smitten enough to defy his family and run away with her."

"I doubt anyone did anything desperate," I said. "In Clover Grove, they must have come from sensible farming stock. I suppose in time they moved on and found a match that met with family approval."

"Then why was this box still hidden away with the ring inside?" Jilly asked. "It's not sensible to leave a big diamond in a hayloft. Henny would have come back for it at some point, wouldn't he? If he were alive?"

Keats mumbled impatiently. Romantic musings bored him at any time. He was ready to move along.

I locked the tin box carefully and slipped it inside my backpack. "We should text Edna."

"Already did," Jilly said. "When you came inside, I sent her a photo of the barn and she's on her way."

"Let's wait to question her about the letters until after the meeting," I said, following Keats and Percy outside. "I want to give this particular mystery some breathing room. It's so..."

"Intimate," Jilly said. We blinked at each other in the bright sunlight, and then nodded. "It seems like the respectful thing to do."

I looked up into the trees. "Where's Picasso?"

There was a streak of red underbelly as he flew off, the movement coinciding with the arrival of the ATV. The bird had no interest in meeting our friend, it seemed, but Edna was a sight for sore eyes to us as she rolled into the clearing.

"The cavalry's arrived," she called over the roaring motor. "What's going on?"

"Full story to follow," I said, as we all hopped on board. "We're late for our meeting."

Edna opened her mouth to argue, but then shrugged and piloted the vehicle over the rocky land and into the swamp. The ride was so uncomfortable that Keats and Percy demanded to be offloaded to make their own way home.

Back at the farm, Jilly and I ran up to the house to change into fresh clothes. Then I moved the birdcage into a utility shed. Using a ladder, I climbed up to the window in the eaves and pulled out the screen. It was big enough for a small bird to come and go as he liked, but would easily block a nosy Langman. Hopefully, we could resolve Picasso's problem to his satisfaction in time to surrender the birdcage for the auction, but it was his for as long as he wanted it.

By the time I slid behind the wheel of the truck, Edna ensconced in the passenger seat with Keats and Percy in her lap. Normally Jilly rode shotgun but she climbed into the rear without complaint. I suspected she welcomed the downgrade to keep her coat nice for mingling.

Edna's fatigues barely showed fur, paw prints or swamp muck, but that didn't stop her from whining about the pets. I let her get it out of her system as we drove under the arching iron sign that said, "Runaway Far." Many had pressed me to get the "m" replaced. Bladesmith Harvey Dunbar had offered to do the job for free, but I liked it the way it was. Someday I might fix it, when the memory faded of how I'd run away "far" from the corporate life I'd hated. A year into my stay here, that great escape was still very fresh in my mind.

Keats mumbled agreement from Edna's lap. He, too, had been happy to run away from Boston—and the criminal who owned him. Life was interesting here, especially now that a small bird had delivered the buzz my energetic sheepdog craved.

"What's he saying?" Edna asked. "It's rude to have a conversation that shuts the rest of us out. Just like it was rude to leave me out of your sneaky mission this morning."

"It wasn't sneaky," I said. "We didn't know it was a mission till we were already in it. Picasso showed up in that old birdcage and then lured us through the swamp."

"Picasso?" she said. "Isn't that pretentious for a bird?"

"He's no regular bird," Jilly said. "I've never seen such spectacular plumage. And he clearly wanted us to follow him."

Edna tried to balance both animals on her lap as she turned to stare over her shoulder at Jilly. "What have you been drinking? Normally you're the one with common sense."

Jilly laughed. "I guess you had to be there."

"Which is exactly my point," Edna said. "I *wasn't* there. I was a convenient afterthought. Just someone to bail you out after the fun."

"It wasn't like that, Edna," I said. "Remember you told us you weren't coming to this planning meeting. 'Too busy for old garbage.' Those were your exact words."

Jilly leaned forward and tapped Edna's shoulder. "What have *you* been drinking? You never miss a significant Clover Grove event."

"Especially one that's pretty much guaranteed to end in fisticuffs," I added.

"I'm a busy woman and something has to drop off my plate," Edna said, patting her tight curls. Her perm and color were fresh, suggesting she wanted to look young and vital for her prepper class. Indeed, she looked far younger than her years, which I attributed to doing what she loved. "In the end I decided I had better come along. The Langman sisters are likely to lose their tenuous hold on reality as antiques arrive."

"We've always dubbed them most likely to murder," I said. "This could be their time."

"Ivy, don't even joke about that," Jilly said. "We want this to be the best fundraiser ever. That can't happen if the Langmans live down to our expectations."

"Wouldn't it be great to lock them away for good?" I asked. "Not in the luxury penitentiary with Myrtle McCain, though. They'd team up and destroy the world."

Visiting Myrtle, the first person in Clover Grove to try to murder me, had been harder than I expected—mainly because she wasn't in the least repentant. I wouldn't be in a hurry to visit anyone else I'd helped put away.

Keats set one paw on my leg to ground me. When I drifted too far down murderous memory lane, he was always there to pull me out. Lingering in the past was a dangerous affair when there were challenges enough in the present.

"Are you going to tell me what you were doing at the old Harlow property?" Edna said. "I deserve to know, after rescuing the damsels in distress. If you'd gone properly equipped, it might have ended differently."

"At least I remembered my go-kit," I said, picking up speed on the highway. "It's not easy when you're swept up in the moment."

"That's one reason you didn't make the cut for my class," Edna said. "Too young and impulsive. People with a few miles behind them gain impulse control." She cracked the window at Keats' bidding. "Not your mother, of course. Dahlia made a good case, and she is improving, but you don't overcome challenges like hers in a day. A flibbertigibbet would be the first to perish in an apocalypse and take the rest of her platoon with her."

"You lumped Jilly and me in with my mother? That's the most insulting thing you've ever said to me."

Edna chuckled. "Really? Then I need to up my game."

As we rounded the next curve, I craned my neck. "Pumpkins! Is that...? It is! A blue pumpkin."

"Ivy, we don't have time for pumpkins of any color," Jilly said.

I was already easing the truck onto the shoulder. "There's always time for pumpkins. And besides, they're *my* pumpkins. It's Vernie Cobbler's vegetable stand and she's one of my biggest consumers of fertilizer."

"She probably wouldn't like to hear you put it quite that way," Jilly said, laughing. "And the pumpkins will still be here on our way home."

"Maybe not," I said. "Blue pumpkins aren't common in these parts."

"God made pumpkins orange for a reason, Ivy," Edna said.

"Oh yeah? What reason is that?"

"Because there's a natural order to things," Edna said. "Humans tamper too much with that nowadays and a blue pumpkin is the perfect example of such folly."

I turned off the truck and pulled the key from the ignition. "Maybe so, but I'm still excited that Runaway Farm manure is breaking new ground. Today a blue pumpkin, tomorrow, who knows? You and your little army would be happy enough to see these crops in your bunker, Edna."

She let the pets out the passenger door and jumped down with a heavy thud. That was a statement because Edna was normally light on her feet. "Vernie Cobbler is about as silly as the name sounds," she said. "She's the crotchetiest woman in hill country, and coming from me—someone who embodies the word—that's saying something."

"Is crotchetiest even a word?" Jilly asked, joining us.

"I'm not afraid to use it," Edna said.

"Well, don't," I said. "At least not before we've got a pumpkin or two in the truck. They're a testament to the power of my manure. I always hoped to achieve something like this."

Edna muttered audibly as she followed me to the vegetable stand. I picked out "aim higher," "head injury" and "permanent brain damage" but decided to let it go. Yes, the concussion I got rescuing Keats left a lasting mark, but more people should find joy in pumpkins.

And what pumpkins they were! There was a trestle table loaded with at least 40 blue orbs of various sizes and hues. In the middle sat a behemoth that likely weighed over 60 lbs.

My client, Verna Rae Cobbler, was sitting on a crate behind a wagon that may have dated back to the pioneers. Over her head was a sign nailed to an oak tree that said "Vernie's Vegetables" in a flourish of fresh red paint. The cart held bushel baskets of potatoes, onions, beets, turnips and cabbages. All seemed to my untrained eye to be unusually large and unblemished. In fact, they looked almost too good to be true. Fake.

"Hey Vernie," I said. "You've got one heck of a crop this year."

Jilly was already picking through the onions. The inn's resident chef couldn't pass up produce like this.

"If you're looking for praise, forget about it," Vernie said. "Your head is big enough already."

"Excuse me?" It was Edna who came to my defense, leaning across some enormous turnips to do it. "You can't speak to my friend like that, Verna Rae Cobbler."

Unlike most locals, Vernie wasn't at all cowed by Edna. In fact, she unleashed a rather nasty cackle that revealed gaps in her smile. Meanwhile, she tucked long, wiry gray tendrils into an unruly twist of hair. Vernie was in her eighties, but unlike Edna, she'd given up on salons. And clothing stores. She wore a dated floral dress under a grimy apron, with unlaced work boots and a stretch of skinny bare leg in between.

These vegetables appeared to be all that stood between her and utter destitution. It made me all the more determined to support her business.

"You can't tell me what to say, Edna." Vernie stood to face my friend across the cart and she seemed to have shrunk since I last saw her. "The crime rate in Clover Grove skyrocketed when Ivy came home. Even an old farmer like me feels anxious."

I'd been reaching for a blue pumpkin but let my hands drop to my sides. "Why would you say that, Vernie? I've been keeping pretty busy helping to put criminals away."

"You're missing the point," Vernie said. "There *were* no criminals before you came back. Well, barely. Other than seizing your mother's driver's license, the police had nothing to do. There hadn't been a murder around here in a decade." She turned to Edna. "I dare you to say otherwise."

Edna's rapid blinking told me she was combing her mental database to come up with a murder to throw back at Vernie.

Jilly didn't wait for an escalation. "Vernie, your produce is awesome this year. How did you manage to grow these gorgeous pumpkins? I'm going to buy a dozen to decorate the inn."

"Limit of two per family," Vernie said. "They're a rare hybrid and it took more than good fertilizer to pull them off. Vegetable stands are a dime a dozen around here lately, thanks to stupid homesteaders, so I need to stand out somehow."

Jilly started rolling around pumpkins on the cart to find the best ones. "Hasn't Ivy earned more than two of these with her manure? I doubt she charged you a cent for it."

"Free delivery, too," I said. "It's my contribution to the community."

"I'd rather pay to have exclusive access," Vernie said. "You're doling that stuff out to every Tom, Dick and farmer."

It was probably the closest she would ever come to a compliment, so I decided to settle for it. "Vernie, I'm glad it's worked out for you this year. If we can only have two pumpkins, so be it."

"Fine, take six," she said. "Two apiece. I've had enough trouble today."

"What kind of trouble?" I asked, grabbing a pumpkin. They were nearly all perfectly smooth spheres.

"The kind that comes when you do-gooders get people to haul out their old treasures and donate them," she said. "Heirlooms flip the crazy switch."

Edna, Jilly and I exchanged a glance. "The Langman sisters?" I asked.

"Those girls should be put in the clink till the auction's over," Vernie said. "Tell that to your boyfriend, Ivy. He's the only one with any sway over them."

"What do you have that Heddy and Kaye want, Vernie?" Edna said.

"And more importantly, can *we* have it?" Jilly added, smiling. "Anything that desirable would raise a lot of money for rescue."

Vernie plunked herself down on the crate and twisted the dirty apron in her gnarled hands. "I was on the fence about donating some paintings but I'm fed up with people trying to buy them for less than they're worth. It's gotten so bad I worry someone will break into my house, so I brought the paintings along in my truck today to keep an eye on them. My Pommy isn't much protection, I'm afraid."

"That's the Pomeranian I saw when I delivered your fertilizer?" I asked.

Vernie nodded. "I got her from Cori Hogan, the rudest do-gooder in the region." Staring around at the vegetables, she seemed to come to a decision. "Pommy means a lot more to me than the art and she could get hurt in a break-in. It's hard to feel safe in Clover Grove anymore."

Edna crossed her arms and seemed to inflate a size. "What's

going on, Verna Rae? Do you need help handling someone? Gertie Rhodes and I do freelance security."

"You do?" I asked.

"Minnie was bored," Edna said. "Wanted to get out more."

Vernie's grin said she was well-acquainted with Gertie's rifle. "I'll be fine, Edna, but thank you. Dispersing my valuables, such as they are, makes sense anyway. I'm not getting any younger and I have no true heirs. I trust the rescue ruffians to do some good with the proceeds."

Edna wagged her index finger. "Verna Rae, don't you dare give up on life. You're barely ninety."

"Ninety! Nice try, you old coot," Vernie said. "Anyway, I just want a peaceful last inning. Don't we all?"

Jilly and I laughed, knowing that was the *last* thing Edna wanted. I expected Keats to chime in, but when I looked down, he was puffed and uneasy. Percy looked disgruntled, too, but he circled Vernie's crate and managed to insinuate himself into her lap.

"Vernie, I want to go down in cannon fire," Edna said. "And I wish that for you, too. In fact, I'm giving you a special invitation to my first survivalist class. With your terrible temperament, you'd be a terrific asset."

For the first time, Vernie's smile seemed genuine. "I can outshoot both you and Gertie. Guaranteed."

"Put your rifle where your mouth is," Edna said.

The two continued their banter, while Jilly and I loaded blue pumpkins into the bed of the truck and tried to secure them from rolling around. Then Vernie handed me the key to her pickup truck, and I moved heavy blankets aside in the back seat to collect her treasures. The framed paintings were wrapped in burlap and tied in twine.

"Be careful with those," Vernie called. "The Langmans would kill for what you're getting gratis."

Jilly walked behind me, arms outstretched in case I dropped the valuables. The paintings fit easily behind the driver's seat in my cab, where I concealed them with my own blankets.

When we were done, I circled back to toss a couple of twenty-dollar bills onto the produce cart. "Vernie, seriously," I said. "Don't hesitate to call us if you're feeling threatened."

She gave a reluctant nod. "Fine. I didn't mean what I said earlier, Ivy. Crime was always around here. Just died out for a while."

"The era of peace has ended, Vernie, here and beyond," Edna said. "Hence my preparations for the end times."

"Don't forget we have a good police force, ladies," Jilly said.

Vernie's sigh seemed to rise from her battered work boots. "Your handsome boyfriends are no match for this, I'm afraid. It's a special kind of crime."

"That's why I'm creating a special kind of militia," Edna said. "Join us."

"I'll think about it," Vernie said. "Take a pumpkin."

I grinned and grabbed one more. "Thank you, Vernie."

"Just don't grow any yourself," she said. "Next year everyone will have blue pumpkins and I'll have to find another way to stand out."

"Next year, you won't care about pumpkins," Edna said, as Keats herded her to the truck. "Gourds will be the least of your worries."

"The way you and Gertie shoot, you won't last another season," Vernie said.

Edna climbed into the passenger seat and bellowed back, "Watch your mouth, Verna Rae."

"What are you going to do? Knock the rest of my teeth out?" Vernie said.

They cackled as I let Keats into the truck, and went back to get Percy, who was assertively headbutting Vernie's chin. "The cat's telling you to keep your chin up," I said.

"Get along now, all of you." She stood so abruptly that Percy almost didn't get his landing gear down in time. Grabbing a spade, Vernie started shoveling onions from a wheelbarrow into a basket.

"My appreciation of your manure doesn't make us friends, you know."

"Oh, it does. We're besties now."

She gave a rude flick of her spade before I turned to walk away. "Choose your friends more wisely, Ivy, or you'll end up as fertilizer yourself."

# CHAPTER FOUR

When we arrived in Bellington Square, dozens of volunteers were milling around, chitchatting and laughing. There were plenty of familiar faces and even more new ones. This fundraiser was getting off to a good start.

Remi Malone was standing on a platform under the massive statue of a fearsome German shepherd. Since the Rescue Mafia had ousted the previous corrupt mayor of Dorset Hills and Isla McInnis had taken over as political leader of Dog Town, city council had stopped adding more statues to the dozens that already existed. Rather than celebrating dogs in bronze, more funds went to supporting real canines.

Even with strong political backing, however, there was always more to be done. There were puppy mills to shut down and floods of dogs into the city that other towns couldn't house properly. It kept the Mafia busy not only rescuing and rehoming but finding the money to do so. The public coffers were spread too thin.

Remi was the right person to spearhead the drive. She'd begun her fundraising career with the hospital foundation but now ran her own business. Like most of the Mafia, she needed time and flexibility for their operations. Holding down a nine-to-five was difficult when you might get a call to drop from a small plane and airlift a stray dog and her pups from an isolated area. That had happened a week ago, and I was surprised to hear Remi's boots were first to touch down. On the surface, she was the sweetest and meekest of the Mafia and used to be painfully shy. Leo, her affable therapy beagle, still dangled from her arm today but I sensed he wasn't called into active duty as much anymore.

Tapping on the mic, Remi got everyone's attention.

"Welcome, welcome! We've never had a better turnout for a planning meeting," she said. "That means our arts and antiques theme is hitting the mark. I've lined up an appraiser from the Houghton Gallery in Boston to put a starting price on every piece donated. The hitch is that he'll only evaluate items that have already been formally surrendered to our cause. If you get second thoughts after hearing the real value of your items you'll need to buy them back at full market value."

A groan rippled through the crowd. It would be harder to pry donations from people's hands now, but it was a clever ploy. Remi, and Evie Springdale, who was filming everything, always had good promotional ideas. They'd helped me salvage Runaway Farm's reputation after the murders that threatened to sink the inn into oblivion. I suspected Isla McInnis had influenced the Clover Grove mayor on my behalf, as well. They had a collegial relationship and quite a few of our guests came by referral from one mayor or the other. Local citizens might not appreciate my sleuthing, but our political leaders did.

After delivering a rousing pep talk, Remi asked everyone to visit the stations throughout the square to sign up for various tasks, from handing out flyers to repairing and polishing donations as they came in.

Cori Hogan cut through the throngs with a few flicks of her trademark black gloves with orange middle fingers. Clem, her sheep-dog, was already managing the crowd for her. Keats swished his tail in fawning admiration of Clem. Normally my dog disdained other canines, but Clem was not only his senior, but a prizewinner in herding trials. He'd shown Keats a thing or two about livestock management that served us well at Runaway Farm and beyond.

"Where's this legendary birdcage?" Cori asked. "You'd better not be reneging, Ivy. I'm counting on it to stir things up with the Langman sisters."

I laughed. "We all are. We've become drama llamas."

Cori offered a rare smile. The tiny tyrant of a dog trainer was quite pretty, with her mop of short, shiny hair and bright, dark, bird-like eyes. I didn't notice her looks often because she was usually berating me for farming or rescue misdeeds.

"The birdcage has a guest," Jilly said, eager to share the story about Picasso. "A painted bunting with a secret."

"Oh? Do tell." Cori came a little closer. She was barely five feet tall—about the same size as my mother, who was currently weaving through the crowd with my sister, Iris.

"I haven't heard the story myself," Edna told Cori. "They took on a mission without me."

"Let's move past that," I said. "You've taken on a whole class without us, Edna. We all go rogue sometimes."

"You won't let them in our class?" Cori said, turning to Edna. "Even Bridie Brighton made the cut."

"Excuse me?" I said. "Cori's in and we're not?"

Jilly glared at Edna indignantly, too. "You took my grandmother over me?"

"Girls, I have my reasons," Edna said. "The main one is that neither one of you could give my class the focus and attention it deserves. You're always running hither and yon after animals, killers or good-looking men. At your stage of life, you can't commit to something as serious as survival."

"And Cori can? She runs after animals all the time, too," I said.

"But not killers or men," Cori said, with a wicked grin. "Especially not men in law enforcement. I have the bandwidth to commit to survival. Plus, I couldn't turn down the chance to teach rappelling. My specialty."

"You will not have my gran rappelling or leaping out of planes," Jilly said.

Edna brushed paw prints from her camo jacket. "Bridie will need to skip the experiential elements until I can head back down south to deliver intensives. Anyway, this is a complex program with high stakes, girls. I can't spend time worrying about people's delicate feelings."

"Fine," I said. "Then Jilly and I will deal with the bird on our own. This mystery is all about delicate feelings."

Cori winced and began receding into the crowd. "Then count me out. I'm a woman of action, not sentiment. Just get us that bird-cage, Ivy."

"As soon as the vacant sign goes back up," I said.

"Edna," Cori called out. "Clem's gathering some of your recruits. Let's have some face time."

Jilly and I stared at each other, bewildered. What had life in Clover Grove come to when two of our greatest warriors could so easily dismiss exploring a new mystery? I guess there had been so many lately that people could afford to pick and choose.

"It's their loss," Jilly said. "Because this is a puzzle that deserves attention." She checked over both shoulders to make sure no one was eavesdropping. "Picasso's tin box of love letters needs to find its rightful home. This is a poignant, private matter, so maybe it's better people like Cori and Edna don't trample all over it."

"True, but I resent Edna suggesting we're silly and distractible," I said.

Jilly just shrugged. "I own being distractible. It's a month till my wedding and probably not the right time to learn how to eke out a living in a bunker."

I had to own it, too. On top of my other diversions, sometimes I found myself thinking about future weddings, in which a certain hobby farmer played a starring role. Jilly's wedding would take place in the orchard, as I had pictured it months ago. Maybe I could make a convincing enough case to hold mine in the barn.

Assuming I was formally asked at some point.

"You only get married once," I said, signaling Keats to guide us away from my mother. "We can learn to rappel anytime."

"Exactly," Jilly said. "So how do we get started with our search?"

"By asking around. Discreetly. Someone other than Edna must have known the owners of the Harlow property. There probably weren't many young men who were likely to hide a pile of love letters and an engagement ring. The box survived better than the barn itself."

"Such a sad story," Jilly said. "Henny and Wren gave up their happiness out of family duty."

"If they're still alive, we'll find them," I said. "And we can do it without Edna. There are some true romantics around who might help."

"I suppose it's not a big rush," she said. "The letters seem to have been there for decades. This is one mystery we can squeeze in between other obligations."

I nodded. "Although I do worry either Henny or Wren might pass away. They must be quite old by now."

"Clover Grove breeds longevity," Jilly said.

"Sounds like I arrived just in time," Evie Springdale said, joining us. "Any discussion of breeding piques my interest. It's inevitable when you marry a veterinarian."

Her strawberry blonde curls were tied back to stay out of the way when she was filming and her blue eyes sparkled with the joy she took in her work to benefit animals. Like me, Evie had spent years in a soul-sucking career and the trauma created a bond between us. Nevertheless, she delighted in exploiting my farming foibles for fundraising goals.

Jilly and I exchanged a glance. Evie was most definitely a romantic and her nose for a good story would send her running to hunt down the thwarted lovers. But how would she use the information? Long ago, two hearts had been crushed under the wheels of hill country convention. Perhaps they may yet be healed and reunited. There was a reason Picasso, the painted bunting, had led us to them.

I decided to throw out a red herring. "We were just talking about breeding the goats for a spring delivery. If we want to expand our line of Runaway Farm soap and lotion, we'll need your advice on promotion."

"Anytime," she said. "Did you bring the birdcage?"

"I want to deliver it to a safehouse," I said. "Which reminds me that Vernie Cobbler sent some donations and they're still in my truck. Where should we drop them?"

Evie beckoned Remi, who came over with Leo cradled like a baby. Jilly was in a similar pose, only with Percy in her arms.

Reaching out, I touched Leo's irresistibly soft ears, causing Keats to complain noisily. My sheepdog sided with Cori in viewing Leo as more of an accessory than a real canine.

Remi gave me the address of a storage unit and the combination on a lockbox to get inside. "Would you mind making some pickups over the next week?" she asked. "I don't have a truck and I don't trust Cori to handle precious antiques."

That made me laugh. "Have you seen my pratfalls? The greatest hits reel is still making the rounds."

There was a ha-ha-ha pant of agreement from below.

"But unlike Cori, you care," Remi said. "You treasure old things."

That hadn't been the case before we arrived in Clover Grove, but it was now. Antiques had stories to tell, and I loved hearing them.

"Sure, I can do some pickups," I said. "Gives me an excuse to poke around places where I'm not always welcome. You'll need to clear it with people so I'm not driven off their land with shotguns."

Remi frowned. "It's wrong that people connect you more with the crime problem than the solution."

"They probably think murder's contagious," I said. The thought crossed my mind sometimes, too. "Regardless, I'm glad to help."

"Don't go alone," Remi said. "Some donations will be worth stealing right out of your hands, but I know you can handle yourself."

"So, you're saying I'm the muscle," I said. The thought actually filled me with pride.

Remi's cheeks flushed. "Not exactly. But some of our volunteers couldn't handle a confrontation with Heddy and Kaye. You and Keats are used to them."

I *was* used to them, and someday I'd welcome the opportunity to give them what they deserved. But I no longer underestimated the passion that blinded treasure hunters like them.

Jilly started to argue on my behalf but Bridget Linsmore, one of the Rescue Mafia's leaders, emerged from the crowd to collect Remi and Evie. She was all business when it came to events that could save dogs, so there was no time for more than a smile before she led Remi and Evie away.

The void they left was filled quickly by my mother and a gaggle of women.

"Darling." She gave me an air kiss on each cheek, although we'd seen each other just two hours ago when she was trying to elbow me out of the bathroom at the inn. Mom shared a roof with me when it was convenient for her. Her apartment in town had become "too confining for her art," which was dressmaking. Or rather, re-dressmaking, since the materials were nearly always thrift store finds. Today she wore a red wool skirt I hadn't seen before with a black jacket trimmed in red velvet. It was striking enough for a formal luncheon and made my overalls look extra dumpy. She gave me the once-over, her expression a mixture of motherly disgust and satisfaction that I made such a good foil.

Meanwhile, I stared around at the group of seven women who surrounded her, four of whom I recognized. Beverly Roxton, the veterinarian's wife, was one of my most vocal detractors in town and never had a kind word about Mom, either. Gwen Quinn had worked for me briefly, mostly in the capacity of a spy for Myrtle McCain. Morag Tanner and Joan Snelling were members of the disbanded Bridge Buddies, a club that had combusted at my inn when they accused each other of murder and other despicable things.

Why was my mother chumming around with people like this? Why was Mom chumming with *anyone*? Normally she considered all women competition for the scarce resources of eligible men. She did not have "friends," per se. Maybe they were clients at Bloomers, the salon she ran with my sister, Iris.

Jilly moved to stand next to me, shoulder to shoulder, and Keats circled both of us warily. Although he loved my mother, my dog had a long memory for people who'd wronged me and the growl deep in his throat proved it.

"You be nice to my friends, handsome," Mom said. Her voice was a trilling purr, worthy of Percy in a fine mood. The cat's mood wasn't fine now, however. He struggled in Jilly's arms till she had no choice but to release him to take his chances in the crowd.

"Mom, we have work to do," I said, allowing Keats to ease me away.

She followed, and the group moved as if they'd become planets in orbit around Dahlia Galloway, former town pariah. It felt like we'd landed in an alternate universe.

"Ladies," Mom said, "some of you know my youngest daughter, Ivy Rose, and my soon-to-be daughter-in-law Jilly Blackwood. Girls, I believe you've met Beverly, Morag, Joan and Gwen."

"Indeed," I said. It took all my HR training to hold back everything else I wanted to say. Sometimes I worried I'd lose those skills but they continued to support me well. "Hello, ladies."

Morag and Joan muttered greetings while staring at the ground, but Gwen looked me right in the eye, sending a chill down my spine. Beverly could barely contain a sneer.

"Darlings, I have some new friends to introduce. Silkie and Satin Carnegie are sisters who've just moved to Dorset Hills. And Mercy Bellweather is a former colleague of mine."

I didn't bother to ask which job, as Mom had been fired from so many. Instead I dug up a smile. "Nice to meet you," I said. Hopefully the Carnegie sisters and Mercy Bellweather were decent human beings, unlike the others.

Rubbing her manicured fingers together, Mom beamed at me. "Everyone's excited to roll up their sleeves and help with this event."

Mom was never excited to roll up her sleeves for anything but sewing, so it smelled fishy to me. Silkie and Satin, likely in their late forties, had hazel eyes and brunette hair with a nearly identical low-maintenance cut. They wore sensible black clothes and looked capable of moving an armoire without breaking a sweat. Maybe their names had been cute when they were toddlers, but they seemed at odds with their image today.

Mercy Bellweather, on the other hand, oozed femininity. She was wearing a full-skirted dress with filmy layers. Her highlighted fair hair cascaded over her shoulders in waves like a vintage movie starlet's, and her makeup was heavy. I could see how Mom might have bonded with Mercy while stocking shelves at the grocery store.

Keats took the measure of Dahlia's new solar system and grumbled loudly, causing the group to ease back. I took his complaint seriously, because his ruff rose and his ears flattened. As if that weren't bad enough, a scraping sound at my feet made me look around for Percy, only to find him raking invisible litter across the pavement. Normally he only did that when someone was about to pass away, if they hadn't already.

"Oh no," Jilly said, grabbing my arm.

"What?" Mom said. "You look like you've seen a ghost, Jillian."

"It's okay, Mom," I said, scooping up the cat. He moved to my shoulder, in his pirate's parrot pose, and scraped at my jacket to drive his point home. "I get a little claustrophobic in a crowd, that's all. As some of you may know, I have PTSD."

"Please excuse us," Jilly said. "I'm sure we'll cross paths again working for this great cause."

"No hard feelings, Ivy," Gwen called after me. "It's all water under the bridge."

"Same," said Morag. "Everyone deserves a second chance."

The words could have cut either way, but Morag's smirk told me I was the one getting the second chance.

"The nerve of them," Jilly said, when we were out of earshot. "As if *you* did anything wrong. They're the ones with tattered reputations."

"Why on earth is my mother hanging with that posse?" I said. "Blood is supposed to be thicker than water."

"Edna has her new posse, too," Jilly said, as we came upon another group.

Our friend was in the center, gesticulating enthusiastically with camouflage gloves. Three graying women had their backs to us, and Keats apparently didn't like the smell of them. He was trigger happy on the hackles today. Percy gave a few more scrapes on my jacket and let out a spooky yowl. Two of the women turned and I saw from their green eyes that they were certainly sisters, if not identical twins. Edna tried to snap her fingers to reclaim their attention. The gloves prevented that so she slammed her palms together and the sisters turned back.

Jilly tugged my arm and we continued to the parking lot, arriving at nearly the same time as Heddy and Kaye Langman. They flitted past us, moving between parked vehicles like secret agents—if secret agents wore khakis and sensible cardigans. Last fall, there had been a fallout between the sisters over a duplicitous ballroom dancer who wooed them both. A thirst for treasure drew the Langmans back together and now they seemed closer than ever. Their joint commitment to bilking good people of heirlooms made them a formidable team. They'd even found a secret cache of gold on Gertie's land, and made the evidence vanish.

Jilly texted Edna while the Langmans skulked from vehicle to vehicle, peering into back seats and flatbeds to scope out potential collectibles. I had no doubt they'd lift anything they thought they could steal. Before long, they'd reach my truck that still held Vernie's donation.

Raising my phone to film them, I called, "I've got eyes on you, Langmans. You heard the lady: you've got to buy things fair and square to benefit the cause. You're already at an advantage knowing the value of collectibles."

"That's how we like it," Heddy said, striking a defiant pose. "Antiques are the Langman Legacy, like the sign over our store says. We've worked hard to get to this point and now your friends are inviting in a stranger to confuse people about the true value of their mementos."

Edna emerged from the crowd and made a show of fumbling in her pocket. "Where did I put that pesky grenade? It's always slipping away on me."

"You'll blow yourself up one of these days if you're not more careful," Jilly said.

"That's how I want to go, Jillian," Edna said. "I've decided against cannon fire. How about you, Heddy? Kaye? Don't just leave these things to chance. There's no dignity in that."

The sisters were already retreating rapidly.

"Say hi to Gertie and Minnie," Edna shouted after them. "They're on the lookout for you."

The Langmans were in good shape from transporting goods, and forced their way through the throngs like quarterbacks.

The sight gave us a welcome laugh as we climbed into the truck and left Dorset Hills. During the drive, Edna practically burbled with delight over meeting her prepper following, although she didn't share any names.

I eased off the gas when Vernie's Vegetables came into view and Keats left Edna's lap to crawl into mine. He rarely did that when I was driving and it meant he wanted to pilot our ship. His mumble was discreet, more of a vibration against my chest. He had business here.

"Not Vernie again," Edna said. "I can't handle more blue pumpkins today. Like I said, it's unnatural."

I pulled onto the shoulder. "Says the woman preparing for a zombie apocalypse. Fully natural."

"I'm preparing for the end times," Edna said. "You're the one throwing zombies into the mix."

"Well, you can wait in the truck," I said. "I just want a quick word with Vernie. No need to aggravate her further."

"*Wait in the truck, Edna.*" Her tone was snippy. "You're always glad to leave me behind like a sack of spuds when you don't need security."

"A sack of onions," I said, jumping out. "You're enough to make me cry."

"Be nice, both of you," Jilly said. "I hate it when my bridesmaids bicker."

"Tell Vernie I said blue pumpkins are the stupidest newfangled thing I've ever seen," Edna called through the open window. "Although I don't blame her for trying to get a leg up on the competition."

When I walked around the long cart, however, I found Vernie wasn't trying to get a leg up on anything.

In fact, her battered boots were neatly crossed as she lay in a pile of smashed pumpkin.

# CHAPTER FIVE

If I had any doubt about Vernie's condition, Percy let me know with assertive scrapes of an orange paw over the gravel that Vernie wouldn't be haggling with anyone over the price of turnips again.

"Dagnabit," Edna said, coming up behind me. "We've lost another good one."

"You hated Vernie," I said, looking around. There was no sign of anyone else and Keats' flags were at half-mast, suggesting we were in no immediate peril.

At first glance, the only thing that had changed since we left nearly two hours ago was the smashed blue pumpkin. Judging by the number of pieces, it was likely the huge one that had held pride of place on the trestle table. There was no way it had tumbled off and rolled behind the long cart. To be crushed like that, it must have been thrown down with force by someone in a rage. And then it seemed Vernie had been thrown down on top of it.

"I didn't *hate* Verna Rae," Edna said. "We were practically friends. People of my generation have a different definition of friendship."

"Meaning it's fine to get all stabby with each other and then climb into a bunker together?" I asked, still trying to make sense of what I was seeing.

"Exactly. Although I'm going to be extremely selective about who ends up in my space. Taking my course isn't a free pass into my bunker."

Jilly gestured to shush us as she spoke to the police. After hanging up, she asked Keats to herd us away from the body. Vernie was lying among so many small bits of blue pumpkin rind that it seemed as if the sky had fallen to frame her. It was artistic in a horrible way.

Since the decimated squash was under her, she hadn't died from the blow. It was hard to know without moving her, but there were signs she'd been struck in the head from behind.

"The spade," I said. "The one she used to refill the onion basket. It's gone."

"Check her truck," Edna said.

"Check nothing," Jilly said. "The police will be here in five minutes tops."

"But I just want to—"

"Ivy, no," she interrupted. "What frustrates Kellan the most is when we mess up a crime scene before he's had a chance to inspect it himself and collect evidence. His job is harder when our tracks and fingerprints and pet hair are all over."

I conceded she was right, with a sigh. "But we saw how everything was set up earlier. We're a great asset to this case." Keats followed Jilly's request to move us away from the vegetable stand and it felt like a small act of mutiny. "Just who do you work for, Keats? I believe I'm the one paying your bills."

He gave me a saucy mumble, knowing he'd repaid me many times over for the costs he'd racked up in kibble and vet fees. In fact, he could fairly demand a salary if money were of use to even the most brilliant sheepdog.

Another mumble concurred with my assessment. It went on so

long that I assumed he was suggesting other ways I could make it up to him. Long walks in the hills, perhaps. More varied livestock. Or more crime-solving. The best reward for a working dog was more work.

He poked my hand hard and I realized I felt light-headed.

"What's going on, Ivy?" Edna asked. "We've seen plenty of situations like this, yet today you look green around the gills."

"I think it's the smell of pumpkin. I'm a bit queasy."

"Me too," Jilly said. All the color had left her cheeks and she was hugging herself with crossed arms. "No pumpkin pie at Thanksgiving this year."

"Percy," I called. The cat was still busy with his elaborate scraping routine, repeatedly pronouncing Vernie's death. "Thanks, buddy. We got the message. Now it's time to do your therapy cat thing for Jilly."

He covered the space between us in a few leaps and hit Jilly mid-back, scaling the rest of the way with sharp claws. It spoke volumes that Jilly didn't make a peep about the damage to her new coat. She simply lifted the cat off her shoulder and lowered him into the crook of her arm, where he flexed his paws, apparently well-satisfied with his contributions.

"You girls need to toughen up," Edna said. "There's no nausea allowed in a bunker."

"I don't want to get used to seeing something like this," Jilly said, rocking Percy. "No matter how many times it happens."

"Me either," I said. "Edna, how can it not affect you more when you claim to have been friends with Vernie?"

"My training. Did you know I was an emergency medic all over hill country before there were paramedics? I don't mention it often because it was the most traumatic work I've done. There was no choice but to toughen up."

A new respect for Edna pushed out my annoyance. There were depths to her that more than explained her rough edges.

"That's awful," Jilly said. "I'm sorry you had to—"

Edna cut Jilly off with an impatient wave. "I hear sirens. I hope you girls won't get swoony over your boyfriends. We may need to help them find justice for Vernie, and there's no room for love in sleuthing."

"Asher would say there's no room for sleuthing in love," Jilly said, sighing.

"Is that ruffian giving you a hard time about this noble work?" Edna said. "Because I'd be happy to set him straight. It is never too late to call off a wedding, Jillian. You won't lose a penny since it's mostly do-it-yourself."

Jilly managed a smile. "No second thoughts. Just wishing we could avoid things like this for awhile. I want to remember my wedding as an oasis of peace."

There was a sound at my knees. A canine snicker. "Don't laugh at Jilly," I told Keats. "It's a perfectly reasonable wish and exactly what I'd want for myself in her shoes." I met Jilly's eyes. "Can you imagine it? An oasis of peace?"

"Nope," Jilly said. "Even when we get a quiet week or two, something nasty is loitering in the wings."

"Like the ugly drunk you don't invite to your wedding who crashes it anyway," Edna said. "You know that's bound to happen with your nuptials, too, Jillian. There must be a few Galloways and Fables who have yet to climb out of the woodwork."

My head snapped around at that. "I thought every family member had surfaced. My parents were both only children. Who could possibly be left?"

Edna shrugged camouflage shoulders. "I forget. It happens at my age."

That was a crock. Edna Evans forgot nothing—not even the reaction you gave at age six to the vaccine she jammed into your arm.

"Edna, if there are relatives that could turn Jilly's wedding into a spectacle, we need to hear about them beforehand. To prepare."

"My brain fog may clear after we've put Verna Rae to rest," she said. "This is a strange time to be talking about the wedding guest list, isn't it? What's next, party favors?"

Jilly shook her head. "Great. Here I thought I only needed to worry about my own crazy family."

"There's that, too," Edna said. "A few people at the Briar Estates are plotting a jailbreak to see you marry."

"What?" Jilly's voice and mine overlapped.

"They can't," I said. "It's not safe."

"It will be by then," Edna said. "I'm virtually training a couple of them in combat, and Gertie and I will have a full security team on the farm itself." She straightened and gave us each a pat on the shoulder. "Don't worry so much. It's going to be the wedding of the decade."

"I don't need to top the list," Jilly said. "Leave room for Ivy and Kellan."

"See? Swoony," Edna said. "Romance is all you girls talk about these days."

"You're the one listing what could go wrong at the wedding," I said.

"Just trying to distract you so that you don't embarrass yourselves by fainting," Edna said. "Anyway, I've come to a new conclusion about you, Ivy."

I willed myself not to take the bait. Poor Vernie was lying dead just yards away and this conversation was disrespectful. Even if it did keep me from fainting.

Jilly couldn't resist asking, "What conclusion is that, Edna?"

Smirking, Edna delivered the verdict. "Ivy should never marry."

"Don't say that!" Jilly was outraged. "Kellan and Ivy are a perfect match."

"Really?" Edna said. "He's trying to bring order to this lawless region and crime runs deep in Ivy's veins. What Vernie said earlier wasn't entirely wrong. There hadn't been a murder around these parts for ages until Ivy came home." She gestured in Vernie's direction. "Yet here we are again."

My mouth dropped open and Keats gave my dangling fingertips a nudge till I spoke. "Edna, are you blaming me for Lloyd Boyce's murder, and all that came after it?"

Something in my voice caused Percy to spring from Jilly's arms into mine. It was a relief to know he was still my cat, too.

Meanwhile, Keats took a dive at Edna's calf. She didn't even flinch, having fortified her camo pants for just such occurrences. Keats figured that out fast and took a leap at her backside, instead. Even seeing her jump and flail didn't bring a smile to my face.

Jilly shook her finger at Edna. "You apologize to Ivy right now, or I'm downgrading you from bridesmaid to car jockey."

"Oh, don't be so sensitive," Edna said. "It doesn't take a rocket scientist to track the rise in cases against Ivy's homecoming. I didn't say it was her fault, though. Lloyd's murder opened the door to reveal an ugly toad on the doorstep. Now the chief has his hands full, and unless he can figure out what's behind the change, weddings are just a distraction."

"A welcome distraction," I said. "Just what we need after Imogen Pigeon's funeral. And now this."

Edna pulled a camouflage hat over her perm and yanked down the flaps. "Ivy, don't you have enough animals to keep you busy till the urge to pair up passes? Because it will, you know. Give it a few years and you'll come to your senses." Squinting down the highway for the first sign of flashing lights, Edna continued, "Your mother was an exception to the rule. Dahlia's urges went dormant for decades but rose again, worse than ever. I hope you and your sisters didn't inherit that, because there are so many worthy causes when you stop thinking about men, and heaven forbid, children. No one should be reproducing in times like these. Keep that in mind, Jillian. If you've got an infant slung over your shoulder in my bunker, you're of no use to me. You can't even cook for the army of good."

Keats came back and mumbled a reminder that we had bigger problems on our hands. I stroked his ears and then leveled a glance at Edna. "I make a lot of allowances for my friends, my animals and my family, Edna. Sometimes it probably looks like I have no boundaries at all. But I do, and you just stomped on one with your combat boots. So I'd thank you to back off."

"Oooh, touchy," she said. "Take all the space you need."

There was a reason Edna was stinging so hard today, and I'd figure it out eventually. For now, I turned toward the sirens, rocking Percy in both arms, while Keats leaned into my shin.

Jilly stood beside me and we watched as Kellan jumped out of one car and Asher from another. Our men didn't acknowledge us before charging over to Verna Rae Cobbler's body and confirming nothing could be done to help her. Edna joined them and her arms flashed, as if giving a grand tour of the murder scene. Kellan's glare was wasted on her. Meanwhile, the investigative team began setting up, and I couldn't help but think about all the practice they'd had since I got home.

"Don't let her get under your skin," Jilly said. "You know what Edna's like."

"But she's been so much nicer lately," I said. "That was a sneak attack when my guard was down."

Jilly's fingers dropped to Percy. He flexed and purred, happily filling us both with comfort.

"The truth always comes out in time," she said. "Don't force it."

Asher slipped away from Kellan a moment later. Even a murder couldn't weaken the magnetic pull Jilly had over my brother. He looked at her with the dazed eyes of a kid holding the rarest of collectible baseball cards, and I had no doubt he always would. With his geniality and brawn, and her shrewd capability, they would do well together.

Even if we all ended up in bunkers.

"Are you okay?" Asher asked, dropping a quick kiss on Jilly's cheek.

"Fine. We're fine," Jilly said. "It's not the first time we've seen something like this, unfortunately."

Asher churned a big hand through his fair hair. "You've seen almost as much death as I have, Jilly, and it's not... It's not good for you. You'll be scarred by it."

In truth, Asher was more likely to be scarred by the calamities we witnessed than Jilly. Under his relentless cheer was a very soft heart. Jilly's heart was soft, too, but an inner shark circled it protectively. I had one, too. That's how we survived the perils of the corporate world. We'd trained for this without knowing it.

Kellan finally came over and our eyes met. The baby goats in my heart still bounced around whenever he came within yards of me, but his furrowed brow stilled them quickly today. His lips pressed into a thin line as he pondered yet another murder in his jurisdiction. He took each crime personally—as a black mark on a record that had indeed been clean when we reconnected over the dogcatcher's body in my rye field.

"What do you know about this incident, Ivy?" he asked. There were no kisses on cheeks or besotted gazes for me. His voice was terse enough to earn a little lunge from my black-and-white bodyguard. *Soul*guard. If Kellan noticed the assault on his pant cuff, he didn't let on.

"We stopped here to buy some pumpkins on our way to a fundraising meeting in Dog Town," I said. "Vernie was cranky. More so than usual. But she asked us to deliver her donation and we left here a couple of hours ago. Keats wanted to stop again on our way back and we found... this."

"Did she mention feeling threatened or uneasy?" Kellan asked. "I can't imagine it was a dispute over a pumpkin."

"Verna Rae rubbed people the wrong way," Edna said, joining

us. "I speak from long experience of doing the same. Many have wanted to clock me for less than a pumpkin."

Kellan acknowledged that with a slight nod. He routinely wanted to clock Edna and one of her favorite hobbies was getting the best of the man she called "Chief Haughty McSnobalot." However, I sensed they secretly respected each other as worthy adversaries.

I told Kellan all I could, with frequent interruptions from Edna, which irritated me more than usual. Keats left his position at Kellan's cuff and eased Edna away so gradually that even the seasoned warrior didn't notice. Before long, she had to raise her voice to be heard and she did just that.

"Stop shouting, Miss Evans," Kellan said. "A crime scene demands a certain decorum."

Edna looked down and realized she'd been bested by a border collie. Color rushed into her sallow cheeks and she tried to dodge around him. He countered the move, nearly managing to trip her.

"Stand down, dog!" Edna's voice was thunderous. "Or fend for yourself with the rest of the strays when the end comes."

Keats taunted her with a pant-laugh and then came back to me. Meanwhile, I looked at Kellan and said, "Chief, how about the rest of us head home and you come by to chat later? I agree with you about decorum."

Kellan's dark blue eyes narrowed. "As long as you'll commit to staying out of this."

"Of course, she will," Jilly said. "We're up to our necks in alligators right now. Not real ones, thank goodness. Between wedding planning and the fundraiser and guests coming, there isn't a spare moment."

"Jilly's right," I said. "We've never been busier."

His expression grew even more skeptical. "So, you'll just go home and shovel manure, correct?"

"Manure's what got me into this mess, actually. But if that's what you want..."

Jilly's hand dropped to my sleeve and she started towing me away. Passing Asher, she whispered, "Could you please have someone drive Edna home? She knew Vernie well, and it's all been too much for her."

My brother morphed into a uniformed sheepdog and herded Edna toward the police vehicles despite her protests.

Her last outraged bellow reached us as we got into the truck. "I refuse to be packed up like an old— Ivy Galloway, what is going on here?"

"Handle with care, brother," I called. "We've ordered a bridesmaid's dress in her size."

Asher wrestled Edna into a squad car among a flurry of fists. "No worries," he called. "I've got four more sisters. Someone's gotta fit that dress."

Edna's indignation cut off abruptly as the car door slammed shut.

———————

# CHAPTER SIX

"Are we really going home so you can shovel manure and wait for Kellan?" Jilly asked, as I pulled back onto the highway and headed in the direction of Runaway Farm.

"Of course," I said, taking the next turn onto a side road. "Right after we run a couple of important errands."

Entering the complicated back country trail system from behind the farming supplies store, I then backtracked around the crime scene to head in the opposite direction.

A smooth ride it was not. Jilly held onto the passenger door handle for dear life and some of the pumpkins in the bed of the truck broke loose and thumped around.

"We don't have time for two errands before Kellan arrives, do we?" she asked.

"Possibly," I said. Based on past experience I guessed it would take Kellan several hours to finish his work at Vernie's Vegetables. Still, there was no being sure.

I geared down so that the trails didn't buck the truck right off, which had happened more often than I cared to admit. Zeb Rogan, a small organic farmer and a big fan of my fertilizer, had twice come with his tow truck and hauled me out of a creek. A promise to supply him with my secret black label manure for life had secured his word that Chief Harper would never know about my back country mishaps.

"Possibly isn't good," Jilly said. "Probably."

"It'll be fine if everything goes smoothly," I said. "Sometimes it does."

Stopping on a hill, I pulled out my phone. No matter how many times I was back here with Kellan, Edna and even my mother, I still got lost. Navigation wasn't one of my superpowers.

After a few more twists, I left the trails and got back on the highway where I quickly found Vernie Cobbler's winding lane. There was a stone fawn right at the end, where the space opened to reveal a classic hill country red farmhouse. Selling vegetables clearly hadn't provided enough money for upkeep, however, as both house and barn seemed to droop in despair. Hopefully a new owner could look past Vernie's misfortune and restore the home to its former glory.

"Tell me you're not planning to break in," Jilly said. "That might be worse than trampling Kellan's crime scene."

I eased the truck into the bushes at the side of the house and opened my door to release the pets.

"Remember, it's not breaking in if you can find a key," I said. "And Keats and Percy always find a key. Or at least, an open window."

"So we're just popping in here to look around when the killer could be doing exactly the same thing?" Jilly got out and followed me. "Maybe I shouldn't have given Edna the boot."

"She deserved it," I said. "We've managed fine without her before, and we can do it again." A sigh slipped out. "She does make things easier, though."

"Maybe she'll show up anyway," Jilly said. "She's curious about what happened to Vernie, too."

"Our visit isn't about curiosity, my friend. We're here on a heroic mission."

"Oh yeah? Good, because we're taking a pretty big risk." Jilly spun to make sure we hadn't been followed. "The rewards had better be big, too."

I headed up the stairs to the front door. "Probably quite small, but that's okay."

Pulling work gloves out of my pocket, I tried the door. I hadn't expected it to be that easy and it wasn't. Jilly's heels clicked on the paving stones as she walked around the side of the house ahead of me. She slipped on leather gloves and tried the back door herself.

My broad sweeping gesture to the pets was unnecessary because they'd already fanned out. Keats was running in serpentine loops with his nose to the ground looking for keys, clues or both. Percy took the vertical route, climbing an apple tree and then leaping onto the roof. He picked his way daintily across the back of the house.

"What exactly do you hope to find here?" Jilly asked, as I ran my index finger along the top of the door frame, and then did the same to the kitchen window. "Do you think Vernie owned anything people would kill for?"

"Possibly, based on what she said about wanting to disperse her property," I said. "More likely she just had secrets. Everyone around here does."

I gave up my hunt with a grunt of frustration. The boys weren't having much luck, either. Vernie was more security conscious than most people in Clover Grove. Then again, standards had probably changed since I drove up the crime rates, supposedly singlehandedly.

Keats stopped his undulating turns long enough to stare at me with his eerie blue eye. It looked like a rebuke and the mumble that followed confirmed it. Self-pity wasn't permitted mid-task, if ever.

When he was satisfied that I understood, he lifted his white paw in a point. There was a mossy stone bench surrounded by wild and weedy lilac bushes. Keats gave me a chance to fumble around trying to find the key myself and then pushed past me to dig it up from under the back leg.

Vernie had wrapped the key in plastic, so it still gave off a bit of a gleam in the last of the daylight.

Jilly took off her gloves and twisted her curls into a knot. I did the same with my own hair. When skulking around the house of a murder victim, it was best not to forfeit peripheral vision.

"Do you actually know what we're looking for, Ivy?" she asked.

Keats looked up and went into another point, and Percy trotted across the shingles toward the front of the house.

"Yep," I said. "Just listen."

In one of the upstairs rooms at the front of the house, a small dog barked.

"Oh right, Vernie mentioned a Pomeranian," Jilly said.

"Pommy, yes. The Rescue Mafia placed the dog with her and that's why she wanted to support the fundraiser."

"So, we're adopting a Pomeranian now?" Jilly asked, while I unwrapped the key and then unlocked the door.

"Nope," I said, stepping into the kitchen. "Working dogs only at Runaway Farm. We'll return Pommy to the Mafia and they'll find a good owner. It's easier for them to rehome a small dog than pregnant goats."

"Or an emu," Jilly said, with a slight shudder. She tried to love all of our animals but the big bird was a harder sell.

"I wanted to get to Pommy before the police did," I said, leading the way from the kitchen to the dining room. "I'm sure they have a process for pets in crisis, but I doubt they surrender animals to vigilante rescuers. Yet that's where Pommy rightfully belongs."

"I guess," she said, giving me a gentle poke between the shoulder blades. "But Kellan won't be happy we're here, Ivy."

"It's fine. We're fine. Keats and Percy would let us know if there was anything to worry about. We'll just take a quick look, grab the dog and— Whoa!"

Vernie's kitchen had been as outdated and run-down as I expected, but the dining room was an entirely different matter. It had essentially been turned into a modern art studio that would be flooded with light most of the day.

The long oak table was covered with sketchbooks, bottles and tubes of paint, and brushes. There were several easels around the room, one of which held a still life work in progress. The models sat on an oak buffet: a trio of blue pumpkins that were different from the perfect spheres she sold at the vegetable stand. These were misshapen, bumpy and scarred. Perhaps she kept the best for paying customers, or just preferred painting flawed ones. The inner workings of the artist's mind were a mystery to me, and judging from what I saw here, Vernie was a talented painter.

"Look at this one," Jilly said. "I love it."

The painting in question featured a spice rack holding some of Jilly's favorites. I could see why it spoke to her. Maybe I could buy it from the estate as a wedding present.

"Seems like we keep discovering people aren't as they seem, yet it still surprises me," I said.

"Me too. When I worked as a headhunter, I thought I knew everything about people."

"Same in HR," I said. "I gave too much credit to my intuition back then. And yet, not enough. I wonder if some of our clients were killers, too."

We walked into the living room, where a painting over the fireplace showed us who we'd likely be meeting upstairs. The Pomeranian depicted was coppery red with puffs of glorious fur. The dog's brown eyes had circles of white that made her look uneasy. Worse, it felt like she was watching us as we moved around the room. Or maybe it was Vernie watching us from beyond. After what happened with the songbird that morning, my mind had cracked open to possibility.

I wasn't the only one fixated by the dog's portrait. Keats had gone into a point and his ears flattened. He had never had much use for poufy dogs, but this seemed like an overreaction.

"Don't worry, Pommy's not staying with us, buddy," I said. "But try to keep an open mind. Small dogs have a valuable job, too. Any pet is a reason to get up every day."

He mumbled something that suggested I was missing his point.

"Oh, I get it," I said. "She's not a real working dog. But we still need to rescue Pommy and make sure she's rehomed."

I turned on a lamp just long enough to capture images of the paintings mounted on every wall in case they came in handy later. When we finally started up the stairs, Keats was still preoccupied by the portrait. His fascination made me a little nervous about meeting the original.

The Pomeranian had stopped yapping around the time we discovered her portrait and there was an eerie silence as we finished the climb and walked down the hall to the front bedroom. The door was wide open and the fluffy red dog was sitting on a pillow. There was a plastic doggie staircase at the foot of the bed, which meant she could have come down and joined us on her own. I suspected she had chosen to stay on Vernie's pillow for as long as she could. Perhaps the little dog sensed something terrible had happened to the woman who'd doted on her. A tremor passed through her, and she whined as we came into the room.

"Hello, Pommy," I said. "I'm Ivy and these are my friends, Jilly and Keats. Percy, my cat, is around someplace, too. We've come with bad news, I'm afraid. Vernie won't be coming home again. But she told us how much she loved you, and we'll make sure to find you another good home. I promise."

The little dog got off the pillow and walked stiffly to the little staircase. It seemed like she wanted to leave on her own terms and I was relieved there was no need to force the issue.

"Poor sweet thing," Jilly said, as Keats fell back to let Pommy precede us out of the bedroom. "It's like she knows."

I nodded. "Hopefully she remembers some good times with the Mafia. She stayed with Bridget for quite a while, I think."

At the top of the stairs, Pommy stopped and her hackles rose. At least I assumed that's why she became even fluffier suddenly. A shrill growl confirmed it.

"She's probably spotted Percy," I said. "Let's take a quick look in the basement and skedaddle."

A deeper growl at my side told me the time for poking around had ended. If there was any doubt, Percy struck me mid-back and began his ascent to my shoulder.

"Ivy," Jilly whispered. "I may not have inherited my family's dubious psychic abilities, but I'm sensing we should skedaddle sooner."

Bending, I scooped up the little dog while Percy initiated a 20-claw alert in my shoulder. We hurried down the stairs and by the time we locked up the house and headed for the truck, both Keats and Pommy had swelled to double their normal size.

"I don't suppose you want to wait around and meet a suspect?" I asked Jilly. "Because that's probably who's coming. Maybe we could wrap this case up straight away and go back to wedding planning."

Jilly opened the passenger door and got in. "I want to live to see my wedding. So if it takes longer to solve this crime, I'm good with that."

I let Keats and Percy jump into the truck from my side and passed Pommy to Jilly. "There's a lot to be said for efficiency, Jilly."

"There's a lot to be said for breathing, too," she said. "This bride doesn't want to collapse among pumpkin shards, even if they're borrowed and blue."

Her ability to joke under pressure was one of the traits I admired most in Jilly. "I guess not, but I'm still proud of the products of my manure. There are worse ways to go."

I turned the key in the ignition and then backed the truck around.

Jilly grabbed the handle again. "When we're safe at home, we can debate that."

I geared up too fast in the lane. The truck stuttered and threatened to stall but cut me a break in the end.

That was just as well, since Keats' posture when we reached the highway gave me every reason to think we were being followed.

# CHAPTER SEVEN

Keats didn't relax even after we reached Dorset Hills, which told me we hadn't yet shaken our pursuer, who stayed far enough back that I couldn't see any lights. Finally, I began using evasive maneuvers. That was easier within city limits because the huge dog statues helped me navigate. I hoped our tail didn't know about all those bronze tails.

Only when Keats and Percy shrunk to normal size did I relax my death grip on the steering wheel. We'd done it!

Jilly had stayed silent throughout the drive, holding Pommy firmly with one hand and gripping the handle with the other. Somehow, she'd also managed to text a heads-up to the Mafia.

"Thank goodness whoever followed us doesn't know Dorset Hills like we do," I said. "I'd hate to lead trouble to Bridget's door."

My friend released a breath she'd probably been holding too long and let go of the handle at the same time. "I'd feel worse if the Mafia hadn't led trouble to us so often," she said.

"True. And while they're not as well-armed as Edna, they know how to take care of themselves."

Cori and Remi were already standing with Bridget in her driveway when we got there. It was dark now, and light poured out of the many windows in the stunning house Bridget's husband Sullivan had designed. It had been featured in magazines, and yet it felt homey because it was full to the brim with rescue dogs.

There was always room for another, however, and Bridget's arms came out to bring Pommy back into the pack. Beau, her black setter, fanned his feathery tail in welcome.

"Poor little girl," Remi said, clutching Leo closer. "She'll mourn Vernie terribly."

"She'll be fine," Cori said. "Vernie was her third owner and her best, but this dog is adaptable. You'd be surprised at how many people are willing to adopt a senior pet. Especially seniors them-selves who can't handle puppy energy or behavioral issues. Since Pommy trained with me, I know she's a gem."

"That's a relief," I said. "A happier ending than I feared."

"Except for Vernie," Remi said. "She was a tough nut but always so generous with pet fundraisers. At first I thought she was in dire straits, but she just didn't like spending money on herself."

"Or the house," I added. "The place is falling apart. I figured she was barely eking out a living selling vegetables."

Remi shook her head. "My connections in the art world said Vernie made good money from her watercolors when she was inclined. She did commercial work under a different name—local landscapes that usually included dogs."

I glanced at Jilly. "We didn't see anything like that at her house. It was mainly still life paintings in oil. At least, I think so. I know very little about art."

"That's what she did for love," Remi said. "The watercolors were for money and I got the impression she felt she was selling out."

"Interesting," Jilly said. "I wish we'd had more time to get to know Vernie."

Cori steepled her gloved hands. "It wouldn't have mattered. I was over there often training Pommy, and Vernie met me with a rifle and a temper every time. She trusted people even less than Gertie and Edna."

"Where was her rifle today, when she really needed it?" I asked.

"Not close enough," Cori said. "Vernie seemed more cautious at home than when she was out in the world. I suppose Chief Hottie will get to the bottom of it."

Cori's statement showed how far her relationship with Kellan had come recently. In the beginning, tension simmered between them because Cori not only flouted the law during pet rescue but flaunted her escapades in front of my boyfriend. Now they had what I'd call an armed neutrality. Cori shared information with Kellan about criminal activities the Mafia saw in their rescue work, and he pretended *not* to see criminal activities in the rescues themselves.

"I hope he can sort it out before the fundraiser," Bridget said. "Vernie's paintings would sell for a good price. Do you think he'll take them into evidence?"

"Probably," I said. "I figure someone must have known their true value already. Maybe they figured out I had them and that's why I was followed."

"Vernie sent me the paperwork to surrender them, so we'll wait and see," Remi said. "If we can't sell now, they'll raise funds for us later. We just need to keep them safe in the meantime."

"Any idea who tailed you tonight?" Cori asked.

I shook my head. "I stayed well ahead, but I'm sure we can make an educated guess."

"The Langmans," Jilly said. "They're aggravatingly well-informed about the whereabouts of collectibles."

Everyone murmured agreement. The sisters' reputation was known all over hill country. I suspected that they made regular rounds, peeping into homes and taking inventory. They were first to arrive at every funeral, shamelessly pressing business cards into the hands of grieving families. Their flower arrangements arrived promptly, no doubt due to bribing the only florist in Clover

Grove. And they hand-delivered a casserole, along with a personalized memento of the dearly departed. It was a well-run operation and quite effective, from what I could tell. The Langmans probably made a secret killing—far more money than they'd ever need—but their appetite was never satisfied.

Bridget set Pommy on the driveway, where she was greeted officially by Beau. He was used to dogs coming and going and served as an elegant ambassador for Bridget's annual Thanksgiving Rescue Pageant.

Clem came out of the shadows to give Pommy a quick sniff. Like Keats, he had little time for other dogs. Leo didn't seem to notice the new arrival at all. His job was providing comfort to humans, not Pomeranians. It never ceased to amaze me how the dogs all differed.

My canine genius stared up at me now with his eerie blue eye, and mumbled. He was urging me to *do* something. That meant there was more to be done here.

"Vernie's art is still in my truck," I said. "Do you want me to take it to the storage unit?"

Jilly raised her hand quickly. "We were already followed, Ivy. Let's get it to the police station."

"Leave it with us," Bridget said, signaling Cori to pull her truck closer. "If the chief wants it, we'll surrender it."

Cori hopped into her pickup and spun it around with a skilled ease I could only dream of achieving one day.

We all stood in the circles of light created by the truck headlights. Remi handed Leo to me, causing Keats to offer an indignant rumble. In this case, the beagle transfer was only meant to free Remi's hands to collect Vernie's donation. She was more knowledgeable than any of us about art. Recently, she'd even become a representative for the works of both Hannah Pemberton and her late mother.

Vernie had wrapped her pieces casually in burlap and twine, but Remi handled them with gloved hands like they were priceless gems.

She set them on the back seat of Cori's truck, loosened the string and let out an excited squeal. "Oh my! There are three pieces from her watercolor series and a couple of small oils." She turned the smallest of the lot to show us. "Isn't it charming? Her work didn't usually run to the fanciful."

The painting was of a grouping of five flawless blue pumpkins.

"Not that fanciful," I said. "Vernie sold us some blue pumpkins today. They're the latest craze."

"We could pull one out of the truck to show you," Jilly said. "But the way they were rolling around back there…"

"Let's not," I said, thinking of Vernie. "I'll hose them into the pastures later. The livestock will be happy."

"Blue pumpkins?" Cori said. "Why can't people leave well enough alone? They're meant to be orange."

"Edna said the same thing," I told her, as I snapped a couple of photos of the art. "You two sound more alike every day."

"That's high praise," Cori said. "Edna and I have been doing target practice, you know. Turns out I'm a very good shot."

"That doesn't surprise me at all," I said. "No wonder she rolled out the red carpet for her survival course."

Cori tipped her head and smirked. "Are you still burned about that? If you really want my place in the course… take it. I don't have all the spare time on my hands you do."

I laughed. "I don't want your castoffs. If I get bored with farm life, I'll take up knitting. You'll be begging for my scarves in your bunker."

"Cori couldn't hack bunker life," Remi said, closing the truck door gently. "No privacy."

"Good point," Cori said. "Lone wolves will need to go it alone when the apocalypse comes." Her black gloves flashed in the head-lights and the orange middle fingers lingered longer on me, no doubt to signify I was one of the lone wolves. "Till then, I won't be packing a gun. Too easy to get it turned on me or the animals we're rescuing."

I nodded. "I said the same thing to Edna... when I was still speaking to her."

There was a collective gasp around the small circle.

"Still speaking to her?" Bridget said. "What happened?"

"You can't break up with Edna, Ivy," Remi said. "You need her protection."

Keats gave an indignant yip and Cori smiled down at him. "We mean you no disrespect, sir. Sometimes opposable thumbs come in handy with adventures like yours."

"Everything's fine," I said. "Edna was extra tactless today and agreed with Vernie Cobbler that my homecoming caused the local surge in crime."

Cori opened the driver's door and glanced back at me. "Maybe it did."

"Cori. Leave it," Bridget said. She was the only one who could ever silence the mouthy trainer. "Crime was always here in one form or another. We've been busy protecting pets for more than a decade. Long before Ivy's time."

"But things are escalating," Cori said. "Someone opened Pandora's box."

"Not Ivy," Remi said. She took Leo back from me with a smile and hugged him. "Nor Jilly. It was just bad timing."

Bridget let Beau and Clem into the back seat of the truck and walked around to the passenger side with Pommy. "Sorry I can't ask you inside," she said. "We're all going with Cori to store the paintings safely."

Remi climbed into the back seat with three animals and the art. "I hate to say it, but Vernie's donation will probably bring in even more money after what's happened."

"Maybe we should sit on it for a while and let it appreciate," Cori said.

"Too risky," I said. "Move it out as soon as you can."

"Think of all the rescues it will fund," Remi said. "Vernie would be happy about that, wherever she's gone."

"I like to think she's sitting with Imogen Pigeon and chatting over a cup of tea," I said.

Cori snorted. "There was no love lost between those two. Vernie had daily dustups with people haggling over produce. Ima drove a hard bargain over turnips, you know."

"Things will be different where they are now," Remi said, with a serene smile. "Vernie's probably counting on you to sort things out, Ivy. Just like Ima did."

Keats mumbled his agreement and gave my shin a poke to punctuate his comments.

"I'll do what I can," I said.

"You mean what Chief Hottie allows," Cori said. She waited while Remi got settled and closed the back door. Then she swung into the driver's seat like a gymnast, despite being about 10 inches shorter than me.

"Kellan and I work like a well-oiled machine," I said, grinning. "He always appreciates my help."

The collective laugh eased the tension building in my throat. I was going to have some explaining to do when I got home. Our errands had expanded into hours and involved a car chase, smashed pumpkins and possible evidence changing hands.

"He really does," Jilly said, letting Keats escort her to my truck. "Long after the fact."

"This time will be different," I said.

## CHAPTER EIGHT

This time, it *was* different.

Shockingly so.

When we got home, Jilly headed up to the house, giving Kellan's SUV a wide berth in case she caught a lecture just by venturing too close. It was 50:50 whether he was waiting for me inside the barn or up at the house. Since Mom's sewing room light was on, I guessed the former. While my boyfriend was uncomfortable being alone with the animals, he was even more uncomfortable with my mother. She was as unpredictable as the llamas and twice as dramatic. Kellan wasn't livestock savvy but he knew how to sidestep trouble of the human variety.

I found him out behind the barn where I least expected... on top of my manure pile.

"Hey," I said, trying to sound casual. "You've discovered the magic of muck."

He kicked the spade into the manure harder than necessary and turned it before flicking gray-blue eyes my way. The glance felt like crackling icicles sprinkling me with chilly particles.

"Might as well make the best of a bad situation," he said, continuing his work.

I wasn't sure if he meant Vernie's departure from the planet, or my interference afterward. Surely a killer on the loose was a bigger concern for the chief of police than a meddlesome girlfriend.

"You're helping to create the hottest fertilizer around," I said. "Vernie Cobbler grew blue pumpkins from that very muck. Some homesteaders are trying to bribe me to supply them exclusively. If I wasn't a hot ticket before, I am now."

Kellan thawed slightly. "You were always a hot ticket. But if people knew how hot*headed*, it would reduce my competition a lot."

"I'm many annoying things but hotheaded isn't one of them," I said. "As the youngest of six I didn't have the luxury of a bad temper. I took whatever scraps trickled down and was grateful. Mostly."

"Okay, I chose the wrong word, although it sounds like you were pretty testy with Edna Evans today. She gave Asher an earful when he was strong-arming her into the car. That woman is a rattlesnake. She shed a layer of camouflage to escape and had a fresh one underneath." Finally he drove the spade into the pile and crossed his arms around the handle. "I pity the poor zombies when she's leading the opposition."

I laughed and relief flooded through me that Kellan could joke again. Keats felt the change in mood, too, and started frolicking around the big pile. The dog didn't like getting his paws dirty there so Kellan's stress reduction strategy had a side benefit of keeping his uniform cuffs safe.

"I let Edna get under my only layer of skin today," I said. "While we waited for your team to arrive, she suggested you and I would be better apart."

"Oh, really?" he said. "It would be convenient to have Edna making decisions for me. She's got plenty of opinions."

"It all started with Vernie, who said there hadn't been a murder around these parts for a decade before I came back to town. Now the bodies are stacked up higher than this hill of manure."

Kellan rested his chin on the spade's handle. "What else?"

"Isn't that enough? Edna agreed with Vernie and basically suggested I do the honorable thing and step back from our relationship. For the sake of Clover Grove and perhaps all of hill country."

"Huh." Stepping back himself, Kellan lifted the spade and shoved it into the manure again. "That's awfully generous of her. Normally Edna doesn't care that much about our citizens. In fact, she's called them pre-zombies."

"And zombie food. And even zombie vitamins," I said. "You make a good point. When did Edna start caring less about me and more about the general public?"

"That's the question." He had fallen into a rhythm that was almost hypnotic to watch. Kellan was graceful in everything he did... unless a certain sheepdog made things difficult. "It must be a red herring. She's tossed me enough of them," he said. "In this case, you're the one she's decoying. Or perhaps both of us."

Leaning against the barn doorway, I stared up at the pinpricks of light in the sky, pondering. "Her survival class," I said. "She's doing something she doesn't want us to know about."

"Then Edna and I are in full agreement for once," he said. "I don't want to know about it either."

"Some of the students are seniors and they can't all be as fit or quick-thinking as Edna. They could get stranded up a tree or down a well without a rope."

Kellan stopped shoveling and shook his head. "I said I didn't want to know. Now I need to start planning for such eventualities, and obviously I've already got plenty to handle with your sky-high pile of bodies."

"Mine! It's not like I killed these people, Kellan."

Keats' indignation overwhelmed his repulsion to manure and he charged up the pile. The dog's last-second dodge would have destabilized a lesser man. My boyfriend just laughed and drove the spade into the muck for balance.

"I know that," he said. "But she's not wrong about the crime rate rising. There hadn't been a murder in ages before Lloyd Boyce passed in your rye field."

"The stars aligned against me," I said, sighing. "I never put much stock in astrology but maybe I should visit the lady who does readings at the farmer's market."

"Save your money and I'll tell you what's going to happen," Kellan said, coming down the manure stairs. "Your boyfriend is going to give you a stern lecture for interfering in his investigation. Especially after you told him you wouldn't." He didn't give me a chance to reply before continuing. "Normally you at least let me take a first pass before you charge in and leave pet prints and hair all over. Instead, you took the scenic tour through Vernie's house and then gallivanted over to Dorset Hills."

There was no point denying any of it. "How'd you know?"

"I had you tailed," he said. "I've got a new recruit who needs the practice. You gave him a good run for his money. Apparently you lost a pumpkin on a sharp turn and he needs a car wash."

He sounded a little bit proud of me and Keats gave a ha-ha-ha of triumph.

"I can't believe you wasted good police resources tailing me when you could have been solving the murder," I said.

"Having you tailed might well help me solve the murder. Depending on what you found at Vernie's."

"Just the dog," I said. "And a lot of art we didn't touch."

"But you have some art you transferred to your lawless buddies along with the dog. Or so I hear."

"Ah. So your new guy found us."

"Eventually, with a little help from me." Kellan came over to study me close up. "He got photos of Remi putting the art in the truck but lost them after they drove off. Cori took the back trails, which did more damage to his car than the pumpkin. I'm calling her in for questioning tomorrow."

"Prepare yourself for some glove theatrics," I said. "But you two will come to some agreement, I'm sure. She speaks so highly of you now."

He refused to be sidetracked. "My recruit got decent photos so I know at least some of the pieces you have. I already knew about Verna Rae's success in the art world."

"That was all news to me," I said. "She gave me the paintings as a donation to the rescue fundraiser before the uh, incident. I didn't know they were originals. She wanted the Mafia to have them because they gave her the dog." I smiled at him earnestly. "I just wanted to make sure Pommy landed in good hands, Kellan. That's why I went over."

"That's it?" He watched me closely, no doubt looking for my "tells." Despite my HR training, I probably had them.

I nodded. "Discovering Vernie's secret talent was an accident and that's when I realized the art in my truck was valuable. I'm assuming someone killed her to get the paintings. Apparently, they're worth thousands."

Kellan started walking back and forth in front of the barn door in a brisk, erratic pattern. Anyone else might have assumed he was agitated, but I knew it was a strategy to avoid sneak attacks by canine or feline. At Runaway Farm, a casual conversation was rarely an option for my boyfriend unless my best furry companions were locked up or exhausted. Tonight they were percolating with energy and he was right to worry.

Eventually, he paused to shrug and then shake his head. "If it sounds too easy, it *is* too easy. The killer could have taken those paintings from her house any other day when Vernie was out flogging her vegetables. She didn't have a security system and you managed to get in easily enough. Instead, they chose to do this at midday in plain view of traffic. That seems more like a crime of passion."

"Vernie was prickly and provocative," I said. "It was like she'd already graduated from Edna's program."

Kellan stared up at the sky for a second and then back down, probably remembering that distraction was a surefire route to punctured pant legs. "Still, attacking her there was a very bold move. Someone that confident—or that deranged—is worth worrying about. Did you learn anything else that might prove useful?"

I shook my head. "No, and I honestly didn't intend to get involved, Kellan. But I feel partially responsible. She trusted me with her art and now she's dead."

He started the intermittent pacing again and Keats watched, belly to the ground, waiting for his chance. "Ivy, you are not responsible for Vernie's death or anyone else's. It's just dirty luck."

"Well, I brought that dirty luck back here from Boston, apparently." I snapped my fingers at Keats to call him off, but the dog was fixated on his prey. "Even you admit there's a spike in crime."

"I never said there's a causal relationship. It's a coincidence. With the history of this region, it was bound to happen eventually. I could feel it gathering to pounce even before I took the job." He took a leap just as Keats launched and the dog missed by inches. "Ha. I'm trainable, too, Keats."

"Leave it," I told the dog. "I'm tired even if you're not."

Kellan walked over and folded me in his arms. Usually—or at least often—Keats would allow me to enjoy a hug after a tough day.

"Forget about what Edna said and figure out her end game," Kellan murmured into my hair.

"Vernie said it, too, though," I grumbled. "And then Cori agreed."

"It has nothing to do with you and your planetary alignments. Crime often goes in cycles. That's one reason I came back when I did. There was an uptick all over the region and I figured it would reach Clover Grove, too."

"I thought you came home to reconnect with me," I said, resting my head on his shoulder.

"Both things can be true at once," he said. "I didn't think they'd overlap in the way they have, I must admit."

"Vernie said it's going to get worse before it gets better. Do you think there's someone in particular pulling the strings?"

"Too random. Although it's crossed my mind. Leave the bigger picture to me, Ivy. Please?"

"You got it. The smaller picture is hard enough to wrap my head around." I sighed. "If it weren't for the concussion I could probably be more helpful."

"Unless you want to train as a police officer, I'd prefer you be *less* helpful. Stay here and stay safe."

Keats offered a cheeky mumble that Kellan answered with one of his own. I couldn't help laughing at the wordless discussion.

It was a good juncture to change the subject by telling him about our discovery at the Harlow barn that morning. I skated lightly over the details so he wouldn't get too interested. This mystery was mine to solve and I didn't want him taking that away from me, too.

"Returning those love letters sounds like a worthy project," he said. "The Harlows were a bad lot in their day, though. Be careful where you step and let me know if anything seems at all risky."

I nodded. "If it's one of the Harlows he'd be close to ninety by now. I could probably take him in a fistfight."

Kellan laughed. "But he could probably still pull a trigger."

"This is about forbidden love, not buried gold. I'm sure we'll be fine."

"I mostly skipped English classes in high school," he said. "But I seem to recall those stories never ended well. Maybe these lovers—or their current families—won't want to be found, let alone reminded of their tragic past."

"Then we'll exit stage left in a hurry," I said. "Remember, I might blunder into things, but Jilly's the soul of tact."

"You're perfect, just the way you are, aside from those daredevil moments I blame on Keats and Percy."

"Be careful," I said. "They've got energy to burn tonight."

Kellan squeezed me tighter and I let myself go limp for a second, enjoying the sensation of being supported.

"For what it's worth," he said, "I think you came to the right place at exactly the right time. I wouldn't change a thing, Ivy." Releasing me, he jumped back suddenly, leaving a chill behind. "Even if I'm constantly replacing uniforms. I have to keep one under plastic for formal ceremonies."

"Let me pay for them. It's my dog's fault."

Kellan looked down at Keats, who readied for another pounce. "Do your worst, pal. It won't stop what's going to happen."

I barely had time to wonder what was going to happen before Kellan screamed.

## CHAPTER NINE

"Was that really necessary?" I said, glancing at my passengers as I drove away from the farm early the next morning. "Percy, I'm speaking to you. And don't swish your tail at me like that. It's disrespectful."

Percy's tail swished harder, lashing Keats in the face as they jostled for the best view out the front and then the side of the truck. Normally Keats won that battle easily, but Percy was full of himself, fresh off his success in making Kellan scream. Dropping from the barn roof had been a stroke of genius on the part of the cat. I had screamed, too. Percy's mastery of his clutch and release maneuver meant there was no harm done beyond some slashes in Kellan's police jacket, and a whole lot of frayed nerves.

"I know you boys enjoy treating Kellan like a plaything, but we're a team and it's all about balance. As a result of your antics, I didn't get the quality boyfriend time I needed last night. I really wanted him to whisk me away to Clover Grove Gardens for an hour. Instead, he couldn't escape fast enough."

Keats panted a ha-ha-ha but there was a note of disappointment in it, too. He liked to be the one driving Kellan and me apart and Percy stole his thunder. The mumble that followed sounded like a reminder we had bigger issues than what Edna called canoodling.

"A bit of canoodling goes a long way to settle my nerves and keep me focused. You boys underestimate the value of romance." Keats started to protest and I held up my palm. "I know... The vet stole that capacity from you." I put my hand back on the wheel. "I wonder how Cliff Roxton is doing. I just heard he split from Beverly."

This time Keats' mumble was unmistakable: good riddance to bad garbage.

"So many people have been harsh to me since I got home but I think Beverly's the worst. Maybe seeing her hanging with Mom is what made me extra touchy yesterday with Edna. I shouldn't have to put up with trash talk from my real friends."

Percy turned from the window, green eyes wide. His tail settled into an occasional twitch and he gave me a purr-meow along the lines of "buck up, little camper." He was fond of Edna because she'd maintained the feral cat colony in Huckleberry Swamp at great effort and expense before he chose to join the mainstream at Runaway Farm. Both Edna and Jilly generally got a free pass from his mischievous exploits.

"Fine," I said. "From now on, let's just focus on the two mysteries at hand. I promised Kellan I'd stay out of his investigation. We all know that only means I'll be discreet about it. Let's give him a day or two to collect the evidence he needs before getting more hands-on." I turned off the highway and into the parking lot at Mandy's Country Store. "It won't be easy to stand down, because helping to solve Vernie's murder feels like a moral obligation." I parked in my usual spot and turned the key. "Romance is all about compromise. That's why I can't have you two stealing the moments of gold that make up for the sacrifices."

Neither pet looked in the least chastened. Their tails were high as they trotted up the stairs ahead of me. I set Percy's carrier down and he stepped inside without complaint. Clover Grove generally wasn't uptight about pets in stores, but a cat roving freely around a café might raise eyebrows. Poor Mandy—or more specifically, her grandmother, Myrtle McCain—had raised enough of those already.

She unlocked the door and let us inside. It would be another 20 minutes until the store formally opened but a cup of coffee was ready and waiting on the long counter in front of my favorite stool. When there was an incident of such magnitude as Vernie's passing, Mandy knew I'd be among her first stops. I needed breakfast pie to get the wheels turning.

"I've only got apple pie and chocolate cream today," she said. "I wasn't expecting this to happen again so soon."

By "this" she meant murder, but the word didn't come easily to her, since Myrtle was the one who'd broken Clover Grove's murder-free record and started a new trend. The fact that it happened on my property gave me a share of the notoriety I didn't deserve. Maybe that was because I was available, whereas the perpetrator was behind bars. Actually, Myrtle was living a fairly cushy life in an institution that was more like a retirement home whereas I'd become a convenient proxy for the community's concerns about safety.

"Sounds good, Mandy," I said, setting Percy's carrier on the floor and hopping aboard the stool.

"Both?" she said, grinning at me.

"You really need to ask?" I took a sip of the coffee and then released a long breath. I'd missed out on quality boyfriend time, but this visit would go far to restore my equanimity.

Keats mumbled something from below and I said, "You underestimate the value of coffee and pie, as well as romance."

"What's that about romance?" Mandy called from behind the counter. "Trouble in paradise?"

"Nope," I called back. "At least I hope not, but Percy and I did overstep yesterday."

She came back carrying a plate with two pieces of pie separated by a mound of whipped cream. In her other hand, she had a bowl of whipped cream with a spoon. After setting the plate down, her fine blonde eyebrows rose in a question and I nodded twice as a signal to add two dollops. I thought about getting her to add one to the coffee but decided to keep it strong and black to cut the richness of the pie.

Not that I considered it rich. There wasn't much I considered too rich anymore. Back in the city I used to watch my weight because my only exercise was taking the stairs at work and by the end, I'd stopped doing that. In Clover Grove I could—and did—eat whatever I wanted. In fact, when I was on a manure drive, I had to eat *more* than I wanted. It was a good problem to have.

"So, what's your going theory about Vernie Cobbler?" Mandy asked, taking the stool beside me.

I swallowed a bite of apple pie as a nod to nutrition before slicing into the chocolate. "Vernie donated some valuable paintings to the rescue fundraiser and it's possible someone tried to take them by force," I said. "But Kellan says that's too obvious. Did you know about her art?"

Mandy nodded. "Only because of running the post office. I shipped things for her and received art supplies."

"Anything suspicious lately?"

Mandy started shaking her head and then stopped. "Only that her visits had dwindled lately. I wondered if she was getting fewer commissions or losing her muse. But when I asked, she bit my head off. You know how she was."

"Yeah. She bit mine off yesterday, too. I wanted to buy too many blue pumpkins."

Mandy laughed. "And she bit mine off because I only wanted to buy orange pumpkins. The flesh from the blue ones is less stringy, she said, but I didn't want to take a chance on them for my baking."

"Vernie was another of the many eccentrics in Clover Grove," I muttered through a bite of chocolate pie. "I'm joining their ranks."

"If so, I welcome you," Mandy said. "I've been here all my life."

Mandy was a naïve and introverted child and teen, which ultimately made her prey to a manipulator like Lloyd Boyce. He'd used her to try to get his hands on the store in which we sat now, and Myrtle had punished him fatally for his presumption.

I washed down the pie with coffee and stared at Mandy over the rim of my cup. "Remi Malone wants to set you up with a nice guy she knows. Asked me to see if you're willing."

"Me? Why?" Mandy sounded horrified. "You have three single sisters."

"Maybe, maybe not," I said. "No one shares their status anymore because of Mom's dating philosophies. Anyway, that's not why. Remi just thinks this guy would be a good fit for you, and Bridget agreed. They both love matchmaking and happily ever afters."

"No," Mandy said, unequivocally. "That's not for me."

"What isn't? A happily ever after? Are you saying that option is gone forever because you made one wrong choice while you were squished under your grandmother's thumb?"

"That's exactly what I'm saying." She set down her coffee cup and twisted her thin hands together. "When romance went to my head I nearly got you killed. So I put it behind me. For good."

I jabbed my fork in her direction. "Don't underestimate the power of love, Mandy. It might be exactly what you need to take your transformation to the next level."

Since her grandmother's incarceration, Mandy had indeed metamorphosed into a confident woman, at least where her business was concerned. Her luscious baked goods had opened doors in the community that seemed permanently shut. Judging by the vehemence of the head shaking, however, her romantic confidence wasn't keeping pace.

"I can't," she said. "Not yet. Maybe not ever."

Her right hand dropped to her side and soft black ears were there to greet it. Keats mumbled something comforting to her and then something harsher to me. A decided "back off."

I smiled and then shrugged. "Keats is taking your side, so forget I asked. Remi can foist her fine catch on any sister of mine who's still on the market."

"I've never known you to matchmake before," Mandy said. Her coffee cup trembled now and I kicked myself for upsetting her.

"You're right. It's not normally my thing because it can backfire so badly." I took another mouthful of pie. "I should have told Remi no right away, but I suppose the mysterious love letters cast a spell on me."

Mandy's fine brows shot up. "What love letters?"

"The ones I'll tell you about in the strictest confidence, but only if you'll get me a refill first." I grinned as she hopped off the stool. Mandy may not be ready to date again but she was most certainly interested in romance.

Her pale blue eyes were eager when she set the cup before me. "Is it a secret admirer?"

"Oh gosh, no," I said. "Keats and Percy would expose such folly in a second. Besides, I only ever had eyes for Kellan, and that won't change as long as he's willing to embrace my ark full of crazy critters. And my even crazier family."

Keats offered something cheeky before Mandy reached for his ears again. Then he focused on infusing her with comfort and courage.

"Then, what happened?" she asked.

I glanced at the parking lot to make sure the coast was clear before pulling the tin box out of my backpack. Lifting the lid, I showed Mandy the stack of letters and the engagement ring. Then I gave her the high points of the story between the forbidden lovers. "They called each other Henny and Wren," I said. "Obviously not their real names. Jilly and I found the box in a barn on the old Harlow property yesterday."

"Why were you there?" she asked.

"A little bird told us to go. Literally. A gorgeous painted bunting led us through the swamp and then worked with Percy to send the box down from the hayloft."

It said a lot that Mandy accepted the account at face value. "Do you think the box belonged to a Harlow? I believe Myrtle mentioned at least six boys, plus a girl. Others have owned the land since."

"These belonged to one of the sons, I suspect. The letters are from a woman and it sounds like their families didn't approve of their match."

She nodded. "That was common back then. In hill country, you married for alliances, just like royalty."

"I figured as much. Do we know who the Harlow family was at war with? That might help identify the lady of letters."

Mandy shook her head. "I expect Myrtle knows more. Is it worth another visit?"

A shudder struck us both at the same time and I set down my fork. Seeing Myrtle in prison had been traumatic, especially because I'd always liked her. Her capacity to commit violent crime had made me question my instincts. Keats moved his ears back to their usual location at my side, reminding me that I could trust his.

"We won't visit your grandmother again unless the stakes are much higher than returning some love letters," I said. "There are other ways to get information. Even behind prison doors, Myrtle would find a way to sully that sweet, heartbreaking story. I was surprised that some people kept in touch with her."

"Me too. If her own granddaughter cut her out of her life, why can't everyone else?" Mandy said. "But there may be a higher stakes reason to visit. It's possible Myrtle has information on Vernie's situation, too. If you think it would help, I'm willing to go."

Mandy had clearly committed to doing all she could to aid me in my sleuthing, even if it cost her dearly.

"No. But thank you." I reached out and patted her arm. "I've barely begun to scratch the surface as far as Vernie is concerned. Kellan asked me to step back, probably because this killer was brazen enough to attack on the roadside in broad daylight. It's hard to believe anyone could be that highly motivated to kill Verna Rae Cobbler."

"Well, she did have detractors, including the usual suspects, like the Langmans." Mandy stared down into Keats' warm brown eye. "I overheard the sisters talking about a particular buffet in Vernie's dining room. They made her what they considered a very good offer for a damaged piece. Vernie refused and told them where to go."

"I saw that buffet," I said. "It was banged up pretty good, but it held her art supplies, and probably had sentimental value." Swallowing the last of the apple pie, I left a bit of chocolate to savor. "Anything else?"

"Everyone else," Mandy said. "Or at least anyone who liked vegetables. So many people who passed through here had argued at the roadside stand. It seemed like Vernie really only wanted to sell to people she liked, but she didn't really like anyone. Most people threatened to buy elsewhere but this year her produce was unrivaled."

I shoved the last mouthful of chocolate pie in my mouth and said, "Manure."

Mandy looked horrified. "What?"

"Not the pie," I said, grinning. "I donated fertilizer for Vernie's crops. Some of the homesteaders refused my manure in case it was tainted with homicide. Vernie took a chance on me."

Mandy laughed. "She took a chance on free fertilizer delivered to her yard?"

"I turned that manure into her soil myself. And thanked her for accepting it."

"And you tell me to value myself more highly?" She gave Keats a last pat and slid off the stool. A blue SUV was pulling into the parking lot.

Closing the box of love letters, I slipped it into my backpack. "Keep me posted if anything comes up, Mandy."

"Absolutely," she said. "Try to be extra careful this time, Ivy. Even Myrtle wasn't brazen enough to attack in public."

We shared another shudder and then Mandy hurried behind the counter. She came back with the usual treats for my fur boys, and I said, "Let me know if you change your mind about—"

"The blind date? I won't," she said. "I'd rather spend quality time with Myrtle."

Keats gave a pant-laugh that told her she was being silly. It was probably lost on her because she was heading toward the door to open officially for the people coming up the stairs.

I was bent over collecting Percy when the customers came in, and when an unfamiliar voice called my name, I straightened in surprise.

Standing at the counter were three of the women from Mom's posse at yesterday's fundraising meeting.

"I recognized those overalls straight away," Mercy Bellweather said. "Your mother never stops talking about them."

Mercy and I certainly didn't share much in common where style was concerned. The dress she wore today was cornflower blue with a very full skirt and a laced velvet bodice. It wouldn't have looked out of place at a medieval festival.

"Mom and I lead different lives." I offered an HR smile, although I hated squandering them in case they were in short supply. "She barely steps foot inside my barn, as you can imagine. Yet that's where I'm happiest."

"Makes sense to me," Satin Carnegie said. She had a genial smile and her voice was almost loud enough to rock the store on its foundations. "Join us for coffee, Ivy? We're meeting early to discuss—"

"Satin," Mercy interrupted. "We don't really talk about business. Leave that to Dahlia when she gets here."

Knowing Mom was on her way lit a fire under me. Still, I couldn't help asking, "What business, ladies? Barbershop secrets?"

Silkie and Satin exchanged a look and the former said, "Dressmaking. Your mom is becoming famous online for her wardrobe rehabilitation work. We're all eager to learn from the master."

Both cousins were again dressed in black casual wear and seemed unlikely candidates for learning thrift store makeovers. Something was suspicious.

Percy apparently agreed because he yowled from inside his carrier. Keats wasn't thrilled with the company either. His ears flattened and he used his blue eye on each woman in turn. I couldn't get a read on which one troubled him the most before the door opened again and Joan Snelling came in.

"Ladies, I've got to run," I said, hoisting the cat carrier. "I suggest you try Mandy's pie. Best in hill country."

"Pie at this hour?" Mercy said.

Joan's lips drew together in a disapproving pucker as well.

"It's never too early for pie in my world," I said. There was something about women like Mercy and Joan that made me as impudent as my pets.

"Is that a cat?" Mercy said. "In a café?"

I shook my head. "A rare ring-tailed raccoon. From down under."

Satin Carnegie laughed. "Mercy, she's teasing."

"Absolutely she is," Mandy said. "I have a no-raccoon policy here. From down under or over yonder. Understood, Ivy?"

I tried to push past the group, but Keats blocked the door.

Joan Snelling stared down at him. "You do know a blue eye comes with genetic mutations? That dog could go blind or deaf or worse."

Keats was puffing so I decided not to correct her. "Good thing we're in capable hands with Cliff Roxton, our vet."

"Hush now," Joan said. "Beverly Roxton just pulled in with Gwen Quinn. She won't want to walk in on a chat about her ex."

Two people were already climbing out of another car. It was the middle-aged twins I'd seen as part of Edna's prepper group yesterday. Mandy's store had become very popular as a meeting place.

I had no desire to talk to any of them, but I was trapped.

Mandy came to the rescue. "Ivy, would you mind giving me a hand in the storeroom? I can't quite reach the coffee beans."

"Ivy is very tall," Mercy said. "Dahlia is so dainty."

"I'll let you out the back," Mandy whispered as we walked toward the storeroom. "You'd need more pie to run that gauntlet."

She opened the back door and released us near the dumpster. "Thank you," I said. "And if you could get a fix on what they're up to, I'd be even more grateful. I'm quite sure this isn't about sewing and it's critical to stay a step ahead of my mother to avoid getting knocked out like a stop sign."

"Her focus has improved lately," Mandy said. "She's a new woman."

"That's what scares me most," I said, heading around the corner.

# CHAPTER TEN

H azel Bingham was standing on the porch waiting for us when we arrived at her old family manor. I felt bad even calling it old now, because under the care of Hazel's nephew, Michael, the place was getting a gradual facelift. Every time I visited it seemed a little younger, and so did Hazel. When we met nearly a year ago, she'd needed a walker. Now she came down the stairs to meet me and her hand barely grazed the railing. While she was unlikely to join Edna's warriors, she was doing very well for someone who'd accepted a one-way ticket into Sunny Acres Retirement Villa.

"You look amazing, Hazel," I said, accepting a hug. I didn't like touching the real fur collar on her jacket but sometimes you had to tolerate different tastes for a good friend. Women of her generation in Clover Grove still loved their pelts. Edna had a set of rabbit accessories that came out of mothballs for special occasions, and even Mom slipped a little reclaimed fur into her designs when she thought she could pass it off to me as fake.

"Thanks in great part to you, my friend," Hazel said, looping her arm through mine and escorting me up the stairs. "If we hadn't met, I'd still be fending off the advances of several lonely men at Sunny Acres. I'm sorry about *how* it happened, but still grateful it did."

It happened after a killer cornered me right here on her property, and I hated turning my back even now on the location where Keats unearthed the bones of Hazel's murdered brother. Some memories of our exploits faded into the mists and only reappeared in dreams. Not this one. The mental image of striding into the police department with a femur tucked under my arm and then being restrained by two officers in front of Kellan trotted out regularly in daylight, too. I'd grown used to choking it down like a bitter pill.

The memory didn't trouble Keats, and he frolicked up the stairs with Percy. They both loved visiting Hazel.

"I'm glad you're home where you belong," I said. "It's wonderful that Michael has settled here. Even if he is dating my mother."

Hazel tried to hold back a chuckle and failed. "My dear, it makes me uncomfortable too, I can't lie. Dahlia is a lovely woman but I don't understand the notion of rotational dating. In my day, a woman made a choice and stuck to it. That said, Michael doesn't seem at all upset over being one of a crowd. I suppose he appreciates having no pressure."

"I hear that's the upside," I said. "Although I try my best not to hear anything at all about Mom's conquests. She finally got the message and simmered down. If she wants to hog two rooms at the inn, she has to zip it sometimes."

"I thought your father's return might change things," Hazel said, leading me into the grandest of grand dining rooms. The antique oak table had been commissioned by her father as a wedding gift to her mother. "I suppose there's no going back after a gap that long."

"No one speaks of it, and whether that's healthy or not, I'm relieved," I said. "Judging by how often Mom's out of the house, I'd say she's redoubled her efforts to stay popular. If my dad starts dating, I'm sure I'll hear about it."

"Oh yes," Hazel said. "Calvin will have his share of admirers. There are so many single women of all ages in Clover Grove now. It's a shame that quality men often leave for jobs elsewhere, whereas the girls want to be close to family. You had better hold on tight to that handsome chief of police."

"That's the plan," I said. "Although Edna told me yesterday that Kellan and I shouldn't marry because crime's increased since my return. I'm complicating his mission in life."

Hazel gave a dismissive cluck as she sat at the head of the table. "Never mind Edna. There's always an agenda with her, isn't there?"

I took my usual seat and sighed. "That's what Kellan said. But her comments still hurt."

She pushed a teacup toward me that was so delicate I hesitated to touch it with my stained fingers. No matter how hard I scrubbed I couldn't quite banish the callouses or the dirty crescents under my nails.

"Drink," she said. "My special blend of herbal tea will settle all that pie you just ate."

My eyes widened in surprise. "How did you know?"

"You smell of fresh baked cookies and I doubt that's your cologne. Although if it were, you'd stand no risk of losing Chief Harper ever."

"You're a genius," I said. "I'll slip a cookie into my pocket on date nights to counter the farm bouquet."

Her surprisingly deep laugh filled the room and the tinkle of bangles added to the joyous sound. No one in town had nicer jewelry than Hazel. That was probably why Percy hastened into her lap whenever we visited instead of going off to explore. He enjoyed the fine fabrics of her wardrobe and the tinkle of quality baubles as she stroked his fur. Before she'd even poured the tea, he was curled up on her dress and purring.

Keats rumbled from his place between us. He liked Hazel's attention, too, but Percy tended to take top billing here.

"What is this handsome dog telling you to do?" she asked. "Interrogate me about Verna Rae Cobbler?"

"Since you mention it, yes." I finally pinched the handle on the teacup and lifted it carefully to my lips. "I assume you knew Vernie."

"Of course. I know pretty near everyone in hill country. Some better than others, and Vernie did not care to be known well. Aside from her vegetable stand, she was a recluse. I rarely saw her at events in town, and if she did show up, she flitted about like a ghost. Sometimes I thought I saw her but couldn't be quite sure."

"Was she always that way? Even as a young girl?"

Hazel stared into her teacup, musing. "Actually, no. We were chums in the schoolyard. But her father didn't believe in educating girls and pulled her out of class after ninth grade. It was a shame because she was bright, and gifted artistically, as you probably know."

I nodded. "Jilly and I saw some of her work when we went over to rescue her dog."

"Pommy? Where is she now? The rare times I saw Vernie of late, that dog was all she spoke about. I was glad they had each other."

"I surrendered Pommy to Bridget and Cori," I said. "Are you interested in taking the dog in?"

Hazel shook her head, running her hand over Percy. "My days of owning a pet are over."

"I don't see why," I said. "Michael changes everything, doesn't he? Pommy would be so lucky to live here."

"Oh, you know men, Ivy. They don't fancy small floofy dogs like that."

"I'm no expert on men," I said. "I assumed they wouldn't like being part of a dating rotation but Michael doesn't complain. He's very progressive and might take to a Pomeranian."

We both laughed and Michael poked his head in from the kitchen. "I'm not sure I like the sound of that, ladies. You're up to no good."

"We are, my dear," Hazel said. "And I think we could use more tea if you don't mind."

"None for me," I said. "We have a long drive down to Wyldwood Springs this afternoon. Janelle could use a hand setting up the store for her grand opening."

"She's a lovely girl," Hazel said. "I chatted to her at Jilly's engagement party and I admired the jewelry her friend Sinda created. I commissioned a ring, you know."

"One can never have too many," Michael said, coming in with a fresh pot of tea. "Who are you going to leave them all to, Aunt Hazel? They won't suit me."

"I'll find good homes for them," she said. "How do you feel about Pomeranians, Michael?"

"Pomeranians? Are those the tiny puffball dogs?" he asked. "If we're adopting, I'd rather have a—" He looked down and smiled. "A genius sheepdog."

"As I thought," Hazel said. "Now be off and leave us to our girl talk."

When he was gone, Keats rumbled again and I nodded. My teacup was empty and I'd barely begun digging. "Hazel, are you aware of Vernie having enemies?"

"Plenty of petty squabbles," Hazel said. "Mostly over vegetables, from what I heard. Sometimes trespassing. Vernie was nearly as quick with her rifle as Gertie Rhodes, but fortunately her property didn't come up as often on the treasure maps of the day."

I was holding a teaspoon and set it down on the saucer with a clatter. "Treasure maps? Were there really such things?"

"Still are, I'm sure. Many speculated about where Frank Swenson buried his gold. If someone thought there was a cache buried on this property, perhaps you wouldn't have been left to find... my brother." Her bangles grew quiet and Percy headbutted her hand to get it moving again. "Verna Rae didn't court major trouble. She valued her privacy too much."

"It's got to be the art," I said. "Someone must have known she was donating pieces to the rescue fundraiser yesterday. They probably didn't realize I'd taken them from Vernie already."

"That fundraiser will bring more disreputable treasure hunters into the region," Hazel said. "Like the Langman varmints. They're nothing but a pair of rats in khaki slacks."

I couldn't help laughing and Keats joined in with a happy pant. Hazel was usually restrained and refined, but Heddy and Kaye had been so relentless in their pursuit of Hazel's brother's collectibles that they wore her down. The sisters had few friends left in the community.

"You'll come out to the fundraiser, though?" I asked.

"Wouldn't miss it for the world," she said. "I don't need my cane anymore, but I'll bring it anyway to give those two a sharp rap if they get too close. I donated a couple of nice pieces. You know my weakness for rescues."

"I do. And that's why I hope you'll give more thought to taking in Pommy. She's not young, but she's sweet and well trained."

"If I took in a pet it would more likely be a cat, Ivy. No offense to our canine companion." His tail swished to assure her none was taken. "What else is on your mind?" she asked, steering me away from the subject. "I can tell it's full to the brim today."

My head did feel too full today and that sometimes brought on a migraine. "It's that obvious?" I said, rubbing my temples.

"To me, yes. You might as well clear the slate. You'll need all your patience for your trip later. It's a long drive with Dahlia."

"Mom's not coming," I said. "Thank goodness."

"No? Michael said she was." Hazel gave an uncharacteristic smirk. "Perhaps it was a little white lie you tell the gentlemen in your stable of admirers."

I groaned. "Oh no. Mom must have cornered Jilly this morning and worked her over with mother-of-the-groom guilt. And if Jilly's willing to expose Janelle to my mom full-on, I guess it's her choice." Rummaging around in my backpack I found the tin box and set it on the gleaming table. "Before I go, there's something I wanted to show you."

Hazel leaned over, causing Percy to leave with a mew of disgust. If the attention wasn't all on him, he wasn't all in.

Sifting gently through the letters and then flipping open the ring box, Hazel's eyes widened. "It looks like a love story gone wrong, Ivy."

"Very much so. I didn't want to read them all, but I had to look for clues if I wanted to put them in the right hands. I didn't find much, though, as the pair were extremely discreet. She called him Henny and signed off as Wren."

"I'm sure someone will treasure them, and the ring is lovely, too." She held up the little box and appraised the ring with a practiced eye. "A full carat. Unusual in a farming town where big stones get in the way of practical things. The gentleman had money."

"There's no engraving, unfortunately. Nothing to indicate where the ring was purchased."

"We never had a proper jeweler in town. If you wanted a nice piece like this, normally it meant a trip to the city." She set the ring back in the tin box. "Where did you find all this?"

"In a broken-down barn on the old Harlow property." Percy jumped onto the table and strutted over to the tin box. "Percy knocked it out of the rafters where it had likely been hidden for decades. I thought you might know more about the family, so that I could track down the proper owner of the letters." I let the cat rub his head against the box and brag with a loud purr. "Henny must have been a gentleman. He wanted very much to keep his word to Wren despite his family's objections."

"And the lady declined?" Hazel closed the ring box with a frown. "How heartbreaking."

"It sounded like he'd begged her to reconsider—offered to run away with her, in fact. But she didn't want that for him."

"It's very sad, but not that unusual," Hazel said. "Marriages were rarely for love at that time. Families made strategic decisions that would strengthen connections in the community. For good or ill."

"Like royal marriages, Mandy said."

"Exactly." She sat back and Percy returned to her lap. "My family stayed out of the politics, so I was fortunate not to be played like a pawn in the hill country marital chess game. On the other hand, no young man ever seemed good enough for my father. He preferred I be unmarried than married poorly." Her sigh fluttered the old letters in the box. "I was relieved, yet disappointed too. Staying home to look after my parents and brother wasn't my dream." She stroked Percy under his chin. "I shouldn't complain, as I've done all right. Perhaps this young lady did, too, eventually. Her heart may have healed."

"Or her family may have dealt her into a different game," I said. "They may not have known about this young man."

"It was harder to sneak around then," Hazel said. "Still, we managed occasionally. And if the young man in question was one of the six Harlow boys, he probably had both means and opportunity to steal some time with his lady love. The question is, which of the six was it?"

"And who was the lady? I see nothing at all here to give either one away."

Hazel read a few lines on the top letter and then glanced away. Like me, she probably felt like a voyeur. "The woman wrote very well, so she was educated. And she obviously had a good heart to give the man up for the sake of his family. It's entirely possible both have passed away by now, Ivy."

"Or maybe they're both over in Sunny Acres right now. Together at last."

Hazel laughed. "Perhaps, but I heard most of the 'how-we-met' stories and there were no tales of forbidden love."

"Tell me more about the Harlow boys," I said. "Did you know them?"

Her smile turned grim. "Not well. My parents considered their family beneath us. All the Harlow men—father and sons—were involved in rumrunning and the usual seedy underworld antics of the Swensen and Milloy crews. Honestly, I'd be surprised to learn any of the boys was as honorable and romantic as this Henny. They were a wild bunch, though quite handsome." She put the ring back in the tin box and closed the lid. "You may be barking up the wrong tree, Ivy, but it's worth asking around."

I slipped the box back into my bag. "Any suggestions about where to start?"

"Yes," Hazel said. "You won't like it, but it is on your route today."

I pondered her comment and then rubbed my head again. I knew exactly what Hazel meant, and visiting with my mother would be a nightmare.

"I can't," I said. "I really can't. If it was about helping with Vernie's murder investigation, maybe. But just to track down old lovers… no."

Hazel laughed till her jewels tinkled. "Wasn't it Shakespeare who said, 'the course of true love never did run smooth'? Besides, I wouldn't be surprised if you learned something new about Vernie, too."

I sank down in my chair. "But at what price?"

"Less than you've paid before," she said. "Now have some more tea."

# CHAPTER ELEVEN

"I do love a road trip," Mom said, adjusting the passenger seat backward until it hit Jilly in the knees. "Thanks so much for inviting me, darling."

"I didn't, actually," I said.

"Oh, I know that, darling." Mom gave the tinkling laugh that got under my skin instantly. "I meant my *other* darling. Jillian is the best of my daughters. Undoubtedly the smartest and kindest, and quite possibly the prettiest."

"Dahlia, don't say that," Jilly said, stroking Percy with one hand and brushing fur off her blue coat with the other. "Ivy is brilliant and beautiful. The other girls, too."

"You do realize you're insulting yourself, Mom?" I said. "Since all five Galloway Girls are knockoffs of the original Dahlia?"

"I suppose all my children are attractive and bright. If I had to choose one—"

"And you don't," Jilly interrupted.

"We all know you'd pick Asher," I said. "Even though I'm putting a roof over your head. Two, in fact, since you've kept the apartment in town and I chip in there as well. Have you thought about letting it go and chipping in on my mortgage?"

"I have not. There are so many other pressing things to think about."

She fluttered red fingernails at me and then shoved her elbow into the gap between the seats. Keats was making his second attempt to force his way into the front to ride in her lap. She was determined to arrive in Wyldwood Springs looking like a million bucks, probably because Janelle and her friend Sinda dressed well. Keats was equally stubborn and I'd put my money on the dog for the win.

Keats gave a cheery ha-ha-ha from the back seat. He liked Mom and relished a challenge. It would make the drive more interesting. There was no way, however, that he'd let Mr. Bixby, Janelle's slightly snotty dachshund, see him arrive in town in the back seat like a regular dog. There was a subtle rivalry between the two and while Bixby seemed to have an edge in some respects, Keats had size, speed and agility on his side. If all else failed, he'd use those to overthrow Mom.

I had insisted Jilly ride shotgun—it was her rightful place as my chief human sidekick—but she had insisted even more strongly on relinquishing the seat to Mom. That annoyed me more than I cared to admit, and not because Mom gloried in it. The fact that Jilly let traditional deference for her mother-in-law rule here suggested she might elsewhere in her marriage, too. Asher was more old-fashioned in many ways than Kellan, which was odd, given that we had no father figure for most of our upbringing. No matter how derelict Mom had been in her duty, she had managed to raise us alone, on her own slim dime. As far as I knew, she'd only accepted occasional help from her parents, and mainly for Christmas and big-ticket items. Our father's checks had piled up in a dresser drawer, uncashed. After he came back, she'd sent me to that dresser repeatedly, perhaps to make sure I saw that stack of sacrifices she'd made. I saw the stack pride made—and the unknowing sacrifices her kids had made. Especially Daisy, our true maternal figure. Come to think of it, Daisy's own kids had occasionally gone without as she funneled money from her household into ours after marrying young. I hadn't given her husband enough credit for putting up with that.

"Can you please let this day be about Jilly and her family?" I said, turning to Mom. "This store is important to Janelle. It will help her integrate into Wyldwood Springs, which isn't as welcoming as Clover Grove."

"Welcoming?" Mom snorted. "I'm still waiting for my welcome and it's been decades since I came back."

"Me too," I admitted. "Hardly a day passes that someone doesn't remind me I brought murder to our sweet town."

Mom smoothed her red wool coat with impatient swipes that tangled her fingers in the chain of the old gold locket she usually wore tucked inside her showy clothes. "That's ridiculous and insulting, considering what you've done for this community," she said. "Our family has given so much."

I couldn't help smirking. Mom's main claim to fame in the charity department was giving generously to the rumor mill and entertainment of the town.

She saw my smirk and frowned. "I'm glad you're staying out of this nasty business with Verna Rae Cobbler. You can't get involved in every case just because you had manure in the game."

"Those blue pumpkins were something else," I said. "I feel invested."

Jilly reached through the seats and patted my shoulder. "The police have things well in hand. We're free to enjoy our visits today."

"Visits plural?" Mom asked. "Why are we leaving the highway here, Ivy? What is in Fleetborough?"

"A bathroom," I said. "I drank way too much tea at Hazel's earlier."

"Pick another town," Mom said. "Fleetborough is a dump."

"Sterling doesn't think so," I said. "Or maybe he does."

"Sterling Fable? I don't care to run into him, Ivy. Let that be clear."

"Understood," I said. "You can wait in the car while Jilly and I go in to say hi."

"Oh no. You can't." She sounded like a plaintive child. There was obviously no love lost between the two.

"Why not? He's my great-uncle on Calvin's side, and a girl can never have too much family. Especially secret family. Are there more relatives I don't know about, Mom?"

She directed a glare at the side of my head. Others may have found it chilling but my brain worked better on the cool setting.

"I wouldn't have let Jilly persuade me to come along if I'd known Sterling was on the agenda."

"Don't blame your darlingist darling," I said. "Jilly didn't know till just before we left. Hazel Bingham suggested Sterling might have some information we need."

"About Vernie?" Mom asked. "Because this visit had better be about murder to justify what it's doing to my nerves." She turned her glare through the seats. "Jillian, did you bring any tranquilizers? A flask?"

Jilly laughed and Keats panted happily, too. "Dahlia, you'll want to stay alert for this, I'm sure. It's a great way to clear the slate so that you can dance with Sterling at my wedding. He told us last time he has some moves, and you're the best dancer in Clover Grove."

"Flattery will get you nowhere." Mom's voice had become a raspy squeak. "I cannot believe you'd betray me like this, Jilly. Ivy, yes, but not you. Please do not invite that man to the wedding."

"It's already been done by my betrothed," Jilly said. "You know how Asher is about family. The more the merrier."

Keats used the hubbub to press his advantage and Mom gave him a firmer swat than I deemed acceptable. I took my hand off the gearshift and caught hers. "Do *not* take out your frustrations on my dog. Or my cat for that matter. When you invite yourself along on a road trip, you need to roll with the punches, not throw them."

She subsided into a silent sulk and stayed that way until we pulled into Sterling's driveway. When my great-uncle came out on the porch with his blue-and-black checkered bathrobe flapping, Mom made a choking sound, perhaps noticing the rifle dangling from his right hand as he leaned on a cane with his left.

"I will stay in the truck," she said.

"Suit yourself, Mom. If you can't play nice, that's for the best."

Keats and Percy beat Mom to the stairs, but not by much. As I had expected, she couldn't pass up an opportunity to prove herself in front of a man who dismissed her as silly years ago, no doubt to her very face.

"Did it occur to you to call first? I do have a phone," Sterling said, bending over the pets to conceal his smile. Keats' white-tipped tail whipped a warm greeting.

"Traitor," Mom muttered. "That dog has no taste."

"Well, you're at the top of his favorites, Mom. I don't always understand his choices myself."

Ignoring that, she marched up the stairs, shoulders straight and chin up. "Good day, Sterling. You're looking... well."

The strategic pause gave her time to give him the once-over. Thank goodness he wore striped pajamas beneath his robe. I wouldn't put it past him to try to shock visitors away.

"I'd say the same if it weren't for all the finery," he said. "Someone's trying too hard."

I wagged my finger at him. "Sterling, you admired Hazel Bingham and she puts effort into her appearance. I just saw her this morning and she looked impeccable."

He grunted. "Hazel has taste. I doubt she splashes red around like it's a crime scene."

Mom was far from chastened. Quite the contrary, since conflict was her comfort zone. "Red is my signature color, Sterling. And my designs are becoming quite well known."

That was more or less true. Mom's designs were discussed often around Clover Grove, although the reviews weren't always complimentary. She had the talent and technique, but her passion for the theatrical—feathers, sequins and satin, for starters—was never going to be a hit in a community of homesteaders. Still, I gave her credit for sticking it out. Or just sticking out. Some of us preferred to blend in, if not disappear entirely.

The old man shook his head and gestured with his rifle toward the front door. "Well, take that design inside, where my neighbors can't be affronted." As she strutted past him, he asked, "Is that a boa?"

Her voice drifted back. "Close enough."

His cane came across the doorway to bar Jilly and me from entering. "Ivy, I don't mind you dropping by with Toots, but if I'd never seen Dahlia again—"

"I can hear you, Sterling," she called. There was a little shriek and then, "That recliner! It's still alive? Take it out back and shoot it."

Shaking his head, he let me lift the cane and walk inside. "Somewhere, someone's saying the same about you, Dahlia."

"And twice over for you, sir," she said.

They faced each other in the front hall and I worried for a second that it might come to blows. Keats got to work tying the four of us together in an elaborate sheepdog love knot, but before he could finish, Sterling let out a loud guffaw. Mom laughed, too, and the tension evaporated just like that.

"I have nothing but disdain for you," Sterling said.

"And I disgust for you," Dahlia said. "Now, sit down in that recliner before you keel over."

"From your mighty wind," he said. "Never did a woman talk more and say less."

"Never did a man bore more and charm less," she countered.

Sterling handed her the rifle and started across the living room. "Just shoot me now. I always wanted to go in this chair anyway."

"If you insist," she said. "I'm a good shot, old man."

He stumped across the shag carpet and fired back, "More lies, Dahlia."

"Total truth," she said. "One of my gentlemen friends takes me to a firing range every week."

"You don't say." He dropped into the recliner and worked the lever until the chair creaked back. "And please *don't* say. I already know about your so-called stable."

"Really?" Mom lost interest in the rifle and handed it to Jilly, who handed it to me. I stepped into the kitchen and set it carefully on the table, hoping it wasn't loaded. "Did Calvin tell you?"

Sterling shook his head. "He's got bigger things on his mind than your dating life."

"I most certainly hope so." Mom perched on the loveseat directly opposite Sterling. "But we're not here to talk about Calvin, are we, Ivy? I'm sure there's a good reason to torment your mother like this."

Sterling laughed again and it sounded sincere. Despite their protests, it seemed that they were enjoying themselves immensely.

Jilly and I sat on the couch, just as we had on our first visit, and Percy disappeared on his rounds. Keats took a position beside Mom and stared at Sterling, who stared back. The dog's intense blue gaze didn't unnerve the old man one bit.

"Didn't anyone teach you staring is rude?" Sterling asked.

"His staring is quite helpful sometimes," I said. "Like when there's a murderer on the loose."

"Like always in Clover Grove," Sterling said. "I hear we lost Verna Rae Cobbler this week. She was a nice girl, but turned crusty eventually, as most do." He looked pointedly at Mom. "There's a reason I stayed single."

"Just one?" Mom asked. "I would imagine many turned down that recliner."

They shared another chuckle over their zingers and Mom went up in my estimation considerably. If Sterling had once dismissed her as a flibbertigibbet, he didn't now. Perhaps that was just a convenient box he put her in when my father left us. Sterling hadn't done a thing to help, and he was probably sitting on some money here.

"So you knew Verna Rae," I said. "Perhaps you have an idea of who wanted her dead."

"If you live long enough someone always wants you dead. Right, Dahlia?"

"Not in my case, Sterling. At least, not yet."

"Can you really be so sure?" he asked.

Mom stared him down and finally shook her head. "I'm sure it's crossed people's minds. Starting with my kids."

"Dahlia! That's a terrible thing to say." Jilly sounded horrified. "Enough of your witty repartee, you two. We can't stay long today."

"Mom, could you make us a cup of tea?" I asked. "I mean, if it's okay with Sterling."

"Make mine a beer, Dolly," he said. "And have one yourself. You were always wound a little tight."

Never in my memory had anyone called my mother "Dolly," but today she got up and went into the kitchen. "I know when I'm not wanted," she said.

"Meaning she's glad to go snoop around my house," Sterling said.

"And plant some poison," Mom called back. "What goes best with beer?"

"Solitude," he said. "Make mine a triple."

She laughed again and ran the water in the kitchen.

"You actually *like* my mother," I said, giving Sterling an accusing stare. "After calling her—"

"Giddy? Or was it gaddy? Either way, she's harmless enough. Except for the unfortunate men she's dating. There's a Venus flytrap quality to your mother, Ivy. None of you girls inherited it."

"How would you know? I'm the only one you've met."

He raised bushy white eyebrows. "Really? Seems like there's a constant parade in and out of here, with and without Asher. Mind you, all you girls look the same so maybe I'm confused."

My mouth dropped open and stayed that way. Would my family never cease to shock me?

"There's a flytrap if ever I've seen one," he said. "Now speak quickly while the kettle's boiling and your mother's going through my cupboards. What is it you really want to know?"

"The Harlow boys," I blurted. "Did you know them?"

He nodded. "Sure. Gangsters to the core. Their father was a close associate of Frank Swenson, and he groomed his eldest boys to follow in his footsteps. They mellowed a bit as you went down the line but I still wouldn't turn my back on any of them. You crossed one, you crossed them all. I learned early to watch my step. Others weren't so lucky."

"Where are they now?" I asked. "I haven't heard of any Harlows in the community."

Sterling turned to stare out the window to the back yard. His gardens were ablaze with fireweed, asters, zinnias and, oddly enough, dahlias. He clearly knew what to plant when and his talent for layout rivaled that of the Clover Grove Garden Club. I admired that skill, especially in a man known for brandishing a rifle at visitors.

"Three of them died too young. One fell down a mineshaft over in Hog's Hollow. The second ran over a cliff with a load of hooch. And the third drowned in Capshaw Lake. Barely enough water in that puddle to take a drink, but there you go."

Jilly reached over and squeezed my hand, but Keats' eyes never left Sterling. "Foul play? In all three cases?"

He shrugged. "Unproven. But no one reached eighty in those days, Ivy. Especially not men. That's why I moved down here where life expectancy was a little higher. I'm not sure what happened to the other Harlows. They were chased out by Frank Swenson's successor, who was a horrible man. Strangely enough the vacuum he left was worse. Everyone and his dog started vying for leadership."

Sterling dragged his eyes from the yard and smiled at Keats. "No offense, my tuxedoed friend."

Keats got to his feet and went into a point at the window.

Sterling turned again. "Why, there's Arty again. Prettiest bird I ever saw. Showed up this morning at my feeder."

A little chill went up my back because Keats—and now Percy—started breathing little circles of steam on the window as they watched a painted bunting outside. The bird was indeed sitting on the feeder, but he wasn't eating. He was staring at me.

At least, that's how it felt.

"It's a painted bunting," I said. "More common in the south, although I've seen one up at the farm recently."

Sterling gave me a strange look. "Is that right?"

"With the environment going topsy-turvy, I'm sure many species are changing their patterns," I said. His thin lips pursed, and his eyes fixed on me, just as it seemed the bunting's had. I decided to press on. "Sterling, can you remember the names of the surviving Harlows? Maybe I can track them down."

"Why so curious about the Harlows?" he asked. "Any survivors would be too old to take out Vernie Cobbler through brute force. You're a smart girl, Ivy, but you're on the wrong trail this time."

Jilly slid forward on the sofa. "This isn't about Vernie," she said. "We found some old love letters in the Harlow barn and want to return them to their rightful owner."

Now Sterling's head tilted. "You were poking around in a decrepit barn for kicks? How did that happen?"

"We followed a credible lead," I said, mirroring his head tilt. "Mysteries aren't always about murder, you know."

"Well, the Harlows weren't the type of men to write love letters. If they could write at all. Every last one of them dropped out of school. Or got dragged out by their dad to join the family business."

"Well, judging by the age of these letters, it seems like one

Harlow boy had his heart broken by a local lady," I said. "She sent his ring back because their families disapproved."

"Maybe it was the one who drowned in Capshaw Lake," Sterling said. "The weak didn't last in that era. But I suppose if any of the boys are still around, they'd thank you for the ring and gamble it away in a retirement villa."

"That would be sad," I said. "Because it meant a lot to two young lovers once. But it won't stop me from trying to do the right thing."

Sterling turned to stare at the bunting, now perched on the railing of the deck. "You got that from *my* mother. She tried to do the right thing and it got her killed."

"Times are different," I said. "Just look at the bird who shouldn't be here."

"Times aren't as different as you and your boyfriend hope," he said. "There are rumblings of new trouble, you know."

"Sterling." Mom stood in the kitchen doorway holding a tray of teacups. "Don't say such things. You'll scare the girls."

"Dolly, I kicked in for your kids' upbringing and I'll say what's necessary to keep them alive."

Mom didn't blush easily, but her cheeks rivaled the red of her coat. "Hush, old man."

Keats came over and my fingers reached for his soft ears. "Kicked in? That's the first I'm hearing of it, Sterling."

He shrugged his checkered shoulders. "Now that you have, maybe you can start adding 'uncle' to my name. I'd have a bigger garden if I hadn't been financing a half dozen hungry Galloways."

"You're rather overstating the case," Mom said. "And if I'd realized you were behind those town council checks that kept arriving back then I wouldn't have cashed them. How exactly did you pull that off?"

"People in high places," he said, grinning. "Everyone had a price in those days."

I pondered for a moment. "I always wondered how Mom

managed to feed and clothe six kids on those minimum wage jobs she kept losing. Sounds like it took an unseen army. Thank you, Sterling. *Uncle* Sterling."

"You'll come to the wedding, I hope?" Jilly asked.

"Jillian, he doesn't leave the house anymore," Mom said. "I bet he doesn't even own a suit."

"Sure do, Dolly. Your son took me out to get measured right after he locked down Toots. I've been in touch with Gertie Rhodes about security. Wouldn't step foot in that town without a detail."

Keats mumbled something and pointed again at the window. Picasso flew at the glass, seemingly pecking at his reflection. The bird was too smart for that, I knew.

Getting to my feet, I said, "We need to get going. But if you think of anything more that could help in Verna Rae's case, I'd love to hear it."

"Don't you think I'd have told Asher when he called yesterday?" Sterling said.

Walking over to the window, I put my hand to the glass and the bird fluttered on the other side. I could feel the whirring energy of his wingbeats. "No. I think you'd tell me, because Asher is a cop and you don't trust cops."

There was a moment's pause from the recliner, and then, "She's smarter than you, Dolly. And Calvin, too."

Mom laughed. "Too smart for her own good. So you'd best tell her what she needs to know, or she'll get in more trouble finding out the hard way. There's a pattern, you see."

"Fine," he said. "Leave that bird in peace, Ivy. I prefer seeing him calm and serene, not all stirred up by your voodoo energy."

I turned and scowled at him. Voodoo was totally the wrong word for the bond I had with animals. It was just a profound connection that improved after rescuing Keats. And getting my brain banged up. "So you do have some intel?"

His checkered shoulders shrugged. "Head over to Sunny Acres

and try Martha Kincaid," he said. "She might be able to steer you somewhere interesting."

"Martha? Okay. I'm always glad to have an excuse to visit her."

The bird flew back to the feeder and Keats shot me a look with his blue eye. I suspected we'd gotten what we came for, and far more.

"Be careful, though," Sterling said. "Martha doesn't know what she knows. So you'll have to draw it out of her with your voodoo powers."

Mom shook her finger at him. "You mean her excellent HR skills. I'm on the receiving end of her interrogations all the time."

"You're an easy mark, Dolly," he said. "You've always shown your hand easily."

Mom got up and smoothed her skirt with a Cheshire cat smile. "*You* don't know what you know, Sterling. And I like it that way." She sauntered the few steps to his side. "I hope you get your wish about that chair. It's the perfect final resting place."

"Not before the wedding, Dolly," he said. "Can I get the first dance?"

"You bet," she said. "I owe you that much."

"And more," he said, offering his cheek.

Mom leaned down and kissed it, while Jilly and I stared at each other. Of all the miracles we'd witnessed, that ranked quite high.

# CHAPTER TWELVE

We never made it to Wyldwood Springs. After leaving Sterling's house, Keats became uneasy and restless, and Jilly made the call to postpone our visit. Mom's protests crashed against unyielding black-and-white fur and eventually dissolved. If the dog suggested we were needed at home, that's where my truck was going and Janelle completely understood when we called.

As much as I liked Jilly's family, I was always uneasy being away from the farm. It didn't matter how many reliable people, not to mention security cameras, I had watching over the place. Clippers had nearly been stolen from the pasture in broad daylight under the noses of Cori and Edna. This time, Cori was away on a rescue mission and Edna was "booked solid." So we drove home and Mom was the only one who seemed sorry about it.

"What does 'booked solid' even mean?" I asked the boys that evening, as we drove over to Sunny Acres. "Edna used to surveil us day and night from the comfort of her own living room. It was her favorite hobby, and became her mission in life. Now she's too busy to keep an eye out for us? I feel... well, abandoned, I guess."

Keats mumbled something noncommittal that suggested he wasn't worried about it. No matter how many times Edna had helped us out of a nasty situation, he was confident we could manage alone.

"I suppose," I said. "But it feels like the challenges are getting bigger and I like having a team with diverse skills. Maybe I'm just tired."

He turned to flash me a cool blue eye that suggested sheepdogs don't get tired, whether in canine or human form. We couldn't afford to let our guard down and depend on others. Looking outside of our core unit of three left us weak. We might even lose Jilly if Asher prevailed and locked her up safely in the kitchen.

Now Keats favored me with his warm brown eye. Jilly was a different story. She'd helped rescue him from his deadbeat former owner. She qualified as part of our true pack. Anyone else, I suspected, was optional in his view.

He murmured something soothing. It had a "let's cross that bridge when we come to it" ring to it. Then he added something in a brisker tone. A "let's focus on what we *can* control."

"Right," I said. "Maybe we can make a difference today. Kill two birds with one stone."

He panted a laugh and I realized how inappropriate that expression had become now that Picasso was guest starring on our team. There had been no sign of him today. If he had been the painted bunting in Uncle Sterling's back yard, it was a long flight back from Fleetborough. Or perhaps the bird felt I had the information needed to take the next step toward finding the owner of the love letters.

Martha Kincaid was waiting in the music room for me when I arrived. She was dressed nearly as nicely as Hazel Bingham, though decidedly lighter on jewels. Her frizzy white hair had grown considerably since I met her during our visits with the Christmas choir and was now at that awkward stage of needing a dozen pins to anchor it. In a few months, it would be long enough for a bushy twist.

"You looked tired, my friend," she said, taking both my hands as I joined her.

"It's a chronic condition," I said. "Despite Keats' reminder earlier that we both have a sheepdog get-it-done mentality, I do feel a bit worn down lately."

Martha nodded and then patted the seat beside her. "Perhaps it's the sheer volume of murders since you got home, Ivy. You've had a big role in resolving them. It must take a terrible emotional toll."

"Sometimes," I said. "But spending time with my animals revives me."

"Thank goodness for nature," she said. "I make sure to take a nice walk in the courtyard when the weather is fine."

I wished she had family who could liberate her from Sunny Acres. It wasn't a horrible place by any means. By all accounts the food was good, the staff caring, and the entertainment higher caliber than our Christmas choir. But it wasn't like being at home. Some needed the assistance Sunny Acres offered far more than Martha, but her family was flung far afield and she had been lonely at home. In my view, what she had needed was a network of appropriate community support. A system that included pets. Clover Grove should have that capacity.

Keats mumbled his agreement and Martha looked from one of us to the other. "What's wrong?"

"Nothing," I said. "I'd like to get over here more often. That's all."

"You come plenty, and take me to visit the farm, which I love. The wedding is coming up soon." She squeezed my arm. "Ivy, I have a good life. A comfortable life, that brings occasional surprises. Today, for example, I saw the most glorious bird at our courtyard feeder. It had a blue head, a red chest and green and yellow wings."

"Ah," I said. "That's a painted bunting. I saw my first at Imogen Pigeon's before she passed, but one's been hanging around the farm, too. They don't belong up here in hill country."

"How curious," Martha said. "It almost felt like a messenger, Ivy.

I hope it doesn't mean my time is nigh because I'm not quite ready to go."

"I doubt it's that kind of message," I said. "Although I do agree the bird might have something to tell us."

"About Verna Rae?" Martha asked. A cool breeze blew through the room and loosened some of her curls. "She was certainly a colorful character. Pulled a gun on me once when I picked up a pumpkin from her cart without express permission."

I laughed. "She was possessive of her gourds. I also learned the hard way. But I can't believe that would lead to someone killing her."

Martha shook her head and the curls bobbed. "I expect that had more to do with her estate. Vernie was sitting on a fortune, I believe."

"Because of her art, you mean?"

"Perhaps that, too. But I meant the property. Her place never made it onto the maps but some thought there was treasure there. Her father had criminal ties dating back to the Milloys and Swensons, and her brother died young in a supposed bear mauling."

"A bear mauling!"

"Exactly," Martha said. "There have been no confirmed reports of bears here in my lifetime. Or my parents', apparently. It was very strange."

"If Vernie suspected treasure, would she be selling vegetables to survive?" I asked. Keats muttered something and I added, "Scratch that. We already know she earned plenty from her art and chose to live a very humble life. People have their reasons."

"I'm not sure she ever recovered from losing her brother to violence. After that, she nearly faded from view. Yet pity galled her and she became bitter." Martha glanced around the music room again. "There are worse things than being too comfortable. I'm not sure Vernie knew what safety felt like."

"Do you think someone was after her property?" I asked. "For the treasure? She said she had no one to leave her estate to, and wanted to donate her things to pet rescue."

"I never heard her mention relatives. But she had seemed stressed lately. Twice a month she visited Sunny Acres to lead art classes, and she went from cranky to miserable and gaunt." She pulled out a handkerchief and twisted it. Percy noticed the gesture from the windowsill and came over to offer his signature marmalade fur therapy. "You will tell all this to Chief Harper?" Martha added. "It would be some time before he thought to query us here, I imagine."

"Not as long as you think." I smiled as she tucked the handkerchief away and ran her fingers over Percy instead. "Kellan is very much aware of the wealth of knowledge within these walls, and our senior community. We both are, and we worry that history will be lost. What we really need around Clover Grove is a documentarian."

"I wouldn't wish that on my worst enemy," Martha said. "Lately, I've had a vague sense of foreboding. Like in the days of my childhood. My father never left home without a gun, and each goodbye felt like it might be our last. Perhaps when Vinnie Swenson died last spring it left a vacuum for other criminal factions."

Keats' blue eye landed on me but I looked away. Martha was unnerved enough without adding the eerie sheepdog prescience to it.

"We'll leave that to Kellan," I said. "He's trained to handle big picture crime. A strategist. I just step in for one-offs where I can help." I dropped my hand to Keats' ears and said, "We actually came about another matter, Martha, believe it or not. Something more romantic, though sad in a different way."

I filled her in on our discovery of the love letters and all that had happened since.

"And Sterling thought I could help?" Her brow furrowed. "I didn't know the Harlow boys well at all, Ivy. My father made sure of that. I must admit the younger two had charisma—Palmer and Lewis —and I was happy they got away when they did."

"Got away? I heard they were up to their necks in family funny business."

She took a deep breath and her eyes glazed as she thought back. "That's what their father wanted, no question about that. But from what I heard, the youngest pair bungled an important heist and put themselves in the crosshairs of old Frank. Accidentally on purpose, perhaps. Or so I always thought. Their father had no choice but to let them run far and fast. I never saw either boy again. I felt for their poor mother. Her daughter married young and moved away, leaving only Dutton behind, and he grew into his father's shoes."

"So many tragedies in our collective past," I said.

Her fingers ran faster over Percy. "By the time I came of age, there were few young men to choose from, I'm afraid. I was lucky to land my Sebastian. He got passed over by the criminal faction because he was short, slight and seemingly meek. That worked very much in our favor and we had a wonderful life together."

My own fingers raked Keats' back. "I had no idea about any of this growing up. It makes me feel a little sick."

She nodded. "It's like boiling a frog, dear. I got into the pot when the water was tepid and it heated up so slowly I barely noticed. Meanwhile, you jumped right in and got scalded."

"Poor frogs," I said, getting up. "You've given me two good leads, Martha. Maybe one of the Harlow boys who escaped in such a hurry left his heart behind in letters. Lewis or Palmer."

"I wish I had more information," she said. "But if anyone can find the right man, it's you."

"Or Picasso," I said. "That's what I named the bird. He seems to be representing the young lovers."

Martha put her hand over her heart. "I'm never too old to appreciate a love story. I hope this one is resolved." She caught my arm with her free hand. "And I do hope your handsome police officer makes you as happy as my Sebastian did me."

I nodded. "There couldn't be a finer prince to turn this frog into a princess, Martha."

Her laughter sent me across the room with a smile in my heart.

"Ivy," she called, and I turned at the door. "Beware of bears."

"There hasn't been a bear in these parts in over eighty years," I called. "Or so you just told me."

She smiled but there was a sadness about it. "Perhaps, but that doesn't mean a nice farmer like you can't get mauled."

# CHAPTER THIRTEEN

I spent the next morning picking up antiques and collectibles for the fundraiser and delivering them to the storage unit the Mafia had rented because of its remote location and high-end security. It was my first trip alone. Remi had asked me to bring backup, but with Jilly in town shopping, and Edna offline, I decided to take my chances. It was good to have something useful to do while pondering our scanty leads. I thought Keats might complain about wasting time but he was curious about the new properties we visited.

No one pulled a gun on us, so I considered it a win.

The storage unit had originally been a cheese factory and still smelled of sour milk a decade after the owner moved to a bigger location down the range. After that, a distributor of small farming equipment bought the property and kitted it up with so much technology I couldn't help but wonder if the business was a cover for something more nefarious.

"I'm becoming so jaded," I said, as we made our last call at the Pefferlaws' home. "I was already jaded as an HR rep, but I came to Clover Grove with high hopes for humanity, and that's gradually being eroded."

Keats' mumble suggested our town was no better nor worse than anywhere else. I had my doubts.

Finch Pefferlaw was a reclusive homesteader who rarely mixed in Clover Grove society. That's why he'd asked me to take the antique birdcage off his hands after it generated too much interest in the community. The Langmans had seen a photo of it online and ultimately stole it, probably leaving Finch worried about the safety of his family.

That would explain the huge brindle mastiff out front that hadn't been there on my last visit. The deep-throated barking kept me in my truck—and I didn't scare easily where animals were concerned. I worried less for myself than Keats and Percy. Regardless, the dog that came down and stood against my door showing me its tonsils was doing exactly what I needed: ringing a canine doorbell.

Finch appeared on the porch before long, and while he didn't smile, his scowl registered about three on the hostility scale, when it used to be off the charts. It was almost neighborly.

"What do you want, Ivy?" he asked, when I rolled down the window.

Okay, so his definition of neighborly differed from mine, but he was armed only with a mastiff and not a gun. "It's a friendly call," I said. "Can we get out of the truck?"

"Only if you want to leave alone. Jaws has the highest prey drive I've ever known in a mastiff." His scowl turned into a toothy grimace. "Choice is yours."

"We'll stay inside," I said. "I only came to confirm you're really okay with giving away that old birdcage. It's a family heirloom."

"Family." His grimace deepened. "If I wanted to deal with mine we wouldn't live out here."

I couldn't help but smile. "I hear you, although as soon as I moved to Runaway Farm mine came out of the woodwork."

Finch stared at Keats, who was standing on my lap and telling the mastiff where to go. I knew his attitude would fade if we got out. Keats was bold but not stupid. The brindle brute could shake my pets like stuffed toys and quickly rid them of their squeakers.

"I've heard," Finch said. "I can hook you up with a real dog. Get a mastiff and watch intruders of all kinds fade away."

"A dog with a high prey drive would be a problem on my farm," I said.

"Emu for breakfast," he said.

"Finch, you don't mean that. I was in your barn, remember? Your animals are healthy and among the happiest I've seen."

He let the façade drop and his smile became more genuine. "That's why I wanted to get rid of the birdcage. The Langmans weren't the only ones attracted to it. When it was in the barn, birds kept flying in there and hanging around. Swallows, sparrows, jays and others I'd never seen before. When it was in our living room, they'd gather at the window and try to peck through the glass to get inside. It was the strangest thing."

I rolled down the window a little more. "Seriously? When I brought the cage out of the basement recently, I had the same problem. A bird that's rare for this area has chosen to hang out in the cage. If there's a bird equivalent to catnip, this cage has it."

Finch's eyes clouded for a second. "My grandmother got it from someone else who kept exotic birds. Regardless, I have no desire to have the cage back. You can sell it."

"Actually, I want to donate it to the rescue fundraiser, if you don't mind."

"Sounds like a good plan," he said. "We'll end our bird problem and our Langman problem."

"And animals in need will benefit."

I stuck my hand out the window and Finch actually shook my fingertips.

"Now get off my land," he said. "And don't come back."

"The next time I come, you'll invite me," I said, putting the truck in reverse.

His dark eyebrows rose in his low forehead. "I wouldn't count on that if I were you."

"Oh, I won't. But I just know your birdcage isn't the only thing that attracts unwanted attention around here. One day you might need a friend."

"We're not friends," he called, as I pulled the truck around.

"Yeah, we are," I called back. "You've just forgotten what that looks like."

"It looks like Jaws dropping scraps of overalls on my welcome mat," he said.

For the first time, his grin looked authentic and I grinned back before driving up the lane.

"He's warming to me, boys," I said. "Really."

Keats gave a hearty pant-laugh but he didn't disagree. I had a strong sense that Finch and I *would* connect again before too long and he'd come to value my pets in a way he couldn't his mastiff.

At this, Keats gave a mumble along the lines of "all brawn, no brains."

Percy, meanwhile, responded with a half-hearted scrape with his claws over the passenger seat. Then he curled up in a ball, signifying any new threat was still a good way off.

That was a relief since our current sleuthing seemed to have hit a wall.

Keats turned his back on me, disgusted, but I wasn't giving up. Not by a long shot.

When the going got tough, there was always manure.

---

I WAS FOCUSING on my black label fertilizer when Kellan came through the barn and joined me a couple of hours later.

"We're going to need his and hers spades," he said, grinning up at me. "The couple that shovels together stays together."

"My mother never told me that," I said, grinning back. "There's so much she didn't share about men."

"Thank goodness for that," he said. "No disrespect for Dahlia intended. She made the best of a difficult situation." He offered his hand to escort me down the manure stairs. "And she made you."

"You say the sweetest things." The last word dissolved into a squeal as he swept me off my feet and swung me around. When my boots touched down, I said, "The investigation must be going well."

"We've got some credible leads," he said. "And I appreciate your staying well away from it, Ivy. One less thing to worry about."

I considered telling him what I'd learned from Sterling Fable and Martha Kincaid but decided not to ruin the mood right away. My mother had taught me a couple of things, namely that timing mattered and blurting never helped. Granted, I learned it from studying her poor example, but knowledge was valuable no matter how it was gained.

Kellan jumped as Keats yet again ambushed his pant cuffs. I noticed my boyfriend's jeans were frayed and his boots lace-free and well worn. This must be his off-duty Keats-proof "uniform." Next it could be overalls. I would have believed that impossible a month ago, but his style downgrade made my heart sing. It meant he was accommodating my animals and lifestyle. What more could a hobby farmer ask?

"Care to come for a drive, my lady?" He pulled off my work gloves and reached up to set them on a shelf. Percy launched from the same shelf and landed on Kellan's shoulder, turning the word "lady" into a strangled squawk. It was no less gallant.

"Sure," I said. "To the gardens?"

He tried to shake his head but all it got him was a face full of fluff. He sneezed and then said, "Something a little less romantic. Probably not romantic at all, if I'm right about what we'll find."

"I'd love to," I said. "Any drive is romantic with you."

Keats made a retching sound, as if he were choking on fluff or flattery. I just laughed. My handsome boyfriend deserved to hear the truth more often. With Mom as my example, I'd rebelled and grown up repressing my feminine side. Working in HR had buried it so far under the manure of corporate expectations that it was a miracle I could exhume it at all.

Kellan led me out of the barn, where I saw a vehicle parked behind my truck that was neither a police cruiser nor his own SUV.

"We're going undercover together?" I asked. "That is totally romantic."

Opening the back door, he gestured for Keats and Percy to jump in. They didn't need to be coaxed.

"I have mixed feelings about your considering a potentially dangerous mission romantic," he said, opening the passenger door for me. "Honestly, I wouldn't put you in this position if it weren't for the boys. I need them."

"I don't know whether to be hurt or tickled that my pets are the main attraction," I said, getting into the car.

"Tickled, please." He leaned inside to kiss my cheek. "They're boyfriend bullies, but they do have unique talents that come in quite handy."

His words lit a fire in my heart as he walked around the car and got in. Percy and Keats *were* boyfriend bullies, and it was amazing he could see them in a positive light.

"Did you hear that, boys?" I said. "You owe it to Kellan to help."

Keats mumbled something sassy, but there was also an eager note that showed he was excited. So much so that the back seat couldn't contain him, and before Kellan even turned the key, the dog was in my lap, paws on the dashboard. Not to be left out, Percy managed to wedge himself in the small space between Kellan's headrest and the door, lashing his tail.

"Careful, Percy," Kellan said, "or we'll wind up in the ditch instead of completing an expedition I'm pretty sure you boys will enjoy."

"Curiouser and curiouser," I said. For this sleuth, it felt like Christmas Eve. My excitement grew when he eventually left the highway and took one of the many secret entrances onto the trail system. The sedan wasn't well suited to the rough ride and it wasn't long before Percy retired in disgust to the rear. Keats was determined to hang in there, which meant my legs took a beating from his claws.

I lost my bearings nearly immediately. My mapping exercise hadn't yet brought me down this far. Wherever this even was. It felt like someplace I'd never seen before, and yet we'd only been gone from the farm for half an hour or so.

Finally Kellan slowed and pulled the car into the bushes. "From here we go on foot," he said. "And quietly. We want the element of surprise." He turned and eyed the dog. "Keats, I'm counting on you to point out trouble. You'll know it when you smell it, I'm sure."

Keats gave a happy pant: *Bring it on.*

The two animals raced into the woods ahead of us and Kellan took my hand. It still felt like fun because tails were up. Keats lifted his muzzle and sniffed the breeze again and again. Finally he gave a high-pitched whine of excitement that probably only I could hear and bolted out of sight. Before I could tell Kellan the dog had found something, there was another sound we couldn't miss: a loud metallic clatter. And then a yelp of distress.

I let go of Kellan's hand and ran.

Nothing in the world scared me more than the prospect of losing Keats. That wasn't to say I didn't care deeply about many people, especially Kellan and Jilly, but my relationship with Keats was different. Primal. Or spiritual. I wasn't quite sure how to categorize it. But I would lay down my life for him, and he'd already done the same for me.

"Wait, Ivy," Kellan called after me. "There's a—"

The last word was lost as I stumbled over a bank and ended up on my behind in running water.

*Cold* running water.

"A creek," he said, kneeling to pull me up and out.

Peering around, I saw Keats climbing a muddy bank. He was fine. Wet, but fine. Water always distressed him, but what about that snapping sound?

I clambered up to join Kellan. By that time Keats had joined us, and lifted one sandy, sodden paw in a point.

"What's that?" I asked, staring down at a strange contraption concealed in the reeds and rushes. It was well over a foot long and appeared to have jagged metal teeth.

Kellan's face flushed in a rare show of anger. "It's a bear trap."

"A bear trap? Martha Kinkaid said there hadn't been bears in this region in her lifetime." I turned to stare at him. "Is she wrong?"

"Nope. And these traps are illegal. It could have..."

My face flushed, too. "It could have hurt my pets."

"Or caught someone's leg. Or injured a child."

I picked up my wet dog and hugged him tight. Keats never enjoyed overt affection and now he thrashed in my arms to get down. "Take it easy. It's just a hug."

"Is he hurt?" Kellan asked, inviting Percy to climb up to his shoulder perch.

I knelt to grope every inch of the dog and shook my head. "Just upset about getting dunked in the creek." Keats mumbled indignantly, so I added, "The snap of the trap probably startled him and he lost his balance."

Then the dog gave a low growl. He didn't bristle but his ears flattened. I sensed he was more annoyed than anxious.

"The trapper is still around, I take it," Kellan said. He reached under his jacket for his gun, and I realized how strange it was that I had never noticed him doing that before. Surely, he had, given all our dangerous confrontations, but I didn't recall seeing it. He cut an imposing figure, aside from the orange cat-parrot on his shoulder.

Keats started to forge ahead. Calling him back, I hooked up his leash. "Sorry buddy, but there could be more traps."

"This time I lead," Kellan said.

Percy held on tight with his tail circling Kellan's neck almost like a monkey's. I had the unaccountable urge to laugh but choked it back. It was hysteria brought on by a cold posterior.

Keats glared up at me with an even colder blue eye. I had rarely seen him so peeved. He was wet, leashed and had barely escaped a trap. Someone was going to pay.

There was a rustle in the bushes ahead of us, followed by scrambling limbs and a hasty retreat.

Kellan started running, dislodging Percy, and Keats jerked the leash out of my hand. The dog passed Kellan easily and a moment later came another high-pitched yelp.

This one didn't come from Keats, because his jaws were full of fabric.

He hung from the derriere of the fugitive and when I saw who it was, I didn't tell him to let go.

Instead, I yelled, "Bite harder."

## CHAPTER FOURTEEN

E dna Evans turned quickly and the dog, still clamped on the seat of her camouflage jumpsuit, swung in an arc. "Get off me, you cur!"

"If you harm one hair on that dog, I will make you pay, Edna Evans," I said. "Don't think I won't."

"Ow! Call him off right now, Ivy. I think he may have broken skin."

"Then I guess you won't be super comfy in your recliner for awhile," I said.

"This isn't a game," she said. "It's a training exercise."

Now Kellan and I flanked her and I finally signaled for Keats to let go.

"An exercise in *what*?" Kellan asked, putting his weapon away. "Trapping imaginary bears?"

I raised my hand and answered before Edna could. "Trapping imaginary zombies, Kellan. I'm guessing we've interrupted her survival class."

Turning, he shouted, "If there are any more of you, show yourselves immediately. Says your chief of police."

"You're not my chief," someone said. A middle-aged woman

crawled out from behind a tree and pushed herself upright rather stiffly. It was one of the pair I saw at the fundraising meeting and again at Mandy's Country Store. The other one joined her.

"Meet Beatie and Alfreda Agnew," Edna said. "Sisters from Crow's Landing."

"You're currently in my jurisdiction," Kellan said. "Who else is around? Mrs. Rhodes?"

Gertie emerged from the shadows carrying Minnie. When she saw Kellan's expression, she let the rifle drop to her side where the poncho enveloped it.

There was another rustle and out came my sister, Poppy, wearing a camo jumpsuit.

"Are you kidding me, Pops?" I said. "She almost killed Keats in a bear trap."

"Your dog wasn't supposed to barge in on my class," Edna said.

"There's at least one more of you," Kellan called. "Come out or I'll send in the hound. And he's a butt-biter."

I had a sinking feeling another family member might appear. Instead, the gray head that emerged belonged to Annamae Muir, one of the disbanded Bridge Buddies. Like the other members of the club, she had treated Edna badly in the court of public opinion. It got even worse when Fleecy, Annamae's cat, chose Edna's feral colony over a cushy home. Ultimately, Fleecy had moved in with Gertie Rhodes.

Annamae and Edna had traded bitter verbal slings, and yet here they were, setting bear traps together.

"Is that it?" Kellan asked, turning back to Edna.

"No," Poppy said, scuffing the dirt with her boot.

As I'd feared, another Galloway soon appeared. My sister, Violet.

I would have deemed Violet the least likely to become a prepper and slayer of zombies. Growing up, she'd been nearly as quiet as I was, and I still didn't know her very well. She had managed to remain pretty much a stranger to her own family and that took some doing. One day I'd tell her how much I admired that, but I wasn't sure she'd appreciate my noticing.

"And now?" Kellan asked Edna.

She gave him a belligerent glare, followed by a reluctant nod.

"We're the only ones who showed up for the course kickoff," Poppy said. "A few people bailed when they realized Edna was serious about the overnight part. I couldn't shake off the cold till after our morning run."

"Morning run?" I looked around at the unlikely athletes. "Edna, is it wise to have people sleeping in tents at this time of year, let alone running in the hills? Someone could get sick."

"It wasn't tents," Poppy said. "It was—"

"Poppy Galloway, shut your trap," Edna said. "You're as bad as your mother with all that babbling. There's a reason Dahlia didn't make the cut for my course."

"Mom really applied?" I said. "Why on earth would she do that? She loves luxury."

"Everyone is starting to grasp that preparedness is no longer a luxury but a necessity," Edna said. "Even Dahlia. But there's no room for divas in a bunker, even those attempting to reform. I fell out with her anyway after she stole my intellectual property."

I blinked a few times, trying to take in the new information. "Mom wanted to start a prepper course?"

"As if," Edna said. "But when I turned her down she not only basically stole the name of my class, she stole some of my potential clients for her own course."

"What course?" Poppy's voice overlapped with both Violet's and mine. At least my sisters hadn't kept that a secret from me.

Edna crossed her arms and her lower lip jutted in a pout.

When she didn't respond, I looked to Gertie. She was no less stubborn, but far more respectful of Kellan, who'd helped her considerably with treasure hunters trespassing on her property.

Turning slightly away from Edna, Gertie tossed her waist-long braid over her shoulder. "This course is called SurvivalDare," she said. "Your mother's is SurvivalDate."

"What?" Again my voice overlapped with those of my sisters.

"It's a how-to on rotational dating," Gertie continued. "Filled up fast, too. A few of Edna's applicants decided a challenge like that was more up their alley than this one."

I rubbed my forehead and Kellan did the same. Keats was still highly disgruntled, despite getting his payback. He was as puffy as a wet dog could get. Percy's tail was lashing, too. The mission hadn't turned out to be as fun as my pets had hoped.

Gertie added, "Dahlia's tagline is 'Survive the worst with someone you love.'"

"And 'Bunker up with the best,'" Edna said. "Wait till you see the class list. No class at all in those ladies, and I know you'll agree, Ivy. Dahlia's turned my noble concept into something tawdry."

Kellan stepped forward. "You call bear traps noble? You nearly caught this dog."

Edna looked at her boots and mumbled, "It's set for fifty pounds. Shouldn't have triggered with a sheepdog."

"But it did," he said. "And it could have been a toddler, Edna."

"I was right here the whole time," she said. "That dog is probably the only creature who could escape my notice."

"Aside from Percy, who was with him, you mean," I said.

Kellan held up his palm to silence Edna. "Keats, show us around."

"You've seen all there is to see," Edna said. "It's traps and snares day. They'll be essential to catch food and enemies when the end comes."

Keats pointed into the bush and there was a gleam in his eye. There was definitely more to see here.

The dog set off with Kellan and the rest of us trailed after them like baby geese. In fact, Edna honked protests behind me nonstop until Gertie threatened to shut her up with Minnie.

It wasn't long before we reached a clearing containing three large shipping containers that had been freshly painted a dappled green to blend into the foliage.

"Aha," Kellan said, as Percy climbed up and onto his shoulder again. "Someone reported seeing a trailer and crane pass at dusk and I put two and two together."

"Dagnabit," Edna said. "I warned them to come in through the trails."

Kellan pulled out his phone. "These will be seized and removed immediately."

"You can't take my property," Edna said. "These cost three grand a pop, and good ones are hard to come by because people are getting wise. Everyone and their uncle wants a bunker at the ready."

"They're bulletproof, you know," Annamae said. "I felt utterly safe in there last night. Uncomfortable, but safe."

"Not enough air circulation," said Beatie Agnew. "We ate beans straight out of a can for dinner."

"If you'd managed to catch a rabbit or build a fire, you'd have dined better," Edna said.

"I'm not killing any animals," Poppy said. "Violet and I hid in the bunker when the rest were firing on squirrels."

"You two will fail the class, Poppy. And you'll starve when the end comes," Edna said. "Survival isn't for sissies."

"I'm fine with learning the lesson in theory and putting it into practice later," Poppy said. "Living off chickpeas and sharing a big airless coffin will be highly motivating when the time comes."

A laugh built in my throat but I subdued it by reminding myself that Edna had jeopardized Keats.

"Shipping containers aren't bulletproof, Poppy," Kellan said. "While your classmates were shooting things up, you and Violet could have become dinner yourself. Is that how you want to go?"

"Chief, I'll thank you not to scare my students," Edna said. "These containers are resistant to bullets. And remember, it's only a simulation."

"What I'm remembering is that your students very likely aren't licensed to carry a weapon at all," he said. "Show of hands if you are?"

Only Edna and Gertie raised camo gloves.

"I'm starting to feel persecuted, Chief," Edna said. "Obviously this is just a temporary setup. A proper bunker would be concealed so people like you couldn't sashay up and invade our privacy."

Gertie caught her friend's arm and tried to quell the tide. Edna wasn't doing herself any favors. Maybe what happened with Keats had unnerved her more than she let on.

"Even if these containers were on your property I'd take issue, Miss Evans," Kellan said. "But they're not. Nor is the latrine you no doubt built."

"I'm simulating a postapocalyptic experience," Edna said. "This is how we'll all be living one day. Perhaps sooner than later."

"Until then, I'm responsible for the safety of my citizens and your actions are jeopardizing it," Kellan said. "I could haul you all in and fine you. And I might."

A gasp went around the circle but Edna squared her shoulders. "You can't stop me from educating people. It's my civic responsibility."

"Edna is playing an important role," Alfreda Agnew said. "Obviously you can't understand what it's like to feel like a vulnerable woman in a world that gets more terrifying by the day. No one knows who the enemy even is anymore."

"Exactly right, Alfie," her sister said. "My confidence is growing, thanks to this class. It takes work, but it's truly a joy."

Annamae Muir looked downcast. "I can barely lift my sword, let alone—"

"That's enough, Annamae," Edna said. "You signed a confidentiality agreement. I wouldn't put it past Dahlia to take up swordplay."

"Swords?" Kellan said. "Miss Evans, that's totally—"

"Awesome," Beatie interrupted. "You don't know empowerment until you joust, Chief. If you haven't tried it, I urge you to have a go."

"It's now or never," her sister said. "Otherwise you might find yourself outmanned—make that outwomanned—when the end comes."

Kellan gave them a look that likely intimidated felons but seemed lost on Edna's crew. The parrot-cat on his shoulder didn't give him the necessary gravitas.

Finally, he just shook his head and fought back a sneeze from Percy's fluff. "Let me put this plainly, Miss Evans. I can and will shut down your program, or at least make it very difficult to run. You'll spend all your time surviving my interventions."

Edna's pout came back. "This is unfair. What about Dahlia's course? Does she get a free pass because she's your girlfriend's mother?"

"If Mrs. Galloway's course is putting daters in danger, I'll most certainly shut that down, too," he said. "I'll speak to her about it."

"When you see the class list, you'll know daters are endangered," Edna said. "There are worse things than beans in a bunker."

Great. Just great.

I pulled out my phone and surreptitiously triggered a butter tart 911—our family's distress call.

Poppy glanced at her phone when it pinged and whispered something to Violet.

"Kellan, I'll catch a ride home with my sisters so you can finish up here," I said. "Unless you need to take them in for questioning."

Normally feisty Poppy stayed quiet while Kellan considered his next steps. "I'll catch up with Poppy and Violet later at the farm to see if their story lines up with everyone else's."

"Ivy, wait," Edna called after me. "A word, please."

"Not right now, Edna," I said. "You nearly snapped my heart in two with steel jaws. I have nothing to say to you today."

"I'm sorry," she said. Those words didn't come easily or often from her lips. Even Gertie looked surprised to hear them. "That wasn't supposed to happen. Obviously, I should have factored Keats and Percy into any survival scenario. Would an apology to the dog help?"

"Not this time," I said.

Keats glanced up at me and mumbled. It sounded like he was willing to let this slide.

"See? He's letting bygones be bygones," Edna said.

"A month ago you hurt his feelings, Edna. Today you could have maimed him, or worse. I appreciate all you've done for me, but you're getting reckless."

Everyone in the clearing seemed to shrink back, even Kellan. We all expected an explosion from Edna, and I was certain she'd throw my own recklessness back in my face. Instead, the camo warrior wilted, which was rarer than an apology.

"It really was an accident," Gertie said, since Edna stayed silent. "You know we both love Keats and Percy. And you, incidentally." She inspected the tip of her braid. "Have you never gotten caught up in a moment and made a mistake?"

I looked from one woman to the other and sighed. They'd had my back so many times. Was I really going to hold a grudge over something that *could* have ended badly, but didn't?

"Let's all talk about it later," I said. "Poppy, Violet and I need to run."

"Good luck getting a straight answer out of Dahlia," Edna muttered as we walked away.

About a quarter mile past the railway shipping containers Keats went into a point. His ruff came up and his ears went down. Percy stalked ahead into the long grass.

"What's wrong with him?" Poppy asked.

I walked after Percy, and within a couple of yards, my steel-toed boot clanged against something.

The dog pushed past and blocked me.

A spade lying in the bushes didn't seem too dangerous, but when Keats rumbled a warning, I listened.

"Just let me take a look, buddy," I said. "It's obviously worrying you and that worries me." He let me bend over the spade and I straightened just as suddenly. "Oh. I see."

I might not need protection from this spade, but someone else definitely had.

## CHAPTER FIFTEEN

P oppy and Violet didn't make it to the family meeting I'd initiated with the Butter Tart 911 alarm call. Like the rest of the SurvivalDare class, they were taken to the police station for questioning and I left in Poppy's car. The spade Keats found appeared to be the same one used to kill Vernie Cobbler, and there was a possibility that someone in the class had used the opportunity to dump the murder weapon nearby. I couldn't imagine Poppy, Violet or Gertie had any motivation to kill Vernie, which left Annamae Muir and the Agnew sisters from Crow's Landing. Or anyone else clever enough to drive out that far and dump it conveniently to implicate them.

"Kellan will handle this," I said, pulling up in front of Daisy's house. "I've got enough on my plate."

The big driveway was already full of vehicles, including the beaters owned by Daisy's elder twins. In the time-honored way of country boys, they spent more time tinkering and repairing than actually driving. That suited Daisy just fine, despite all the dirt the lovable troublemakers brought into her meticulous house.

One of the boys scooted out from under his car on a wheeled cart and startled me. It was Sutton, technically the eldest of the lot. He'd had his nose broken twice in rugby, which made him easy to identify at a glance from his twin Weston. When they were young, only Daisy could tell them apart.

"Hey, Ivy," he said. "How come you're driving Poppy's car? Did you finally smash the truck? We all took bets on the date it would happen. Including Mom."

"I appreciate that vote of confidence," I said, deliberately stepping on his shirttail as I passed. "Which twin are you, by the way? The A student or the C student?"

He laughed. "We're identical geniuses. One of us just has better things to do than study."

"I heard about your girlfriend, Sutton. You know I love being the coolest aunt, but I'm also the high achiever in the family."

He propped himself up on one elbow. "The one who has a rep for pushing her manure on complete strangers on Main Street. You gave up on cool a year ago."

Percy walked up to my nephew and hissed in his face. Sutton laughed, but started easing back under the car again.

"Sorry, Sutt," I said.

"For what?" he asked, popping his head back out. "For being embarrassing? For having weird pets? Or for what you're about to do inside?"

"Inside?" I summoned an innocent smile. "We're just having a friendly family conversation. I called the meeting. No one even knows what it's about."

He slid back under again. "Yeah? Well, I'm staying under here to evade the shrapnel."

I glanced at Keats and found him pant-laughing. Whatever Sutton knew, the dog suspected, and neither was telling me.

"How about a heads-up for your favorite aunt?" I said, bending over to peer under the vehicle. "I hate surprises."

"Liar," he said. "You *are* my favorite aunt because you love surprises. Or at least surprising deadbeats. I want to be just like you when I grow up." There was barely room to move under there, but he managed to whack something with a tool and create a loud clink. "Mom wants me to be a cop like Asher, but I'd rather be a renegade like you. All that lame farmer stuff and the driving disasters are just a cover. Right?"

I laughed and straightened up. "Correct. I'm a renegade to the core. Now, tell me what you know."

He hammered some more under the car before answering. "You're the detective. You figure it out." And then, "I do take bribes."

"Forget it. I'll let Keats figure it out. He works for kibble." The dog mumbled indignantly. "Sorry, buddy, I misspoke. Keats works for the sheer joy of doing some good in the world. There's your role model, Sutt."

The clanging under the car stopped and he called, "Remember, Mom doesn't allow swearing in the house."

"She doesn't allow swearing anywhere," I said, heading up the stairs. "But sometimes, it's the only thing you *can* do."

"That's what I keep telling her. So let 'em fly."

"Should I be worried?" I asked Keats before opening the door.

He mumbled a negative, which my nephew tried to shout down.

By the time I finally let the pets into Daisy's front hall, I was nearly as anxious as I was in Edna's outdoor classroom, which I'd now dubbed Bunkertown.

I kicked off my wet boots, found my socks even wetter and peeled them off, too. I couldn't do the same with my overalls, however, and Mom gave a little shriek when I walked into the kitchen damp and bedraggled.

"Ivy Rose Galloway, what on earth happened?" She tipped a little on her bar stool at the counter. Despite the availability of sturdy chairs around the kitchen table, she loved teetering above the rest of us. Well, most of us. Asher, who dwarfed the entire family, was leaning against the fridge as usual. Somehow, he looked even taller in uniform.

"What's this meeting about?" Daisy said, busily buffing the counter with vinegar spray and a microfiber shammy. "And where are Poppy and Violet? Pops answered ages ago that they were coming."

"They got held up," I said. "Detained might be a better word, since Kellan took them in for questioning."

Asher looked as shocked as everyone else. I had assumed Kellan would let him know but he must have wanted my brother out of the way. "Detained? What for?" he asked.

Normally Keats darted off with Percy to search for the younger twins' ferrets, but today he stuck by my side mumbling advice on how to play my hand right.

"What's he saying?" Jilly asked.

"He's not saying anything," Mom said. "He's just being odd. And judging by his muddy paws, you both fell in a creek."

"Up to no good?" Asher asked.

"At your boss' invitation," I said. "He suspected someone was setting up an illegal camp in the back country trails and wanted Keats and Percy to find it."

"And did they?" Jilly asked, scooping up Percy as he rushed past.

"Yep. There are three shipping containers out there serving as bunkers. Turns out Edna Evans is simulating a postapocalyptic environment as part of her prepper course."

A snicker caught fire, zipped around the room and ended with Daisy, the worrywart. "Where do Poppy and Violet come in?" she asked. "Please tell me they're not taking the course."

"I can't lie to my big sister," I said. "They both made the cut, whereas Mom did not."

"Mom!" Daisy's squawk sounded like a flustered hen.

"Oh, I didn't really want to take Edna's stupid course," Mom said, smoothing the slick red skirt of her dress. It seemed to be yet another new one, but it was hard to know when there were so many. "Could you see me in satin in a shipping container?"

"We've seen you in satin in many unlikely places," I said. "Maybe it's what the fashionable zombie hunter wears these days."

"Very funny." Mom reached for the multicolored mug Daisy typically assigned her to avoid waxy red lipstick prints. "You haven't explained what happened with your sisters. Poppy used to be my most rebellious child, until you turned into a—"

"Renegade, according to your grandson. And a role model." I waggled my eyebrows at Daisy. "Anyway, Kellan was going to let Edna's crew off with a warning. As we left, however, Keats found what appeared to be the spade used to kill Vernie Cobbler. Since it wasn't far from Bunkertown, one of Edna's students may have dumped it there."

"Certainly not my sweet Poppy," Mom said. She looked nonplussed when everyone laughed, even Jilly. "Well, she *is* sweet. Once in a while."

"A long while," Asher said. "Almost never." Poppy had always teased Asher mercilessly and probably left some deep wounds in his psyche from childhood. We all had them. They took many shapes and sizes.

"Well, Violet is sweet, then," Mom said. "At least I think so. She's always been a still-waters-run-deep girl."

"But not a murdering girl," Daisy said.

"How would we really know?" Mom said, still deflecting. "She doesn't share."

Jilly jumped in to steer the conversation. "Poppy and Violet will be fine. They have an alibi. We all saw them at the fundraising meeting. Right?"

A silence fell over the kitchen as those of us who'd been there tried to remember and the rest waited.

"Honestly, I can't remember seeing them there," Iris said. "But neither one would have a motive to hurt Vernie. They never said a bad word about her."

"Untrue," I said. "We probably all said unkind things before we knew better. Vernie made herself hard to like."

"Ivy, surely you don't believe your sisters had anything to do with this," Mom said.

"Not unless it was a class assignment, and even Edna wouldn't go that far," I said. "SurvivalDare probably attracts some weird characters, though."

"Poppy and Iris are no weirder than you are, and possibly less," Mom said.

"No wonder none of us are sweet," I said. "There's a deficit in the gene pool."

"At least you got my sense of humor," Mom said. "Now, who else was there?"

"Gertie, Annamae Muir and a couple of sisters from Crow's Landing," I said. "But what I really want to know is who's in *your* class?"

All eyes turned instantly to our mother, who squirmed on her bar stool and nearly slid off. Iris stuck her hand out to bolster Mom, though it was always tempting to let her topple.

"What class?" Asher asked. "Sewing?"

"You read my mind, son," Mom said. "I have so much knowledge to share about my seamstress work."

"Kellan wouldn't worry too much about sewing," I said. "But he does want to talk to you about SurvivalDate. Your other class. The one Edna's up in arms about. She said you've stolen her prospective clients."

Mom made a flicking gesture that nearly tipped her coffee mug. Daisy darted in to whisk it away and buff the counter in case a drop of coffee had spilled. She stared at our mother and said, "Is this true? Are you offering dating lessons?"

"More like group coaching," Mom said, smoothing her skirt again. "So many have asked about my strategies for keeping a strong and healthy dating rotation. I decided it wasn't right to keep this information to myself anymore."

Asher raked a hand through his fair hair. "Mom, no. Just no. You already made a laughingstock out of me by killing stop signs in your old car. Now you're encouraging women to date around? It's a small town. Everyone will be dating the same people."

Daisy groaned, too. "I won't be able to show my face. I'm supposed to be the sensible daughter who keeps her mother in line. Along with the rest of you and four teenage boys."

"It's just a personal development class," Mom said. "I'm not selling drugs to minors in the schoolyard. Get some perspective."

"What I'm trying to get is a class list," I said. "Edna thought I'd be interested."

"I don't know why." Mom tapped ruby fingernails on the countertop until Daisy restrained her hand with one rubber glove. "It's just a bunch of middle-aged people like me. Women who want to break through the constraints of our repressive upbringing. You should be happy for us."

"Maybe we will be, once you spill the details," I said.

"It's confidential," Mom said. "Privacy guaranteed."

I crossed my arms. "Fine. We'll wait till Kellan asks you about it. Edna suggested there was something fishy going on."

Mom slid off the stool and stared up at me. "There's nothing fishy about a few nice ladies meeting to talk about dating. I know you're going to be touchy about Beverly, that's all."

"Beverly Roxton, the veterinarian's wife?" Asher asked. "You're advising people to step out on their husbands?"

"Of course not. Beverly and Dr. Roxton separated. That mishap with Ivy last Christmas tore their family apart."

I used my height advantage to try to cow her, to no effect. "Are you suggesting I contributed to that breakup?"

"Always jumping to conclusions," she said. "I'm only noting

that's when they hit the rocks after a long marriage. And Beverly's asked for my help to get back in the game."

"Mom, Beverly is a nasty piece of work, and I don't say that lightly. I try to see the best in people, truly I do. But she was harsh not only to me but also to Dr. Roxton's aging father."

"Who turned out to be deranged, didn't he? So maybe Bev wasn't entirely in the wrong," Mom said. "Regardless, does it mean she shouldn't find love again?"

An entire chorus of "yes" echoed through the kitchen.

"Unless she reforms, Dahlia," Jilly said. "She really did treat Ivy and the senior Dr. Roxton terribly. I witnessed it myself."

"That's what my course is about," Mom said. "Not just the ins and outs of dating, but about transformation. About discovering one's own self-worth and potential. If I deem a participant to be a hazard to the eligible men of Clover Grove, I'll expel her immediately. It helps no one if good men get burned." She climbed back on the stool and a classic Dahlia smirk appeared. "Beverly hasn't said one unkind word about you, Ivy. Neither has Gwen Quinn."

"Gwen?" My voice shot up a notch. "From the Clover Grove Herding Club?"

"Also known as the herding harpies," Jilly said. "They actually protected Myrtle McCain after she murdered Lloyd Boyce. That's how she was free to attack Ivy."

"Mom. Myrtle tried to drag me to the dump behind my own tractor." I reached for Keats' ears and found them exactly where I needed them. "And now her friend who spied on me is in your class."

"It wasn't personal," Mom said. "Women of that generation always have each other's back. I hope you won't speak so harshly of Anne Rezek."

My mouth dropped open. "Her husband tried to kill me, too. If she hadn't been competing with you for the attention of that dance instructor, it would never have happened."

"Anne was never competition for me, darling, you must know that. And now we're one big happy club."

"What about Joan Snelling and Morag Tanner?" I said. "They were hanging with you too, the other day."

"The Bridge Baddies?" Asher said. "They should be put away."

"Actually, they should be in relationships, changing and growing into the people they could be," Mom said. "That's where I come in."

I spun in a little circle, evading Jilly's hand as it came out to comfort me. "You're collecting a who's who from my past as your dating posse. What are you thinking?"

"Darling, be reasonable. You've had dealings with half the people in town by now. It would be hard to attract enough participants if I got that choosy."

"Mom, you're incorrigible," Daisy said. "Why do this class at all? If you want to give back to the community, teach sewing."

My mother patted her dress almost as fondly as I touched Keats. "I considered it, but there's little money in showing people how to revive thrift store finds. You kids have always given me a hard time about not paying my way and now I can do more."

Asher straightened and waved. "Show of hands if you want Mom to teach sewing instead of rotational dating. I'm willing to kick in more for her budget."

Everyone raised a hand and I raised two, plus one bare foot. "I'm voting for Violet and Poppy, too. Keats is on our side, too."

At least, that's how I interpreted the dog's repeated nudges. He'd been trying to get my attention for some time and when I looked down he went into a point. I raised my eyebrows questioningly but he just mumbled a half-hearted warning. Then his mouth opened in a happy pant. Was I missing an inside joke?

"Do stop fussing, darlings." Mom's red lips opened and released her trademark tinkling laugh. "Have some faith in me, please. Because when it comes to men, I know *exactly* what I'm doing."

There was a movement in the front hall that made all of us turn and some of us gasp. My father was standing in the kitchen doorway and there was no telling how much he'd heard.

"Did I come at a bad time?" he asked. His blue eyes crinkled, suggesting he'd at least heard Mom's last outrageous claim. When it came to men, she certainly hadn't known what she was doing with Calvin Galloway, who left her to raise six kids entirely on her own.

At least according to her original version of the tale. Now I knew her parents had chipped in for our upbringing, as well as Dad's uncle, Sterling Fable. Dad himself had sent a pile of checks Mom refused to cash out of pride. It was always hard to know where the truth ended and fiction began with Mom. That's why I suspected there was more to SurvivalDate than she had revealed.

"Yes, you came at a bad time, Calvin," Mom said. "This is a family meeting."

"And Dad's family," Asher said. "So I invited him."

"You *invited* him?" Mom's limbs flailed and she teetered for real on her stool. No one made a move to help her except Calvin. He was swift and graceful, two gifts I hadn't inherited. He wove through his children like so many sheep till he caught Mom just before she hit the floor in a pool of red satin.

She let him steady her on her stilettos and then brushed away imaginary cooties where his hands had touched her. "You had no business hearing that conversation, Calvin. And Asher had no business issuing an invitation without clearing it with us first."

I tended to agree with her on that score. What came out at family meetings—Butter Tart 911s in particular—was raw and unvarnished. Some of us, including me, didn't feel comfortable sharing everything in front of Calvin, yet. We'd only known him a few months.

Asher was Calvin's biggest fan, but today he flushed and shifted uneasily. "How was I to know we were being summoned about Mom's class for teaching women in town to be players?"

Calvin flushed, too. "Her... *what*? Should I leave?"

"Do as you like," Mom said, patting her hair. "I'll say nothing more about the subject. I consider it my private business."

"Only they're talking about your private business down in Bunkertown," I said. "Even the preppers are all over this hot gossip."

"Bunkertown?" Calvin said. "What's that?"

"Edna's set up an experiential learning program to prepare for the apocalypse," I said. "SurvivalDare, she calls it. Mom ripped off the name for her course, SurvivalDate."

"Never mind, Ivy," Mom said.

"There are some catchy slogans," I said. "Like, 'Survive the worst with someone you love.' And 'Bunker up with the best.' Edna said Mom turned her noble concept into something tawdry."

"Oh, well then," Calvin said. He was never one for small talk and now he was way out of his comfort zone. "I suppose dating is all about surviving these days." He closed his eyes. "That didn't come out like I wanted. Since the last woman I dated *didn't* survive."

"But Mom sure did," Asher said, with his toothy grin. "First surviving and now thriving."

Mom leaned over to grab the coffee mug Daisy had moved out of reach. She tipped it back and gulped, no doubt wishing it held something stronger than tea. Patting her lips with a tissue, she stared at me. "Nobility is in the eye of the beholder," she said. "And Edna would be better off focusing on zombies than me. I'll speak to the chief about her slanderous claims."

"I'd like to be a fly on the wall for that conversation," Iris said.

Asher shook his head hard. "Not me."

"Me either," Calvin said, circling back to the fridge.

Reaching out, Asher pumped Calvin's hand. "It's good to have you here. Do you have any idea how much I've suffered being the only guy in this family?"

My dad scuffed his white sports sock on Daisy's floor. It had been spotless until Keats tracked in dirt from the creek. "I do, Asher. And it could be far worse than a group of wonderful women."

That gave my brother pause, and as usual when he was flummoxed, Asher headed over to drop a hand on Jilly's shoulder. "I guess we might have girls, too," he said. "I wouldn't complain."

Keats didn't enjoy small talk, either, and he herded me to the door ahead of the mass exodus. In my haste to escape, I barely noticed the misery of sticking bare feet into wet boots.

Percy beat us out the door and by the time we reached the old beater in the driveway, the cat had hopped on Sutton's stomach. My nephew propped himself up and grinned mischievously.

"You could have told me Calvin was coming," I said, bending to swat his legs with the wet socks that dangled from my right hand. "I figure you owe me after that shoplifting incident. Plus a couple of loans."

His grin didn't fade one bit. He gave the cat a one-armed hug and Percy submitted willingly. Despite the rough edges on both sets of twins, they loved animals and that gave me hope they'd do some good in the world.

"How'd it go?" he asked. "Did Dahlia freak right out?"

Mom preferred the boys using her first name over being seen as old enough to have grandsons who could drive.

"Meltdown still in progress," I said. Reaching into my pocket, I pulled out a twenty-dollar bill and slapped it in his free hand. "Try to send her off with Calvin, okay? Prolong the torture."

Everyone was scattering to avoid driving Mom home. Asher almost tossed Jilly into the police SUV. Iris pulled a hard U turn and booted it up the street in her car. That left Mom with Daisy's fleet, Calvin, or springing for a cab.

Sutton pocketed the money and got to his feet, after gently dislodging Percy. "Shame none of our vehicles are operational right now. You can count on me, Aunt Ivy."

"Twenty bucks and the 'aunt' title," I said, grinning at him as Keats pressed me forward to Poppy's car. "What a steal."

# CHAPTER SIXTEEN

The next morning, I drank two extra coffees to get rid of the bad taste SurvivalDare and SurvivalDate had left in my mouth. I couldn't afford to let silly things like that distract me from such serious matters as Vernie's murder, the rescue fundraiser, and the mystery of the love letters. In my corporate job, I could toss a dozen balls in the air and juggle like a circus clown. Nowadays they rained down on me.

"I used to be really sharp, you know," I told Keats and Percy as we walked down to check on the birdcage. "You didn't know me then, but I was wasted on Flordale Corporation. If you don't believe me, ask Jilly. She thought I was destined for great things. Lately, I can barely keep track of which livestock I've fed. Good thing they all yell at me if I forget."

Keats offered his humble mumbled opinion that I was being too hard on myself. Maybe he was right. I had expected my brain to be fully recovered from the concussion long before now. Maybe it was time to accept it never would, and make my peace with being both less and more than I once was.

Percy climbed up and over my shoulder and then dropped into

my waiting arms without a moment's hesitation. He knew I'd be ready to receive him. That was what trust was all about.

A purr boomed out and his paws kneaded the air as if to say, "Relax. Let things unfold and just enjoy the ride."

"I wasn't born with a 'relax' setting, Percy," I said. "I came wired for work, like a certain sheepdog we know."

Keats chimed in from below. It sounded like a reminder that while both of us liked to be occupied, only one of us sweated the details. The sheepdog nonchalance was far superior.

"True. I do envy you that," I said, unlocking the utility shed where we'd stashed the birdcage. Picasso had been coming and going at whim through the little vent under the eaves. Sometimes he was waiting when I arrived in the morning, but mostly he was already out on official bunting business.

Today when I opened the door, there was no sign of the bird.

There was also no sign of the bird*cage*.

The shed was completely empty.

"Oh no! Where is it?" I spun around the small space as if it might magically reappear. The door had been locked and the vent was far too small for anyone to fit through. As far as I knew, only Charlie and I had a key.

Percy investigated inside but Keats herded me back out the door, where we found Picasso fluttering and twittering overhead in a vibrant swirl of agitation.

"I'm coming," I said, following the bird around the small building. Keats urged me on from behind with little nips that were entirely unnecessary. By the time we reached the back, Percy had pushed a board aside and popped his head out to stare at us with sharp green eyes.

Kneeling, I discovered four other boards had been pried loose with a crowbar and propped back in place without so much as a nail to hold them. When I pulled them all out, it created a space large enough for a human to fit through, as well as a birdcage.

"Well, that's the how," I said, sitting back on my heels. "We know the why. But we don't know the who or the when. There's only a security camera on the front, unfortunately."

The bunting hopped down into the bushes and ramped up the volume on his chirping. Then he dropped right to the ground and pecked at what appeared to be a scrap of dirty fabric. Leaning over, I pinched the scrap between my index finger and thumb and held it up in a sunbeam.

"Khaki. The uniform of the Langman sisters. One of the antiques Cinderellas has a hole in her pants and we're going to see if this fits."

I got up and shoved bushes aside till I found the tire tracks. A few yards further along, Keats went into a point that drew my attention to a streak of white paint on an oak tree.

"More evidence," I said. "The sisters drive a white van and the tracks look pretty fresh."

Keats mumbled an order to get moving.

"They wouldn't be stupid enough to take it to their store," I said, jogging to the truck with the cat and the dog running alongside. "Would they?"

The dog hopped inside and propped his paws on the dashboard. Another mumble suggested they just might. Although the Langmans were far from stupid, they often got sloppy when treasure fever struck. That had bitten them in the khakis when they stole the cage the first time last winter. Maybe we'd get lucky again.

"Meet you at The Langman Legacy," I called out the window to Picasso. "I don't know why you want that cage, but I'll get it back for you if I can. I promise."

The truck cooperated fully as we raced into town. It seemed to sense my determination to catch the despicable sisters before they could pass the birdcage onto someone else. There was usually a customer waiting for their best scores, and for whatever reason, this cage was worth stealing not once, but twice.

"Maybe it's solid gold underneath," I said. "I didn't take a good enough look at it when I had the chance. I thought it was just one of their odd notions, but there must be something special about that piece."

Keats agreed, sounding a little worried he'd missed something, too. That seemed unlikely as very little slipped by my genius sheepdog. Still, the bunting was as obsessed with the cage as the Langmans. If I managed to reclaim it, I'd go over it with a magnifying glass.

Heddy Langman was standing in the big front window flipping an ornate closed sign to open when I arrived. I pulled the truck up onto the sidewalk outside the antiques store. When she saw me, she turned the sign again and ran to the door. I leapt out of the truck in what was intended to be a superhero bound but turned into a long stumble that almost sent me headfirst through the glass. Just in time, I braced myself with one hand and pressed down on the door latch with the other. Heddy gave up trying to turn the lock inside and simply held the door closed. Both Langmans were fit but they were no match for this manure-turning farmer. I planted one boot on the frame and yanked.

The door opened suddenly and spit Heddy out onto the sidewalk along with part of the door handle. She landed on her hands and knees, giving me a convenient look over the rear of her pants. They matched the color of the fabric Picasso had found but appeared intact.

"Get up and give it back before I call the police, Heddy."

"In case you haven't noticed, you're the one assaulting me," Heddy said, springing to her feet. "You've blocked the sidewalk and broken our lock."

"I'll replace the lock just as soon as you return my property," I said, pushing past her and going inside the store.

"What property is that?" I sensed she chose her words carefully. There was a good chance some of my other belongings had found their way into her possession, too. I hadn't wasted a second taking inventory before following the sisters into town.

"You know very well," I said, staying ahead of her. It wasn't easy to hold onto my lead given the display tables of porcelain, glassware and picture frames. I felt like the proverbial bull in a china shop. Luckily Keats moved with stealth and speed under the tables, while Percy jumped up and ran along the shelves he already knew well from previous visits. By the time I circled the counter and went into the back room, both animals were signaling disappointment. The entire area was packed with boxes and freestanding items waiting to be catalogued and either shipped or shown. There was nowhere to hide something as oddly shaped as a birdcage.

Nevertheless, Keats went into a point and I picked my way through the clutter to the back door and opened it. A white van sat in one of two parking spots, and as I walked around it, I noticed a long gouge on the driver's side.

I tried the sliding door and then the double rear doors, all the while fending off Heddy. She managed to get her hand through the straps on my overalls and haul back till she severed one of them. I shoved her aside and went around the other side of the van.

Locked.

Catching my phone as it was about to slip out of my sagging front pocket, I flicked on the flashlight and shone it inside.

Crouched in the back of the vehicle was Kaye Langman. I let the light run over her slowly, lingering for a satisfying moment on the white flesh gleaming through a gaping hole in her pant leg.

The birdcage was wedged between her sneakers.

"I'm only going to ask you once to come out with my cage, Kaye," I called through the glass. "Otherwise I'll hire someone to pry your van apart piece by piece."

"It's not your cage, Ivy," Heddy said.

"Finch Pefferlaw surrendered it to me and I have that in writing," I said, walking back around the truck to the driver's side.

"Should we get him to come down here with Jaws to confirm? I was afraid to get out of my truck with that mastiff around, but you two don't lack for courage."

"The birdcage doesn't belong to Finch, either," Heddy said. "Someone gave it to his grandmother, now deceased. Only we know its true provenance."

"Who gave it to his grandmother?" I asked.

"It was before your time and you have no right to know. Or to claim this piece," Heddy said.

"Look, I need that cage back right now. We can call the police and do it the easy way. Or we can do it the Edna way. Your choice."

It gave me a pang to remember Edna and I were on the outs. Would she still come and help me out of this bind? Probably. But I hated not being sure.

"I'm not afraid of Edna Evans," Heddy said.

"You should be." I let my index finger trail over the contact list on my phone. "But Gertie Rhodes is closer. Let's call her instead. She'll get things sorted out."

Gertie really was the better choice in this case. She had a deep and abiding hatred for the Langmans since they'd stolen not only her cat but also an object of deep sentimental value. The grudge was definitely personal.

Heddy blanched when I said Gertie's name. Normally the sisters were utterly shameless, but I sensed even Heddy knew they'd overstepped in pilfering one of Gertie's most precious mementos.

Holding up one hand to stop me from calling, Heddy rapped three times on the side of the van. The sliding door opened and Kaye emerged, moving rather stiffly. She'd probably been squatting over her "kill" for some time.

"Good morning, Ivy," Kaye said, with a grimace. "How can we help you today?"

"First, you can hand over the birdcage. Then you can hand over the cash to repair my utility shed and replace whatever else you stole." Heddy started to whine and I added, "Minus the cost of your lock."

"We didn't steal the birdcage," Kaye said. "Because it doesn't actually belong to you or to Finch Pefferlaw. It has a long history that should be preserved, not squandered in a silly fundraiser."

Heddy touched her sister's arm. "Just let it go. We'll scoop it at the sale. No one else will know its true value. Not even the stupid expert Ivy's friends hired."

I signaled for Keats to press both sisters back against the brick wall of the store. Percy strolled up the windshield to stare at them, unblinking, from the roof of the van. Only then did I feel safe enough to lean inside and collect the birdcage.

My fingers closed around the smooth metal, and my throat finally eased. I set it upright and looped my arm around the stand. The domed cage swung gently long after I stopped moving. "Tell me more," I said.

"We're not telling you anything," Kaye said. "Do your own digging, Ivy. Aren't you known for your insatiable curiosity? How are you different or better than us?"

"That one's easy," I said. "I don't profit from my insatiable curiosity."

Heddy crossed her arms. "Don't you? Poking your nose where it didn't belong landed you a farm, did it not? You barely need to work at all now."

I let out a guffaw and showed them the palm of my free hand. "Those callouses don't come from sitting by the fire doing needle-work, ladies."

"And yet you find time to run around interfering with systems that worked just fine before you parachuted in with your equally nosy pets," Kaye said.

"I have interfered with your plans to bilk families of their cherished heirlooms, and I can't say I'm sorry about that. But someday soon that behavior is going to get you in big trouble, ladies. Don't come crying to me when it happens. Now, if you don't mind, I've got to get back to my chores."

The sisters exchanged a glance and there was an almost imperceptible shift in the atmosphere. Keats and Percy had felt it before I did and gathered themselves, ready to react on my cue when the Langmans pounced.

Just as the two women started to move toward me, a brilliant flash shot down from the eaves. It was like a rainbow on wings. Heddy and Kaye squealed and shielded their eyes from wings, beak or both.

"Ow!" Heddy called. "What on earth?"

Kaye managed to get the door open and they backed into the store.

"Do you have your own personal air force now, too, Ivy?" she asked, through the screen.

"The cage has a temporary guest," I said, tucking the stand under my arm as best I could. "That's why it may not be available for the fundraiser."

The sisters released a joint sigh of relief. No doubt they figured if they were the only ones who knew where it was, they could still get at it. I would need to build a better mousetrap.

"Ivy, you'll never know the story of this cage if you let it go to strangers," Kaye said. "There's more at stake than a few dollars for rescue."

"No one ever appreciates the value of our regional history," Heddy said. "Verna Rae Cobbler's paintings, for example. The ones you talked her into donating should be stored until they appreciate."

"I didn't talk her into anything. Vernie wanted to contribute to the cause."

"We know your ways, Ivy," Heddy said. "You double talk until people think it's their own idea to do exactly what you want. Vernie might be alive right now if not for you."

The comment hit me in the chest hard enough to steal my breath for a few seconds. Keats' muzzle swiveled from me to the sisters as he assessed whether he was needed more for attack or comfort. I nodded to let him know I was all right. What they'd said had already crossed my mind, but I knew it was untrue. Vernie had taken those paintings with her to the vegetable stand that day. I didn't plant the seed for the donation.

"Ladies, you overestimate my powers of persuasion," I said. "And I expect you know by now that Vernie mentioned being worried about the two of you. Apparently you'd already tried to part her from her belongings."

"We took a liking to a certain piece, yes," Kaye said. "Vernie refused to sell and that was that."

She peered around for the bird and then cautiously opened the screen door again, probably preparing for another attempt to seize the cage.

"We've explained everything to the chief," Heddy said. "And there were plenty of witnesses placing us at the fundraising meeting during the approximate time of Vernie's passing. Thank goodness we decided to go early that day. You can always count on the Langmans to pitch in."

They exchanged a smug grin that got under my skin. Percy picked up on my irritation and decided to launch himself at them from the roof of the van. He aimed to miss, shooting between their heads like an orange missile. They were still screeching when the cat reappeared through their feet.

"I don't suppose you had to be there in person to do the deadly deed," I said. "You could buy a service like that with the treasure you stole from Gertie's land."

"Oh Ivy, you're letting your imagination run away with you again," Kaye said.

"And you're getting as lazy as your mother," Heddy added. "Whenever something goes wrong you Galloways want to blame it on hardworking Langmans. How about you dig a little deeper and help your boyfriend do the right thing by Vernie?"

I picked up the cage and walked over, dangling the scrap of khaki in front of Kaye's eyes. "Let's make a deal. A scrap for a clue."

"I don't deal with people like you," Kaye said, covering the hole in her slacks with one hand.

"Try Beverly Roxton," Heddy said, snatching the fabric from my fingertips. "We overheard her fighting with Vernie at the grocery store."

I backed away with the cage into the laneway. "Over art?"

"Over cucumbers," Heddy said. "What would Beverly know about culture?"

"I think it was zucchini, actually," Kaye said. "Something irrelevant, anyway."

"Produce was highly relevant to Vernie, just as it is to me," I said.

Their joint snigger was like nails on a chalkboard and it drove me further down the lane.

"Ask her why she visited the vegetable stand on the way to the fundraising meeting," Heddy said. "Maybe they finally came to an agreement over the cukes. Or zukes."

"Thanks for the lead," I said. "I bet my mom can help you mend those pants, Kaye. Are you two in her class?"

"We don't have time to learn to sew," Kaye said. "Collecting is beyond a full-time job."

"I suppose so," I said. "Keeping track of you collecting is a full-time job on top of my other job."

"Just keep that pretty head of yours buried in the manure where it belongs," Kaye called after me.

"Safe drive," Heddy added, laughing openly now.

When I came around the front of the store, a tow truck was easing away from the curb with my pickup on the back.

# CHAPTER SEVENTEEN

"It's fine, boys," I said, as we walked along Main Street. "We'll finish our business here and take a cab to the impound yard. Granted, it's a bit awkward carrying a birdcage around, but awkward has never stopped us before, has it?"

Keats mumbled that it had not. Indeed, awkward was a feeling I'd known from childhood and if anything, it spurred me on. I never managed to outrun it, but knowing it was nipping at my heels kept me moving forward.

"I've got to hand it to Heddy for managing to text parking patrol under pressure," I said. "It'll cost me to get the truck out, so I'm not paying for their lock."

Keats gave a laugh-pant. He was enjoying his day immensely thus far and it was still early.

"Wish I'd had a chance to grab my coat from the truck," I said, clutching the torn strap of my overalls with my free hand. I didn't dare stop and try to knot it together, because it would mean using both hands. The Langmans were no doubt lurking to try to snatch the cage.

I kept my chin up and pretended not to see people watching me. There was a T-shirt under my overalls so it wasn't like I was flashing anyone. Except maybe I was, in the back. The drooping was causing a little breeze where the shirt ended and my undies began. Often, I wore shorts under my overalls. Shame today wasn't one of those days.

A flash of color drew my eyes to the wires overhead. Picasso was keeping pace with me and he was hard to miss. So now people would talk about how I was strolling around town chatting to my dog and cat while trying to court birds into cages, like a pied piper.

Keats dismissed public opinion with a mumble as we stopped outside the grocery store.

"Is Beverly working today?" I asked Keats, who responded by raising one paw in a point.

There was a big "No Pets Allowed" sign on the door, which I was happy to flout with my therapy dog. Percy was another matter, and yet I couldn't leave him at the mercy of two sisters who'd exploited cats for gain before.

"Parrot up, Percy," I said, patting my right shoulder. "Let's try to keep a low profile, okay?"

Percy scaled my back and then kneaded my T-shirt briskly. Perhaps no one would notice the torn overalls with a cat on board.

I directed an open palm at the bunting, who took a seat on a streetlamp and twittered something that I took to mean good luck.

Opening the door, I checked to make sure the cashier was occupied before heading inside with the birdcage, the dog and the cat.

"Find Beverly," I whispered to Keats. "We'll only get one chance to surprise the truth out of her."

He led me past the fancy organic pastas and sauces, across the frozen food section at the back, and then halfway down the dairy aisle. When he lifted his paw again, I peeked into the produce section and saw Beverly Roxton stacking pale tomatoes into a neat pile.

A stealthy approach was nearly impossible with the heavy birdcage, drooping overalls, and a cat bracing himself with 20 claws, but

I did my best. Hoisting the cage a little higher, I tiptoed up behind Beverly and then set it down heavily. She turned quickly and when she saw it was me, two tomatoes slipped from her fingertips. Both hit the floor and rolled away.

"Those aren't local, Mrs. Roxton," I said. "Otherwise they'd have been ripe and made a splat and a mess."

"You're policing produce now, Ivy?" she said. "Surely you have more on your plate than green tomatoes."

"My point is that this store's claim to fame is the finest in local produce and there's plenty of it to be found. I don't know why you'd settle for hothouse tomatoes at this time of year."

"And I don't know why you care," she said. Her blue eyes glinted at me behind stylish new glasses. Her hair was dyed a flattering shade, now, too. Mom's work, I suspected. SurvivalDate must come with a makeover included.

"I care because my manure has been a boon to farmers and hobbyists alike this year. I'm sure the owner would be happy to shop local."

She scanned me and then took a step sideways. "I'm no stranger to eccentrics, Ivy, but you really take things to extremes. Your poor mother."

"Mom's not a big fan of my style choices," I said. "It sounds like you're becoming quite close these days."

"Dahlia? Not really." Beverly's eyes got shifty. "We have little in common."

"Except being single and happy," I said. "Although I was sorry to hear you'd split from Cliff. He's a wonderful vet."

Her face flushed brighter than the insipid tomatoes. "I have you to thank for that. We were doing just fine till you and your donkey stomped all over everything. Cliff actually believed his deranged father over me. Now he visits him in jail. So I lost a home, a husband and a job because you put the old man away."

"Someone *died*, Mrs. Roxton. And I didn't put him away, the police did."

"They deserved to die, at least according to public opinion. There was no reason to disrupt our perfectly happy life." She turned back to the tomatoes and started slamming them into rows. They held up remarkably well under pressure. Almost like plastic replicas.

"Well, now you can get a fresh start with SurvivalDate," I said. "There's probably someone far better suited to you out there. Or five someones. That's what a good rotation is all about."

She turned on me again, raising a tomato. "You hush now. I've been the innocent victim of enough gossip in this town. I just want to live a nice, orderly life and it all starts with making neat piles of vegetables."

"So that's why you like hothouse products." Keats brought me one of the tomatoes that had rolled away and I inspected it. "They're almost fake and probably genetically modified. No wonder you and Vernie Cobbler argued."

"I didn't argue with Vernie, I just told her I had no interest in selling her vegetables here. There was too little consistency, and you can't create a proper display with mismatched goods."

"You mean a natural, locally grown and tasty product. People still want that, Mrs. Roxton."

"Stop calling me that. I go by my maiden name now. Beverly Snorken."

"Fine, Miss Snorken. I heard that you and Vernie had it out over cucumbers."

"Summer squash, actually. Never saw a shabbier bushel of goods, but she wouldn't take no for an answer. I had to get security to see her out."

"And then what happened?" I asked.

Beverly put the tomatoes down, set her hands on her hips and glared at me. "I'll tell you what happened. Every day I drove by her blasted vegetable stand. And every day she hurled rotten produce at my car. It was the only route from the pathetic excuse for an apartment I rent in the outskirts. Vernie figured out my shifts somehow, and hid in the bushes. I never knew where she'd be or what she'd throw. One day I nearly went off the road when a cantaloupe hit the windshield. I reported her for reckless endangerment. All it got me was a watermelon the next day."

"Farming kept her strong," I said. "It can't be easy to hurl a watermelon at a moving target."

"The tomatoes were the worst," Beverly said. "They actually damaged the paint."

"Is that why you stopped at Vernie's stand right before she died?" I asked. "Obviously it wasn't to buy blue pumpkins."

"I don't know what you're talking about," Beverly said, turning away. "Blue pumpkins? We'd never sell such a thing here. Pumpkins are meant to be orange."

"The Langmans said they saw you there when they were on the way to the fundraising meeting."

"I was merely dropping off a bill for a professional car wash after she pelted my car with putrid onions. All that got me was an acorn squash between the shoulder blades when I left." She rubbed the spot where it had probably connected. "I wanted to press charges for assault and was disappointed she died before I could."

"What a sad waste of produce," I said. "I always asked Vernie to save the seconds for my animals."

"Move along, Ivy," Beverly said. "If you came in to accuse me of killing Vernie, I've already presented video evidence to the police of her savage squash attack that day. But I'm not surprised someone gave her what she deserved."

"Vernie didn't deserve to die, Miss Snarken."

"That's Snorken." Her chin tipped up and she added, "Not again!"

There was a bright flash overhead as Picasso flew past.

"Birds keep coming in through our receiving door, but I've found a solution." She bent and pulled a long pool net out from under the shelving. "I'll swat it down and wring its neck like the last five."

"Beverly! You'll do no such thing. That's a rare painted bunting."

"I don't care what it is, the filthy beast," she said, swinging the net at Picasso and missing. When she was getting ready to take another swipe, the bird turned back, hovered and unloaded droppings on her head.

I had the distinct impression he was thinking, "Take that for Vernie."

"Oh dear," I said, picking up the produce hose. "Let me rinse that off for you."

She dropped the net, grabbed the sprayer and fired on me. Normally Keats would have taken great offence, but anyone holding a water weapon was the automatic winner as far as my dog was concerned. Percy wanted to launch at her but I held him on my shoulder as I hustled out of the store with the birdcage.

By the time I reached the sidewalk, my other overall strap had slipped off my shoulder and I added a memorable scandal to my long list by briefly flashing passersby.

"Maybe I should try that again at impound and the guy won't charge me," I said, once my straps were up. "I deserve a silver lining."

## CHAPTER EIGHTEEN

J illy and I both took a deep breath before opening the door to The Tipsy Grape wine bar that evening. Our nights out were few and far between, and it was a shame we had to use one this way. It was going to be excruciating. I had no doubt about that.

"It might not be that bad," she said, as if reading my mind. Between the pets and Jilly, I had turned into an open book.

Keats was caught up in his own thoughts. His nose was up and his ears down. Even from outside, the place reeked of something. Quiet desperation, perhaps.

Or not so quiet.

Stepping into the bar, I heard Mom's tinkling laugh, followed by laughter from at least half a dozen women.

"Again," Mom called out, and laughter followed. "Lighter, ladies. Bright and breezy, remember? And now a giggle, please."

Mom gave a demonstration that sounded like the baby doll I received for my fifth birthday. The poor thing suffered extreme neglect as I far preferred my farm set, complete with livestock hand-carved by my grandfather.

"Oh my gosh, she's teaching my enemies how to giggle," I said, dropping my fingers to Keats' ears. "How is that possible?"

"It does make me uncomfortable," Jilly said. "These women should require a license to date."

"At least local men will be well aware of their pasts," I said. "They couldn't avoid hearing the gossip. With single men being in short supply, they should have their pick of more worthy candidates."

Jilly looped her arm through mine and pulled me forward. "Let's get it over with. At least Dahlia said we could join the fun."

I didn't reply as I stared over at the round table.

"Ivy?" Jilly said. "Dahlia did say it was okay, right? Tell me we're not crashing SurvivalDate night."

"She's my mother. I'm always welcome, just as she takes over my best room at the inn whenever she likes. I expect her to pick up our tab with her earnings, too."

"Oh my," Jilly said. "If you'd warned me, we could have done a few shooters and cabbed over. Keats is the only one who needs to be sober for this."

"That's right, and with any luck, he'll tell us what we need to know before our second cosmopolitan."

"Since when did you drink cosmopolitans?" Jilly asked.

I swept my free hand to the table. "Since tonight. There's one in front of every lady. It's the drink of choice in the dating bunker."

Mom's hands flashed as if directing traffic around a highway collision. She was so caught up that she didn't see us coming. That made her little squeal all the more satisfying when Keats greeted her with a love nip on the thigh.

"Stop that, you mongrel. This is my lucky dress." She batted him away. "You're not allowed in a restaurant so I suggest you leave before I have you thrown out."

"I'd like to see you try it." I bent to kiss her cheek. Although my public displays of affection were rare with Mom, I wanted to remind her class that her first debt of loyalty was to me, her youngest child. Jilly, her favorite child-to-be, dropped a kiss on her other cheek.

Mom pulled a handkerchief out of her purse and wiped the affection right off.

"Go away, girls," she said. "This isn't the time for your games. My classes are serious business."

I pulled out my best HR smile before looking around the table. "Serious business? We heard gales of laughter as we walked in. No one could resist coming over."

Jilly turned to look for available chairs, but all the neighboring tables were full.

"See? There's no room for you," Mom said. "Perhaps you could try the pub down the road."

A young man halfway across the bar got to his feet and brought Jilly a chair. When none of the ladies made space at the table, he shoved it between Gwen Quinn and Beverly Snorken. Then he repeated the move for me. Jilly gave him a sweet smile before taking a seat and letting him push the chair in for her. I thanked him and got myself settled before the group could squeeze me out again.

"Is this where we giggle, Mom?" I asked. "Or do we wait for someone to buy us a cosmopolitan?"

Mom pressed her red lips together. "Save your jokes, Ivy. This group isn't about free drinks."

"Hardly," Mercy Bellweather said. "I can afford my own drinks."

"Then what is it about?" Jilly asked. "I can't imagine any of you ladies need any help finding a date."

"You'd be surprised," Satin Carnegie said. "It gets harder to find quality men when you pass a certain age, especially in hill country. I've heard the ratio is eight to one in favor of the men."

"At least you're new to the region," Joan Snelling said. "Fresh blood."

"Most men probably don't meet quality standards, anyway," Mercy said.

"By this point, I just want a man who's healthy and able to support himself," Satin said.

"Exactly the right attitude, Satin," Mom said. "This is about setting your standards low."

"Why aim low, Mom?" I asked. "That's not what you told your daughters."

"This is a different approach," she said. "It's a numbers game. Our goal is to amass a fine stable of interested men. Then we can simply lean back, sip our cosmos, and allow them to impress us. The cream eventually rises to the top."

"Where does the giggling come in?" I asked.

"Men enjoy the company of women who are happy and living a full life," she said. "The busier I am, the more popular I get. You and Jilly are the rarity for being able to attract quality men while being so dour."

"Dour!" Jilly was horrified. "We are not dour."

"Ivy most certainly is," Mom said. "I hardly ever hear her laugh anymore."

I laughed at her all the time but that must not count. "Maybe that's because I keep stumbling into crime scenes. I used to giggle, too." I turned to Jilly. "Didn't I?"

"Not really," my best friend said. "That wasn't in our repertoire."

"You never giggled even as a baby, Ivy. You were a very serious infant who started reading before the age of three."

"A prodigy," Silkie Carnegie said. "It's no wonder you've gone on to have a remarkable life, Ivy."

"And met a quality man," Satin said. "Giggling isn't always necessary."

"It is for people like us," Joan Snelling said.

"Speak for yourself, Joan," Beverly said.

"No offense, Bev." Joan looked chastened. "I'm just saying my reputation needed a makeover after I divorced my husband. I spent plenty of time reading self-help books but nothing has helped me more than Dahlia's class in just three short weeks."

Mom inclined her head graciously. "That's so kind of you, Joan.

And we all need a helping hand sometimes. I struggled for years to find my way while raising my children alone. Now I am enjoying life to the fullest and you can, too."

"Ivy, your mother's program is working wonders," Mercy said. "The first modules are all about self-care and fostering your own interests. I've taken up painting and piano again."

"I joined a choir in Dorset Hills," Beverly said. "That Christmas fiasco at least proved I have a fine voice and Dahlia's questionnaire reminded me of that."

"I got a new puppy because of this class," Gwen said. "And met a nice man in the dog park in Fleetborough."

"Fleetborough?" I said. "That's a hike."

"Sometimes we need to fish in new water," Mom said. "We all deserve a fresh start, Ivy."

I wasn't at all convinced Gwen deserved a fresh start, and neither was Keats. My fingers rested on his neck so that I could feel his mumbled commentary. When Gwen spoke, a growl rolled in his throat.

Silkie raised her hand to go next. "I'd given up riding horses, but thanks to your mother, I'm taking lessons and volunteering to lead pony rides for children's parties. I haven't met anyone at the stable to add to *my* stable, but it's only a matter of time."

"That's right," Mom said. "When you're happy, you magnetize men. There aren't enough days in the week now to see my regulars because I need time for my sewing."

"Dahlia, can your techniques win back our exes?" Mercy asked. "I'm not sure I want to close that chapter of my life."

Mom took a sip of her drink, leaving a red lip print on the martini glass. "It's entirely possible. My techniques could attract an old love as well as a new one. I've recently started dating a man who fancied me back in high school, when I only had eyes for... But never mind. In the end, none of this is really about dating. It's about becoming the best version of yourself. If you do that work, the right man will follow."

"I agree," Joan said. "My ex showed up randomly the other day and mowed the lawn. We hadn't spoken in two months."

"He can feel your energy shifting," Mom said. "It's as simple as that. Well done."

Beverly leaned on the table and stared at Mom. "Would you take Calvin back, Dahlia?"

Mom's ruby fingertips tapped the table, a sign I recognized as discomfort. "It's usually better to look ahead, ladies. Falling back into old relationships can make you fall back into old habits, too. This is about creating new habits. Becoming our highest self."

"Is that a no?" Beverly persisted. "If so, it means Calvin is available."

"He is a fine-looking man," Gwen said. "Perhaps a little young for me."

"But not me," Satin said.

"Or me," Silkie chimed in.

"I called it first, Silkie," Satin said. "Just because you're a year older doesn't mean you come first in everything."

Mom switched from tapping to rapping the table. "You two bicker worse than my own kids. I say this with love, but negativity is going to repel men."

"You're just saying that because we're arguing over your ex," Silkie said.

"Yeah," her sister said. "If you don't want him, he's fair game."

My throat squeezed shut as I pictured Beverly or Gwen or any of the others sitting beside my father at the dinner table surrounded by my family.

Jilly reached under the table to grab my hand and our fingers rested on Keats' back.

Mom's hand stilled and she smiled. "New class rule, ladies. I want us all to succeed and we can't do that if we're competing with each other for available resources. During our time together, we must agree not to date the same men."

There was a disgruntled murmur around the table. "There aren't enough for all of us, Dahlia," Satin said.

"Of course there are," Mom said. "We're as different as snowflakes and what appeals to me certainly won't appeal to you or Joan, for example. I've provided a comprehensive list in your packages of places to look. Class reunions. Cultural and fundraising events. Seminars, and so on. Start by pursuing your own dreams. Even female-dominated interests like sewing can take you somewhere good. I did a dress fitting last week and the client set me up with her brother. Easy peasy. You just need to be open and receptive."

"I don't believe you answered my question," Beverly persisted. "Would you take Calvin back?"

Mom hesitated so long that I turned to stare at her. I expected a quick no. Or a slow no. But most certainly a no of some flavor. She had avoided my father for months, and redoubled her efforts to date widely. If Mom was interested in heating up the cold porridge, as Edna described it, she had hidden it well.

"Sometimes too much water has passed under the bridge," Mom said, before swallowing the rest of her drink in a single gulp. "But I pledged to be honest with you, so I'll admit I'd like Calvin to appreciate what he lost."

"He already does, Dahlia," Jilly said. "How could he not?"

Mom blinked a few times. "I hope you're right, Jillian." She patted her lips with a cocktail napkin. "We all look back sometimes, but whenever I find myself regretting the past, I know it's time to add a new gentleman to my rotation. A good one who will distract me. When you're starting out, it's about quantity. At my stage, it's about quality. I learned my lessons and now I only want to spend my time on the finest men, who will value my company."

"How can you juggle them all, Dahlia?" Mercy asked. "I only have three in my rotation and I can't keep the details straight."

"Spreadsheets," Mom said.

I couldn't help laughing. "Spreadsheets? Is that why you wanted my old laptop?"

"Darling, you have no idea how complicated this is. I keep detailed notes on every gentleman—his hobbies, children, professional history. They need to feel unique and special before they can make us feel unique and special. I know we're all highly motivated to do the work."

"Definitely," Joan said. "Verna Rae Cobbler's passing was a terrible wakeup call."

"How so?" I asked, feeling Keats come to attention.

Beverly scowled at me. "None of us wants to end up like Vernie, obviously. Old, alone and hurling vegetables. She was a textbook case of what to avoid."

"Bev, please," Mom said. "Negativity only attracts the same. Light and breezy, remember."

"It's not Vernie's fault," Joan said. "I'm of nearly the same vintage and it was even harder to find suitable young men in our day. Seemed like everyone was tied up in ill-doings. My family chose my husband and look how that turned out."

"Vernie had a choice not to become bitter," Mom said. "Or at least to shrug off bitterness later, as I did. I'm not saying it's easy, but it is possible."

"We didn't know her," Silkie said. "But she sounds like a miserable woman."

"Not always," I said. "No one is what they seem on the surface, are they?"

"I am," Silkie said. "And so is my sister. We take pride in being authentic."

"Which is why this class is difficult for us," Satin said. "It feels like we need to be, well, fake."

"At the beginning, yes," Mom said. "Fake it till you make it. Eventually your peace and contentment will shine through, fully authentic."

"If Vernie had learned to fake it, perhaps she'd have come to a better end, instead of a bitter end," Beverly said, taking another kick at the departed. It was tacky, and only the thought of Picasso pooping on her head kept me from doing so verbally. There was no topping the job he'd done so well.

"Vernie's passing galvanized us all," Gwen said. "It reminded us that life is short. One moment you're shoveling potatoes, the next you're under them fertilizing."

Mom winced at that. "It is about seizing the day, no question. We can turn anything around by working hard enough."

I stared at my mother, realizing she *had* changed. This wasn't just lip service. She was throwing herself into her interests and living what she taught. As a result of making herself happy, it seemed she never lacked for male company. Increasingly, judging by the whirring of her sewing machine in my best suite, she preferred her own company and interests.

Keats nudged my hand. He was growing impatient.

I glanced at Jilly and we shoved our chairs back at the same time. My friend pulled a stack of business cards out of her pocket. "Ladies, as Dahlia said, volunteering is a great way to meet new friends and we could use your help at the rescue fundraiser."

I took the cards from her, and Keats led me around the table. As I handed one to each woman, I kept my eyes on the dog for telltale signs of trouble.

It proved more difficult than expected because Keats was disgruntled with the whole affair. His ruff was up and his tail puffed and only Mom and Joan got what I'd consider a free pass from canine judgement.

We said our goodbyes and left the bar.

"I guess that was a bust," Jilly said.

I shook my head. "There was plenty to worry about at that table, but answers aren't going to be served up to us on a silver platter."

Holding up her left hand, Jilly angled her emerald engagement ring under the streetlights. "Thank goodness for your brother, Ivy. He's a quality man and I only need one."

"I feel the same about Kellan," I said. "I'm going to try a giggle on him later and see if a ring comes out of it."

She offered a good impression of Mom's tinkling laugh. "There's still time to make it a double wedding, my friend. Or a triple if your mom surrenders to her feelings about Calvin."

I shook my head as we got into the truck. "You had to go and ruin that moment, didn't you?"

"I'm looking out for myself, now," Jilly said, fastening her seatbelt. "I expect to cook every Galloway holiday dinner for decades to come. None of those women will be at my table if I can help it. My children will never call Bev or Gwen 'grandma.'"

Turning the key in the ignition, I tried a giggle on for size and Jilly gave one back. That made us both giggle for real.

"Have I mentioned you're my favorite sister?" I said. "I mean, I love my bio sisters but you make bad times fun."

I expected Keats to join in the merriment, but he shot us both blue-eyed reprimands.

That drained the fun out of the moment. When Keats couldn't spare a laugh, it meant trouble was closing in.

# CHAPTER NINETEEN

The next morning was crisp and clear. Normally I loved feeling that bite of fall in the air, but today I wasn't happy. How could I be when we weren't a single step closer to solving either mystery?

"Maybe I've burned out and lost my mojo," I said to Keats when I came out of the henhouse. Collecting eggs was my absolute favorite chore of the day—even more so than turning manure. There was something so zen about hunting for eggs and I loved seeing the mix of sizes and colors in my basket. It was like Easter every day, and now all the eggs were mine. As a kid, Asher had left precious few of those for me.

Keats gave a noncommittal mumble and led me into the barn. He was more annoyed than concerned that things hadn't fallen nicely into place for us. Patience wasn't his strong suit.

Even waiting for me to finish in the henhouse each day was tough. For him, that chore was incredibly boring. He left it to me and spent the time greeting his colleague, Byron, and their various charges. I had worried about the two dogs getting along but there was a mutual respect and a seeming understanding that there was plenty of work for all. Keats had slept better since Byron took on the overnight shift. At midnight, two and four a.m., Keats gave an inquiring bark and Byron answered in kind, saying all was well. It put the dogs' minds at ease, but often I stayed awake afterward and got a head start on worrying. Today, I'd been racking my brain since the two a.m. call and answer.

Keats, on the other hand, had pep in his step as he turned out the animals. He wanted to get the job done and move on to new challenges. I expected to receive my marching orders from him shortly. Percy was already waiting on the hood of the truck so I was apparently the last to know.

"I hope Picasso is okay," I said after we escorted Elaine, the emu, to the pasture she shared with Alvina. "I wonder where he sleeps now."

The birdcage was back in the basement, where I knew it was safe. Charlie had installed bars on the windows for me and the rare times we were all out, I turned on the alarm. Never had a farm been so well defended.

Yet nothing made me feel safer than my black-and-white security guard.

He gave a humble mumble and then offered a point into the thicket near the barn. The painted bunting hopped out onto a branch and gave a musical warble. I recognized the tune from our first meeting.

"He wants us to follow him," I said.

Keats rounded me up and headed for the truck.

"Driving? Keats, I can barely keep this beast on the road without trying to track a little songbird, no matter how colorful."

"How about I drive, you track?"

The voice startled me. My father was standing in the doorway of the barn and his truck was nowhere in sight.

"Where's your truck?" I asked. "Did you sleep here?"

"Truck's in the shop," Calvin said. "And yes."

I shook my head. "Where, exactly? I've been in and out a dozen times already and didn't see you."

"Ask Percy. He came up and said good morning, just like always."

"You sleep in the loft regularly? Why?"

He shrugged. "I like to keep an eye on things."

"On the animals? Should I be worried?"

"There's no reason to worry if I'm in the loft. That's kind of the point."

My father walked to the truck, easily snatching the keys out of the air when I tossed them.

"Calvin, you can't sleep in the barn all the time. There are plenty of spare beds inside. The inn is never at capacity, unfortunately."

"You're at more capacity than I can handle," he said, with a wry smile. I imagined he meant my mother but decided not to ask. Their business was their business. "I've been on my own a long time, Ivy."

"But you do own a house, now."

He'd purchased the Galloway homestead after Kellan released exactly enough of the treasure recovered from the family property to cover the sale. Yet, Calvin preferred camping out here.

"I sleep better with livestock around," he said, getting behind the wheel. "The downside of being a longtime ranch hand."

"Keats, Percy and Byron didn't see fit to tell me we had an overnight guest," I said, hopping into the passenger seat. Keats got into my lap and Percy took the back lookout.

Calvin gave the dog a pat before turning the key. "We all have an understanding. A farm runs on good teamwork."

"Then why buy the house at all?" I asked.

"To keep anyone else from getting it?" He pulled the truck around and started down the lane. "Is that a good enough reason?"

I laughed. "Sure. Plus you've got an original, high quality bunker over there. Beats a shipping container."

"Don't know about that. The idea of being stuck down there if someone drops in a grenade doesn't appeal."

"I need to learn more about bunkers," I said. "Just not from Edna."

"There are other experts around," he said. I started to ask, but he raised his hand to cut me off. "Maybe I'll get used to the old house eventually. It's too full of ghosts right now."

"Ghosts?"

"Bad memories," he said. "Of my father, mostly. He was a difficult man."

I rolled down the window and stuck my head out. "Picasso! Show yourself!"

The bird shot out in front of us and did an aerial spin, like a multicolored Ferris wheel.

"Spectacular," Calvin said. "Did he just follow orders?"

"I'd say he's just making it easier for us to follow *his* orders."

I pointed left at the end of the lane and my father raised his eyebrows. "Any idea where we're going?"

"None. Nope. Nada."

My father laughed. "Any idea *why* we're going?"

I pondered whether to share the story. I still didn't know my father well and wasn't sure exactly how deep I wanted to go. Or how deep he was capable of going. It was easier for Asher and some of my sisters, it seemed. Mom would probably say Calvin and I were too much alike and just thinking about it made my inner hackles rise. I'd never abandon my kids. Or even my animals.

Keats mumbled a suggestion to chill out. I gave him a squeeze and said, "Quiet."

"Just like my mother," Calvin said. "Always chitchatting to her dogs. I love animals but I don't understand them the same way you do."

"You do great," I said. "No one can handle Drama Llama and the thug donkeys like you. It seems like they're calming down lately."

"Now that you mention it, I do speak thug," he said.

Keats gave a pant-laugh and I joined in. If the dog was enjoying himself, it was probably okay for me to let down my guard a little.

I gestured for Calvin to turn right just after we passed Vernie's Vegetables. The cart still stood where it had, only now it was covered with wreaths and bouquets. There couldn't be a formal funeral as yet, so people paid their respects in a way they hadn't in Vernie's lifetime. She wouldn't have welcomed it anyway.

"Looks like we're hitting the trails," I said. "I can't imagine how that will take us any closer to solving our puzzle, but it's not my job to question."

"What puzzle? Vernie's death?"

I shook my head. "That's Kellan's mystery to solve, although I do a little poking around where I can. My number one mission is finding the proper home for some love letters and a big diamond ring."

"You don't say." Calvin sounded intrigued. I hadn't expected him to show much interest in an old romance. "And how is the bird connected with this?"

"That I don't know. But he led Jilly and me to a broken-down barn on the Harlow property. The bird pointed out a metal box and a key, and the letters and ring were inside. There's no clue about the identity of the lady writer, but I'm assuming one of the Harlow boys was the recipient."

"You asked Sterling when you dropped by, I assume?"

I nodded and gestured for him to enter the trail behind the abandoned forge. It was one of many buildings the township hadn't gotten around to either refurbishing or demolishing. The decision of trash versus treasure was tough in Clover Grove.

"He said three of the Harlows had already passed, probably under suspicious circumstances."

Calvin gave a bark of laughter. "Few lasted long enough to die of natural causes in those days."

It was a touchy subject as his mother had been murdered, and perhaps his father, as well.

"Well, I'm guessing at least one of them is still around or the bird wouldn't have bothered revealing the box. My job is to try to speak bunting well enough to execute his wishes."

"Bunting? Is that what it is?"

"A painted bunting, yes. Picasso."

He took the bumpy trail at a pace I would never have dared. "Picasso. Interesting. How'd you come up with that one?"

I shrugged. "I don't know how I come up with my own name sometimes. I feel like a…"

"Medium?"

I laughed. "I was going to say puppet. But yeah. I watch and listen and try to figure out what they're telling me. Sometimes it's easier than others."

My father stopped looking for my signs and picked up speed. He made a dizzying series of turns, looping back twice and running through a creek several times. As far as I could tell, the bird was nowhere to be seen.

Finally I asked, "Do *you* know where we're going? Because I don't."

"I think so," he said. "I keep getting a glimpse of the bird."

I was reasonably sure he was *not* getting a glimpse of the bird, because Keats was staring out the passenger window. If the bird was in easy view, he'd be watching for it.

"You don't see that bird," I said.

"I do. At least, I think so. It's in my peripheral vision."

It was in his imagination, I suspected. But he was most definitely going somewhere with confidence, and it was all uphill on a trail that grew incredibly twisty and then faded to nothing more than a hint of tracks through heavy brush.

Finally, he drove out onto a broad plateau and parked. We all jumped out.

Sure enough, Picasso was there, soaring out over a ledge that overlooked a picturesque valley below. Clover Grove was nestled in hills to the left, and Dorset Hills was barely visible to the right.

"Where are we?" I asked. "I've never been here before, but you obviously have."

"Garnet Point," he said. "More than a century ago, a prospector came looking for gold and found garnets instead. They became the stone of choice around here for decades to come. Worth very little, but they're pretty." He gave me an impish grin that made him look years younger. "There was a myth that if you gave your girl a garnet out here, and she accepted it, you were promised for life. The diamond was just a formality."

"Why don't I have a garnet?" I said.

"The myth probably died with my generation. Those little things meant more back then. We had to sneak around, you see. Boys didn't just take a girl on a date. We were more likely to be shot by protective fathers. Including your grandfather."

"Does Mom have one of these garnets?"

"Of course. Several. I staked her out early."

"The locket," I said. "I thought it was her mother's."

"It was *my* mother's," he said. "I had a jeweler down in Fleetborough embed the garnets inside so her parents couldn't see she'd been claimed. We were so young."

I watched the bird soar and dive, and a spacious feeling opened in my heart. This was where he wanted to be. I was quite sure of that.

Finally I turned to Calvin. "She still wears that locket, you know."

He nodded. "I saw it one day. Sentimental value, I guess."

It was more than that. When I came home the locket had been dull, always tucked away inside her dresses or blouses. Then one day it shone again. She must have had it professionally cleaned—perhaps after Calvin came home.

"Huh. Well, I suppose that's why red is her favorite color. Garnet Gush is her signature lipstick."

Calvin's face flushed a different shade of red. I didn't know how he felt about Mom these days, but our conversation was making him mighty uncomfortable.

"So, why do you think your feathered friend wanted to come out here?" he asked, changing the subject.

"There are four little red stones in the engagement ring we found," I said. "I'm guessing the gentleman in question observed the rituals of the day. Maybe he proposed here." I looked around, smiling. "The scenery is stunning and the air is so fresh."

"Like champagne, we used to say. Best view in all of hill country to my mind. But there are probably few alive who know how to find Garnet Point."

"You knew the route like the back of your hand," I said. "You drove so fast I'd never find it again."

He led me to the truck. "It wasn't by memory alone. Your mom and I came so often I marked the way. When I got home last spring, one of the first things I did was refresh my old routes."

As we drove back, he pointed to small splashes of red paint on oak trees far above eye level. He must have brought out a ladder and painstakingly dotted dozens and dozens of trees.

When we got down the hill, he showed me a series of similar markers in blue, and then various other colors.

"I've been using an app to try to map out routes back here," I said. "Meanwhile you've been doing it the old-fashioned way."

"I'm an old-fashioned guy," he said. "Everyone has their own way to go back here. These are my trails. Some I even cut myself."

"Kellan told me about that tradition," I said. "You try to leave the trails better than you found them, he said. There are banks of trees he planted with Asher."

My father smiled. "I'm glad. I never got a chance to show you kids around. Sounds like Asher found his way."

I sat in silence for a few minutes, until Keats mumbled something encouraging. "Would you mind showing *me* your routes?" I asked, at last. "I might need them more than Asher does now."

"Sure. That's why I refreshed them, actually. It seemed like you might need to make a quick getaway sometimes."

"More often than I'd like," I said. "Edna has her routes, and even Mom drove us out of here, once. It was the strangest thing. She's the worst driver on the planet but she became one with this truck when we got near Potter's Bog."

"That's my yellow route," he said. "Easier to see at night. We'll make that one a priority because most who go into the bog don't come out without help." After a few beats, he added, "I'm proud of your mom."

"Me too. She has her moments."

We fell into a comfortable silence that lasted till we were about 15 minutes from the farm.

"There were worse things than bogs in my day," he said. "You know about some of them, Ivy, but not all."

"Did people have help to get out?"

"Sometimes. If they were very lucky."

"Like an underground railroad?" I asked.

"I suppose, yeah." He crisscrossed the stream in what I now realized was a strategic maneuver to throw pursuers off the trail, or at least slow them down.

"So, someone got you out. You didn't just..." I caught my breath and Keats shoved his head under my hand. "Just leave."

"I was encouraged and supported to leave," he said. "Before there was trouble that affected all of you." He slowed to a crawl and wove among a series of carefully placed pine trees that some enterprising young man had planted at least 40 years ago, judging by their height. It reminded me of running a dog through an agility course. "Sterling had help before me."

"Really? Uncle Sterling went underground, too?"

"For a decade or more, yes. By the time he settled in Fleetborough, the coast had cleared."

"Specifically, people had died off."

Calvin gave a reluctant nod. "More or less. But it was never safe for him to move home to Clover Grove."

"But it's safe for you?"

He shrugged. "I'm not sure. I decided it was safer to be here than away right now. Something's percolating." He raised his hand to stop a flood of questions. "I don't know what. If I did, I'd tell Kellan and your brother. It's just something in the air."

"Not champagne," I said.

"Something more toxic, I'm afraid. We'll just need to wait and see."

We emerged from the trail at the old forge again and I noticed a spot of brilliant color perched on its peaked roof. "Calvin," I said. "Dad. Is it possible a couple of the Harlow boys took the underground railroad out of here? Martha Kinkaid suspected they bungled a heist and wanted to leave."

"Possibly," he said. "None of the, uh, passengers know about each other. Officially. That's part of the contract, such as it is."

"But can you find out? Are your railroad conductors still around?"

He shook his head. "I wouldn't risk exposing anyone, Ivy. Not when so many protected me."

"Not even to give a happier ending to a tragic love story?"

He reached out to pat my arm, thought better of it, and patted Keats instead. "Not even for a love story. Especially not for a love story, I suppose. Usually we left the region to protect those we loved. That's probably what happened for your lady of letters."

"But it's such an old story. How can it be dangerous now?"

"Are you *really* asking me that after what you've been through? You know full well how these things work."

I hugged Keats a little too tight and he grunted in disgust. "I'm going to figure it out. There's a reason this bird showed up when he did."

Calvin sighed. "That's why we're putting back country navigation on the schedule. And if you don't mind, I'd appreciate a cot in the loft. These old bones like a few luxuries now."

Percy came over my shoulder and purred loudly as he head-butted me. "I agree, Percy. We deserve garnets, too. Are there any still around, Dad?"

"Ask your friends. The Langmans. If anyone can hook you up with vintage garnets, it's them."

Keats let out his dog version of a raspberry. "Forget that," I said. "I'd rather go down in Potter's Bog than ask them for help."

Calvin laughed as we turned into the farm lane. "Two things I definitely didn't miss while being on the lam: Heddy and Kaye."

# CHAPTER TWENTY

"Where to now, boys?" I said, as we headed back down the lane half an hour later. "Calvin and Charlie have everything under control so we've got the day free. Let's make a difference."

Keats mumbled a reminder that he always made a difference and I pardoned the bragging because it was really just a statement of fact. Percy, meanwhile, curled up on the passenger seat with his tail over his face, content to be a cat. While he most certainly made a difference, too, the pressure to do so didn't keep him up at night checking in with Byron and Calvin. This chill feline dude had plenty to teach me about keeping my cool.

The fluffy tail lifted and he directed the full force of his green eyes at me before dropping the orange curtain again.

"That wasn't particularly helpful, Percy. Today is our day to move things along. I feel it. I just don't know how or where, and you two could probably give me some insights."

Keats kept his paws propped on the dashboard and his eyes straight ahead. If he knew our next steps, he wasn't saying.

"Fine, then, pie it is," I said. "It's later than usual though and we won't have Mandy to ourselves."

The parking lot outside the country store was half-full when we arrived, and while I didn't feel like talking to anyone I went inside anyway. When in doubt, it was always best to apply sugar and caffeine to a situation.

Mandy gestured to the round table at the far end of the café area instead of our usual spot at the counter. That meant she had something of interest to share and needed privacy to do it.

Keats' ears came forward and he trotted past the other customers like a dressage horse. Beverly Snorken and Mercy Bellweather had their heads together whispering at one table and only looked up when Keats gave a little bark likely intended to startle them.

It worked. Mercy jumped and smiled. Beverly jumped and frowned.

"Good morning, Ivy," Mercy said. She was wearing another elaborate dress, this time in dusty rose with plenty of tulle and ribbon. I was surprised Mom hadn't gone through everyone's wardrobe already. She would most certainly have vetoed the dress as well as Bev's old stirrup pants. On the other hand, every student was a special snowflake.

"Good morning," I said, watching Keats. He didn't like either woman, but they may only have been guilty of poor character. "Working on a class assignment?"

Mercy put a finger to her lips and glanced around. "We're going to do our mandatory volunteer hours today. Satin and Silkie suggested we help the rescue people refurbish and repair donations."

I smiled at the idea of Mercy lifting a finger in that dress, but Mom was a good role model for being present while doing little.

"Maybe I'll drop by later and help," I said. "I have errands to run first."

Mandy came along carrying a plate with a double slice of coconut cream pie in one hand and a coffee in the other.

"Oh, Ivy, you're not," Bev said. "That's a heart attack waiting to happen. What would Kellan think?"

"He'd be jealous," I said. "I outeat him, most days."

"Well, I've become a vegan since leaving Cliff. The store gives me a discount on produce."

Mercy looked at me questioningly. "Do single men take cooking classes, Ivy?"

"Don't ask me. My mom's the expert on male-kind."

"You seem to have done all right for yourself," Mercy said. "Appearances to the contrary."

Bev snorted into her coffee cup. "Ivy was different in high school when she bewitched the chief, Mercy. I remember thinking she was the best of a sorry lot."

"Aw, thanks, Miss Snorken." Keats gave a big sniff and I took his cue. "I do smell something strange, Keats. Is it rotten vegetables or bird guano?"

Beverly flushed to the roots of her freshly dyed hair and I moved along feeling more inspired. A double dose of pie would push me right over the top.

Setting Percy's carrier down, I took a seat and accepted the fork Mandy held out to me. It was a ceremonial offering, like the passing of a torch. Or a sword.

"What's up?" I asked, digging in without further ado. "Did the rumor mill serve up something tasty?"

"Yes, and hopefully no." Mandy perched across from me and set her elbows on the table. "I've heard nothing new about Vernie Cobbler," she whispered, "but Teri Mason was in here yesterday sitting right where you are, with her sketchbook and colored pencils. When she flipped through it, I saw the same beautiful bird over and over again. A painted bunting, Teri said. It used to visit Imogen before she died. Now, it's back and visits all the time."

"Picasso," I said, around a mouthful of pie. "I wondered where he went when he left in the morning."

"It's got to mean something, right?" Mandy asked. "Teri seemed very taken with it."

"I'll head over there shortly and find out more," I said.

Mandy leaned in as I told her about what had happened with both Edna and my Mom. Nodding, she said, "SurvivalDare and SurvivalDate. I figured they'd give you and Kellan a headache but I have to admit both classes have brought me more business. Your Mom's students survive on caffeine alone and Edna's leave nothing for anyone else."

"And here I thought the preppers were existing on canned beans."

"Edna, maybe. The rest are beefing up before the end comes. I've introduced a new stick-to-your-ribs spinach and egg dish your sisters love. I call it my Apocalyptic Strata."

"The end is going to come as a great disappointment to these folks," I said. "Because you won't be catering to them."

"I wouldn't even survive the training," Mandy said. "Violet sprained her wrist during combat training and Poppy dislocated a finger. Edna patched them up."

"They did that to each other? They must be as clumsy as me."

"It was a duel against the Agnews," Mandy said. "Sisters on sisters. And the Agnews apparently play to win."

I shook my head. "I thought my sisters would quit the class after their trip to the cop shop. Especially when Kellan specifically told the group to disband."

"It's still going strong. At least from what I've heard."

She looked down as she said it. I knew Mandy hated to expose Edna, whom she now considered a friend. The people who gathered at the inn to celebrate occasions with us had become an unlikely, ragtag family. But she put Kellan first. Or at least, right after me.

"They must have their reasons," I said. "Although it certainly proves I don't know my sisters that well. You wouldn't catch me sleeping in a bunker with strangers. There's not enough pie in the world to get me through that."

"I don't like those sisters from Crow's Landing, the Agnews," Mandy said, lowering her voice. "Or the Carnegie sisters for that matter. They're unusually close. Like the Langmans."

I nodded. "There's a reason I moved away from my family. I love them but I think I always knew our branches would get twisted if we were all reaching for the sun at the same time. Everyone needs space to grow."

"Hard enough to get enough light and love as an only child," Mandy said. "But I'm happy to have friends, now. Will we see you at the storage unit later?"

"Possibly, after my errands," I said. "Can you set me up with some of that bunker food to go? We're going to be on the move."

I took the long way to the counter to avoid Beverly and Mercy, and I was glad to get out in the fresh air. Poppy's car drove in as I was pulling out of my parking spot. Edna stuck her camouflage glove out the passenger window and waved. I waved back, but it made me sad our close connection had been reduced to that. Were we on a waves-only basis now?

Keats mumbled something reassuring, and my fingers rested on his back as I watched Poppy and Edna join the Agnew sisters and head inside.

"I hope you're right, buddy," I said, pulling out of the lot. "Because I miss Edna's salty temperament in my day. More like cayenne pepper. Either way, I need something to offset the sugar I eat."

Pushing the pedal down, I headed over to Imogen Pigeon's house, which now belonged to Teri Mason. She did most of her design work in the refurbished garage, and only went into her store, Hill Country Designs, in the afternoons and on weekends.

I found her in the workshop and she happily joined me on a walk around the property. Keats and Percy romped off, but I looked up at the house and sighed. I missed Imogen and wasn't ready to go back inside with those memories quite yet. I suspected Teri felt the same, and that's why she did her work in the garage.

"It's great to see you," she said. "I assumed you'd be busy helping Kellan with Vernie's case."

"Kellan prefers not to have my help, although he isn't above consulting my pets. Still, I keep my eyes open, and what I've been seeing a lot of lately is a painted bunting. I call him Picasso."

Teri turned to me quickly. "You mean the bird who visited Nan? She called it Carl, and thought it was the spirit of my grandfather."

"That's the one. It hasn't left the area, so I figure it's trying to tell us something."

She turned and led me back to the workshop, where she showed me several watercolors she'd painted of Picasso. The bird's plumage resembled the brilliant caftan she wore. This artist was always inspired by nature, and especially the tropics.

"He's here every morning doing an aerial show," she said. "I don't speak bunting, but he brings me comfort. I haven't seen him yet today."

"He was otherwise engaged," I said. "Led Calvin and me on a merry chase to Garnet Point."

"Ah! I was there a couple of times with Nan," she said. "That's where my gramps proposed."

"My dad locked Dahlia down there, too. It was supposed to be good luck if you sealed the deal with a local garnet. Didn't stick in their case."

Teri beckoned to me. "I inherited a brooch from Ima that had plenty of garnets. It wasn't my style, so I took it apart to create something new. Or many things new."

She showed me a tray with various pieces of jewelry. One was a tiny bird pendant with a garnet chip as the eye.

"Picasso has a circle of red around his eyes," I said.

She handed me the little bird and selected a chain from another tray. "Take it for good luck."

"Teri, I couldn't. Ima already gave me a ring, remember? The garnets belong in your family."

"We have all we need, and the bunting only appears for you and me," she said. "Maybe I should head out to Garnet Point, if I can find it again. I haven't had a date since... you know."

Keats circled back and pressed into Teri's shin. He had predicted her last boyfriend would turn out to be a loser and that's exactly what transpired. It would take a strong man to match this vibrant woman with her rainbow of hair and caftans.

"We'll go together," I said. "My father gave me his secret code to find the way."

"Won't that mean we're dating?" She grinned at me. "It was the make-out spot of the day, according to Nan."

"In our case, it'll just lock down our friendship," I said, grinning back. "But it is very romantic and the scenery is spectacular. I can see why young lovers flocked there."

"Back then, it was about privacy too," Teri said. "If you were lucky, you could have a nice drive with your beau. If you were less lucky, your dad followed with a shotgun. That happened a lot, Nan said."

"There were so many factions. Hazel Bingham said young women were played like chess pieces to form alliances."

Teri sat down at her drafting table and picked up a pencil. That happened often when we were chatting. Sometimes Keats or Percy appeared in her sketchbook, other times it was someone in overalls who looked just like me, and yet seemed a stranger. In my head, I was still a miserable exec and I feared I'd awaken one day from this wonderful dream and find myself in a suit again. I wanted to ask Teri not to tempt fate by drawing me, but she couldn't help herself.

Today, however, the person who appeared on the page was far older than me, but not as old as I remembered.

"Vernie Cobbler!" I said.

Teri nodded. "She used to teach a free art class in the church basement on Thursday afternoons. Vernie was a tough critic. So tough I cried all the time. But I stuck with it. I got better. And I highly doubt I'd have a career today without her."

"No wonder Picasso sticks around here," I said. "Maybe it has something to do with Vernie, since you had a connection."

"As much as she allowed connection," Teri said, continuing to bring Vernie to life on the page. "She did have a beau once, long ago. Ima and Carl were at Garnet Point the night Mr. Cobbler caught them together. Her dad tried to shoot the young man and Vernie threatened to throw herself off the cliff if he did. Her beau escaped and left town, apparently. Vernie's heart was broken for good, I guess, because she stayed single the rest of her life."

"Wow, what a story," I said, as gears started turning stiffly in my brain. I glanced down and found a blue eye staring back at me. "Incredibly sad. Did you get the young man's name? Maybe he'd want to know she passed."

Teri shook her head. "Vernie didn't know anyone saw it happen. My Nan, as you know, could keep a secret like no one else."

"Poor Vernie," I said. "I guess she decided to dedicate herself to her art after that."

"That wasn't easy to do around here, especially for a woman. Yet she mastered her craft and became quite famous with fanciers of hill country oils and watercolors."

I nodded. "She donated some pieces to the rescue fundraiser."

Teri's face lit up. "I'll bid on them. Maybe that would help make this old house feel like my home."

"Ima would be happy you're here and creating." I touched the little bird that now perched on my collarbone. "She was proud of you and your work."

Gesturing to the rear of the workshop, Teri grinned. "I have a cot back there. Sometimes I just sleep out here, surrounded by art."

I laughed. "You and my dad have something in common. I just found out he camps in my hayloft."

Teri laughed, too, as she walked me back to the truck. "You're going to figure out who killed Vernie, right?"

"I'm sure going to try," I said. "But first I need to figure out who loved her."

# CHAPTER TWENTY-ONE

I started up the highway to visit my grandparents, figuring they might well know what had transpired at Garnet Point the night Vernie parted from her beau. But we hadn't gone a mile before Keats scratched at the passenger window and mumbled a request to pull over.

Perched on a road sign that said, "You are leaving Clover Grove. Come visit us again, soon," was the brilliant bird I'd expected to find at Imogen Pigeon's house.

I steered the truck onto the shoulder and rolled down the window. "Hey, Picasso. I was thinking of heading up to Mt. Wilshire. Want to go for a fly?"

The bird twittered something unintelligible, at least to me. He hopped from the sign to a branch and then another branch, moving in the general direction of Clover Grove. Keats stuck his head out the window and then turned to suggest with a longwinded mumble that we follow Picasso's lead.

"Well, you'd better navigate then," I said.

The dog's tail swished an affirmative, and Percy jumped into the back seat to lend his expertise.

Thanks to the trio's teamwork, I found myself parking on a side street outside the Clover Grove public library about 20 minutes later.

Picasso sat in the crabapple tree near the door, chirping what I presumed to be advice as I walked up the stairs with my furry boys. "Sorry, I'm not sure what you're saying, my feathered friend. I wish you could come in, but there are windows all around you can use if you need to point me in the right direction."

As a child, I'd enjoyed my trips here. Books had been portals into other worlds, where I didn't have to share my bedroom with various sisters. It was always overcrowded at home, which was why I couldn't get enough space now. The more my family was around, the more I thought about expanding.

The first time I came to the library after my return to Clover Grove, librarian Dottie Bridges had been openly hostile about Keats accompanying me. Worse, she'd let Myrtle McCain know I'd been poking around into the town's history and was at least partly responsible for my nearly getting murdered later that day.

Dottie and I had mended our fences just a month ago when her secret archives helped me solve a murder. She had not only permitted Keats inside, but Percy, Bocelli and Clippers, too. The miniature horse had trapped Dottie behind her checkout desk but she'd proven surprisingly limber despite the cane she used.

We were square now, but I still didn't feel exactly fond of her. One good turn didn't fully wipe out a move that nearly ended in my death. I wasn't sure how many it would take but today she'd have another chance to wipe the slate clean. One day, it might stay clean.

"Good day, Ivy," she called, letting her glasses slide down her nose. "I'm relieved to see you're without livestock, today. Your donkey left quite a load in the self-help section. It felt like a statement."

"I bet self-help doesn't see much use in Clover Grove," I said. "Although we need help here as much as any town."

"Oh, more," she said, with a prim smile. "Present company included."

"Guilty as charged," I said. "I need to pick an issue of the week and focus."

She got up from the desk and came around. "I'm a work in progress myself, Ivy. Now, how can I help you, today? Are you here on business... or business?"

I laughed. "You're right if you're suggesting I don't have much time to read for pleasure anymore, Mrs. Bridges. In my downtime, I'm usually online learning about livestock."

She reached for a stack of magazines and books on a shelf labeled "Reserved."

"I put these aside in case you came in," she said. "These are the most popular resources among successful homesteaders." Going back around the desk, she opened a drawer. "I even took the liberty of making you a card."

I flipped through the pile and said, "These are great and I need all the help I can get. Thank you, Mrs. Bridges."

Glancing toward the door, she said, "You can call me Dottie. As long as no one else is around. I like to preserve a certain decorum."

"All right, Dottie. I appreciate your kindness. And perhaps you'll be able to direct me to the right material today. I'm looking for—"

"Information about painted buntings?" Now her smile was more genuine and it was actually quite nice. It looked like she still had her own teeth, which wasn't that common for advanced seniors. Our region had little access to good dental care until the last few decades.

"How did you know?" I asked.

She gestured to the window. "That pretty fellow just arrived. It's the first time he's shown up here, although I've seen him in my yard before. I've always considered birds to be messengers."

"Me too," I said. "At least, I have since Imogen Pigeon planted that idea. But this one has me puzzled."

"I assume it has something to do with Verna Rae Cobbler,"

Dottie said. She settled onto the edge of her desk and used her cane to point at the window. "He showed up on the day Vernie died." She watched Picasso fly to the next window and peck at the glass. "Maybe it is Vernie. Did you think about that?"

"He arrived at my place before that happened," I said. "So my money was on Ima. Regardless, he seemed to want me to come in here today so I'm guessing you might have something to tell me about Vernie."

"Like what?" Dottie got up and stumped to the window to meet the bird eye to eye. "I don't believe she's mentioned much in my archives. She preferred it that way."

Dottie was being coy, but two could play that game. "That's a beautiful brooch you're wearing," I said, joining her. "Are those stones from Garnet Point?"

She turned so suddenly she would have hit me in the foot with her cane if Keats hadn't eased me out of the way in time. Percy had already wandered off to do his own research.

"How do you know about Garnet Point?" Dottie said.

"My dad told me. And then Teri Mason gave me this."

I held up the little bird pendant so Dottie could see it. "The garnet was one of many that Carl Pigeon gave Ima."

"It's a pretty pendant but the stone doesn't mean a thing if it doesn't come from a man, according to local legend." Dottie sighed. "It didn't always mean anything if it did. Too many women relied on those semiprecious stones when it all came to naught."

"From what I've heard many relationships came to naught because of the politics of the day," I said. "I've heard most families tried to arrange appropriate marriages for their kids, whether the kids liked it or not."

She pulled out a chair at one of the long tables in the reference section and collapsed into it heavily. "I'm afraid so, yes. And if you didn't fancy the gentleman on offer, you were lucky if you got the choice to go without."

"I assume many hearts were broken that way," I said. "Possibly Vernie's."

Dottie ran her fingers over some lettering carved into the table. On my first visit, I'd noticed my brother's name and all four of my nephews. All of them had been in trouble at one time or another for graffiti. There was something about big families that made you want to scream your name with a penknife or paint, I suppose.

"I wouldn't know about that," she said. "What happened at Garnet Point stayed at Garnet Point."

"Not always. I heard that Vernie nearly flung herself off the cliff after her father threatened her young admirer. And soon after that he disappeared from town."

Dottie's eyes darted around and then landed on the bird as he took dives at the glass.

"If I knew anything that I thought related to Vernie's murder, I would probably tell you," Dottie said. "But a decades-old love story gone wrong couldn't possibly be tied to a modern-day murder at a vegetable stand."

"Can you be so sure?" I asked. "In my experience, one thing leads to another. In this case, a very handsome bird is trying to tell you something. Or else he's trying to tell you to tell *me* something."

She shifted uncomfortably in the hard wooden chair. "You're a strange girl, Ivy. You always were."

Percy landed gently on the table, strolled across it, and stepped into Dottie's lap, careful to avoid the cane. His purr boomed out in the old building and the librarian visibly relaxed. While Keats usually galvanized people, Percy could and did function as a feline sedative.

"I don't like cats," she said, as she began patting Percy. "You really can't trust them. How do you know he won't eat that bunting?"

"I do trust him, and I've become a bit of an expert on trust lately." I pulled out another chair and sat down. "I trust you, Dottie. You want to tell me about Vernie and her young beau, regardless of whether it relates to the murder."

"Why would you think that?" she said, lulled by Percy's best purr. Her fingers slowed and she stared into his big green eyes. "I'm a keeper of the town's secrets."

"You must have been a young girl yourself when Vernie began seeing this fellow," I said. "The Harlow boy." I took a guess on the name, knowing I had a 50:50 chance of being right. "Palmer."

Dottie's eyes widened. "You know."

"I know some. Not enough," I said. "I know the Harlows were considered dangerous business. Vernie's father wanted better for her."

"Palmer wasn't like his older brothers. He was polite. Kind. Respectful. I saw a lot of him in here even before he met Vernie. He wanted to do more with his life. If he'd had the right support, he could have become a good man. A leader. Instead, he got chased out of town. Probably long dead by now."

I was watching her carefully and I already knew Dottie's "tell." When she was lying, she picked at the brown paint on her cane and made a little pile of the chips. And that's exactly what her gnarled fingers were doing now.

"So Vernie and Palmer met here, as well as at Garnet Point," I said. "Because no one suspected the library of being the place for liaisons."

Her eyes came up and she smiled. "Yet there have been many matches made in these stacks. Some more boisterous than others. Vernie and Palmer only met here a couple of times, to my knowledge. But they wrote letters and left them for each other."

"Where did they leave them?" I asked.

Dottie glanced at Keats and Percy and smiled. "In with the romantic poets, of course. I looked for the letters, but I never read them. I was naïve enough to be rooting for Vernie and Palmer and romantic enough to be excited when a diamond and garnet ring was on her hand one day. She sat at this very table and wrote a letter and tucked it into a volume of Wordsworth."

"Then what happened?" I asked.

"A week later the ring was gone and Vernie was on the floor back there crying." Tears filled Dottie's eyes as she told the tale. "After she left, I found the ring in a little blue box behind a collection of Lord Byron's work. I patrolled that section like a security guard until Palmer Harlow came in and got it." She pulled an embroidered handkerchief out of her sleeve and dabbed at her eyes under her glasses. "I never saw him again."

"And Vernie?" I asked.

"She was here all the time. Reading books about art. Sketching. Staring out the window where that bird is now. Perhaps she hoped Palmer would come back one day." Dottie sighed and went back to patting Percy. "Little did she know how men operate."

"Palmer married someone else," I said.

She picked at the paint on the cane again, adding to her little pile. "I never saw him again, like I said."

"But you know where he is, Dottie. He's still alive, living his happily ever after, while Vernie—"

"I didn't say that, Ivy. I didn't say any of that."

"But he's not dead because you keep track of such things. I know that. So you can tell me where he is."

"If he wanted to be found, I suppose he would have let Vernie find him and not you," she said.

Keats looked up at me and mumbled. "Good point," I said.

Her eyes landed on mine. "You're just going to leave it at that?"

I grinned at her. "Do you know me at all, Dottie?"

"Well enough by now, I suppose. You're going to get help from someone I didn't name to find someone I didn't name."

"Exactly. And *your* name need never come into it." I got up and checked the windows. The bird was gone, which suggested I had what I needed.

Except for one thing.

I got up and headed for the stacks. "Can you direct me to the books about Picasso, Dottie? Something for beginners."

She eased Percy off her lap and got to her feet. "Picasso made easy for hobby farmers. Coming right up."

# CHAPTER TWENTY-TWO

"Not a chance," Sterling Fable said, pulling his rifle out of his robe and pointing it in our general direction.

"Oh, come on now, Uncle Sterling," I said, from the bottom of his porch stairs. "You know I can't go alone to see this guy. He might actually use a rifle on me."

"You'd deserve it if he did," Sterling said. "He doesn't want to be found, Ivy. And you wouldn't be asking me to join you if you knew where he was."

"Untrue," I said. "We'd ask you anyway. Jilly and I need more than charm to deal with this guy."

Keats mumbled an objection. "Charm, plus Keats and Percy," I added.

"And the bird, I suppose," Sterling said.

"No sign of Picasso today," I said. "He's not a creature you can rely on. I tend to communicate better with domesticated species, anyway."

"You're doing just fine," Jilly said, and then turned the full force of her smile on my uncle. "Sterling, I only have one question. Are you going to change first, or meet this guy in your robe and jammies?"

"Don't get smart, Toots," he said. "I have a certain influence over your intended and there's still time to call off the wedding."

Jilly laughed. "You do have some pull with Asher, I admit. Hopefully I have a little more."

"How about I text him and tell him what you two are suggesting?" he said. "I could copy Chief Haughty McSnobalot."

I had been about to walk up the stairs but stopped with one boot in the air. "Edna's been here, too? She's the only one who calls Kellan that."

"Edna and I go way back, so she comes down the odd time looking like an old toad in her camouflage. When she showed up in a dress a few days ago, I knew she wanted something."

"Help to hide Bunkertown from the chief?" I asked.

"Bunkertown?" Sterling sounded innocent, but he'd had a lot of practice living a lie.

"That's the experiential learning site where she's teaching people how to survive the apocalypse," I said. "She almost caught Keats in a bear trap." The dog slunk between my legs. "He was so startled he fell into a creek, which he considered the greater offence."

"From what I heard, it was an accident and there was no harm done," Sterling said. "You're overreacting, girlie."

A spark ignited in my gut and it wasn't over his chauvinism. "This dog is—"

"Oh, spare me." He turned to shuffle to the door in his slippers. "I know you got stuck with my sister's dog-crazy genes, but sometimes you've got to let common sense prevail."

"Where's the common sense in bear traps and shipping container bunkers?" I asked, following him.

"If you'd survived the circumstances of our youth, you'd have a bunker or two in your back forty already. Edna has every right to look out for herself. Looking out for others is a bonus. She's not charging a dime over costs for that class, you know."

"Bear trap. Beloved therapy dog," I said, as he went inside.

He shut the screen door in my face. "Hysterical overreaction. Even the dog said so, apparently."

Keats mumbled an affirmative behind me and Sterling laughed. "See?"

"Edna has some nerve coming down here to whine to my uncle. Whose side are you on?"

"The side of common sense, always. Many sources—some more reliable than others—say that Edna's done plenty to help you." He looked past me. "Am I right, Toots?"

Jilly shrugged. "I'm holding Edna's spot in my wedding party. But it's Ivy's decision."

I turned to stare at my friend. My righteous indignation at Edna seemed fully justified, but I hadn't calculated the fallout for Jilly.

"There," Sterling said. "Common sense just descended on you like a flock of locusts and devoured the hysteria. Now that you and Edna have healed the rift, you can take *her* on your foolhardy mission."

I pulled the door open. "Do you really think you and Edna are interchangeable? She's awesome in tactical situations but this one is a political landmine. I need someone with panache."

He backed away, gesturing to his robe and pajamas. "Is this really the best you got?"

Jilly and I both laughed as we walked inside. "You're all we need, Uncle Sterling," I said. "What say you, Toots?"

"I say Sterling should go and put on something dashing while the two of us fight over the recliner," Jilly said.

We lost that battle before it started, because Percy had slipped through our feet and was already curling up in my uncle's favorite spot to watch the birds in the yard.

"Don't shed on my chair," Sterling called as he headed into the bedroom. "Orange goes with nothing."

I hadn't expected him to care about his attire, but when he

emerged 10 minutes later, he was wearing gray wool pants, a white dress shirt and a nicely tailored sports jacket.

He held up two ties for inspection and Jilly shook her head. "Neither," she said. "The jacket signifies respect, but the tie would be obsequious. Mood is everything."

Sterling smiled. "Asher batted out of his league. He's not as smart as Ivy, but it's a good thing Calvin and Dahlia kept reproducing long after common sense vanished. There are exceptions to my rule, I suppose."

He switched on a security system as he locked up the house. I noticed he leaned more heavily on the cane as we left and his breathing became strained. Leaving his safe haven was taking a toll.

"So, where exactly are we going?" he asked, following me to the truck.

"You tell me," I said, opening the passenger door for him.

He stopped in his tracks. "I knew you didn't know. And I don't know."

"You're right I don't know... yet. But I will. Trust me."

"I didn't survive this long by trusting people." He held out his hand, palm up. "Key. I've heard about your driving. As bad as Dahlia's, minus the stop signs."

"I resent that," I said. "I'm getting better every day."

"She is," Jilly said, climbing into the back seat with Percy. "I barely have to hang on anymore. Unless we're getting tailed. Or tailing someone else."

"Reckless. Utterly reckless, the pair of you." His hand stayed out. "No key, no Sterling."

Sighing, I handed him the key and got into the passenger side with Keats. "I hope this ends better than it's starting."

"If my pistol comes home fully loaded, I'll call it a success," he said.

"You're armed?" Jilly said. "We're going to a senior's home. Aren't we?"

"You tell me, ladies." He turned the key in the ignition and backed quickly and skillfully out of his driveway. "The whole point is that he doesn't want to be found. There are two or three places I think he might feel safe enough to retire."

"Name the towns," I said, putting a hand on either side of Keats as the dog found his balance. Sterling was a good driver but he took the corners way too fast. I got the feeling he liked handling my truck.

"Farthingdale and Brookfield Heights," he said. "Possibly Port Perry. Known for having no port, being on a sad excuse for a lake."

"Onward to Port Perry," I said. "That's where he is."

"And how do you know this?" he asked, keeping his eyes on the road.

"You said his brother died in Capshaw Lake, so it makes sense he'd want to be there."

"Or as far away as humanly possible," Sterling said. "I hope you have a better reason than that."

"Do you really want to know? There's an element of woo-woo that men who use terms like 'girlie' and 'toots' generally find uncomfortable."

He turned and glared at me. "Smart aleck. Ungrateful smart aleck."

"Oh, I'm grateful," I said, as Keats got into navigating position and fanned his tail in my face. "You can turn right at—"

"I've got it," he said, turning off the road and entering yet another tributary of the hill country trail system. "Anyone who's spent their life on the run knows both the shortest routes and the most convoluted. Today we'll take our chances on the shortest because I want to get this over with."

"I thought you'd enjoy—" Jilly stopped as his hand came up.

"Quiet, Toots. Sometimes a man needs to be alone with his memories."

We covered the drive to Port Perry in about half the time I expected, but it was such a rough ride that my brain hurt when we pulled into a long, unmarked lane. At the end was what appeared to be the classic red farmhouse of our region. Behind it, however, was a large addition, not unlike Runaway Inn, but more dated. The property was fully fenced in brick and barbed wire, and there was a security gate with an intercom.

"It reminds me a little of The Morgenstern Institution," I said. "Where Myrtle McCain is detained."

"It's the price of a peaceful retirement," Sterling said. His knuckles whitened on the gearshift. Perhaps he was wondering if a place like this was in his future, too.

I wasn't sure Palmer Harlow would agree to see my uncle, but after a short wait, the doors swung open and we parked around the side. Sterling let me take the lead, which meant Keats and Percy escorted us in the front door to a desk clerk.

"Mr. Harlow went out the back to receive you," she said.

Behind the facility was a courtyard that rivaled Clover Grove Gardens for expert layout. The fall flowers were in full bloom and Sterling's face lit up when he looked around. Safety might not feel so much like prison in surroundings like this.

Keats and Percy trotted ahead to the table in a sunny corner, where an old man sat in a hard metal chair. He was wearing a tan cardigan big enough for two people. It was reminiscent of Gertie's poncho, and I wondered if it concealed a rifle, too.

The man stared at the dog and then sat back suddenly in his seat as a fluffy ball of orange made an arrival in his lap.

"That's presumptuous," he said. "Some people don't like pets."

"Mine know where they're welcome," I said, offering my hand. "But if you want Percy to get down, he will."

"It's a cool day. An extra layer never hurt." He waved my hand away. "I don't care to make it official, thanks." He looked over my shoulder and added, "Sterling. I thought better of you."

My uncle scuffed at the patio stones with a polished oxford. "Palmer, I thought better of me, too. I defy any old man to stand up to these girls. My great-niece, Ivy, is a force of nature, like my sister."

"Polly was lovely," Palmer said. "This one's trouble. I still read the paper."

Sterling took a seat opposite Palmer without waiting to be asked. He rested one hand over the other on the handle of his cane. "She's doing good work. Bold work."

"The work of a fool who's going to end up in a place like this... and that's if she's lucky." Palmer shook his head. "If I'd known how things would go, I'd have made different choices."

"And ended up like your brothers," Sterling said. "Who didn't get a chance to sit among the asters wearing the ugliest sweater I've ever seen."

"I care more about warmth than style these days," Palmer said, eying my uncle's snazzy threads. "Nice of you to make an effort, Sterling. I watched you get out of that truck and thought, he's done all right. Living like a man with no regrets."

"Oh, I have plenty of those," Sterling said. "My time on the run didn't pass soon enough to have a family, for example. Ivy says you got all that."

Palmer's eyes settled on me for the first time. "You got your facts wrong. I was married for about a year and then she left me. She came from a family with a similar background to mine, and I suppose we both thought it might work out. Living in hiding took its toll, though, and she bolted."

Keats sat like a statue beside me. His cool blue eye never left Palmer's face, and while the old man didn't acknowledge the dog, he eventually angled his chair slightly away.

"Maybe there was more to the story," I said. "Did your wife find out she wasn't your one true love?"

Palmer's eyes flitted to the flaming wall of fireweed. "What are you talking about?"

I stopped waiting for an invitation to sit down and pulled out two seats for Jilly and me. Then I reached into my bag for the tin box. "I presume this belongs to you?"

His eyes flitted back and his Adam's apple bobbed once. That was the only giveaway. "Haven't seen that before," he said. His voice lost its note of irritability and became calm, cool and steady. This man was accomplished at hiding his emotions.

"I found it in your old family barn," I said. "Well, I didn't find it. *He* did."

I gestured to a pear tree that was stooping under its heavy load of fruit. There was a flutter of green and yellow wings over a red belly.

"Painted bunting," he said. "It's been hanging around lately. Must like pears."

"It came by my farm the day Verna Rae Cobbler died," I said. "Led us over to your family's property and we found your old letters."

His eyes flitted from the bird to the box. "The lock isn't broken."

"Picasso gave us the key, too."

His eyebrow twitched. Another giveaway. "Picasso?"

"That's the bird's name." I slid the key across the table. "You'll find everything here, from the letters to the engagement ring, set with Garnet Point stones. The only thing missing is the broken twine."

When he didn't move, I opened the box for him and lifted the lid. He turned away as I did, his lips pressed into a thin line. His Adam's apple bobbed again as he swallowed whatever he might have wanted to say.

"I figured you should have these," I said. "Maybe your children or grandchildren would like to keep them."

"No kids." His voice was a dry rasp. "It was like you said. My wife found the letters and blew up. I took them home to the old barn. Hid them away and told her I'd destroyed them. That it was all behind me. But she left anyway." He reached out and touched the ring box with his index finger. "No one wants to be second best."

"I heard Vernie's father chased you out of town," I said.

He nodded. "Didn't blame him, with my family history. But I wanted Verna to come with me. She said her family would never give up the hunt and it was no way to live." He hooked the box a little closer. "I kept hoping she'd change her mind. Waited fifteen years till I finally gave up and got married. Then I waited all over again after my wife left. Guess I always thought Verna would come around. Till now. If you could find me, Verna could, too."

"That is so sad," Jilly said, her eyes filling with tears. "It would have been safe long ago, right? Sterling came back. And Calvin Galloway. All the old villains have died off."

He gave a single shake of his head, and strands of staticky gray hair drifted in the breeze. "Different stakes for different folks. My mistakes may have faded into the past, but not my father's, nor my brother Dutton's. They made some terrible and long-lived enemies. I wouldn't get complacent, Sterling."

My uncle patted his sports jacket. "I never do, Palmer. All it would take is one person to start that ball rolling again."

Palmer tried to slick his hair down and failed. "It's rolling. When Vinnie Swenson died, it started something."

"I figured," Sterling said. "I felt something shift. Like a mudslide."

"Exactly." Palmer pushed the letters back to me. "You keep these, Ivy. Sell the ring for your animal causes. It can't do Vernie any good now." He gave a heavy sigh. "The garnets were supposed to bring luck. That's what people said."

"I'm counting on it." I showed him my little bird pendant and then gestured to Picasso. "It's modeled after him by an artist who studied under Verna Rae."

"It's only the second painted bunting I ever saw," Palmer said. "Verna's mother kept one in a birdcage for years. I only saw it once through the window but we both thought it was wrong to keep a wild thing like that caged. When we broke up, Vernie told me she set that bird free."

"Just like she wanted you to be free," I said. "She wrote that in those letters."

"But she stayed caged all her life." Palmer's stoic voice gave way to emotion and Keats turned his brown eye on him to infuse the old man with comfort.

"I don't see it that way," I said. "At least, not entirely. She lived freely through her art."

Finally he smiled and I realized he must have been a very handsome man. His jawline was still strong and his eyes a clear green, rather like Jilly's, only lighter. "I always tried to encourage Verna. Give her confidence. That's the only reason she kept the painting I gave her when she returned everything else."

"What painting?" I asked. "She just donated a few to our rescue fundraiser but I thought they were her own work."

Palmer stared at the bird, who left the pear tree and perched on the iron fence that surrounded the patio. "It was an original Picasso," he said. "Got it from old man Langman for Vernie's eighteenth birthday."

"How'd you manage that on a blacksmith's wages?" Sterling said.

"I borrowed against my inheritance." Palmer grinned at Sterling. "One I knew I wouldn't stick around to receive. Or live to receive. Most of Dad's bad genes skipped me, but I was darned good at picking locks. There were a few items in the family bunker Mr. Langman wanted badly enough to make things happen for me." He reached out for the box again, running a finger along its rusty lid. "Vernie wouldn't give that painting away. It meant a lot to her, I know that."

"The paintings she donated definitely weren't Picassos," I said. "Which means your gift must still be around. And if someone knew about it, like Heddy and Kaye Langman, that could be why she was killed."

"Mr. Langman gave me his word that he'd never say, and he was a decent sort of man," Palmer said. "Unlike his spawn. They took after their mother and I hear they're worse than ever."

I nodded. "Very much so, I'm afraid."

My brain was working so hard it felt like a car about to overheat. Keats' blue eye cooled it off and he came over to set a paw on my shoe. It was time to go and figure these things out together. That wouldn't happen under the watchful eyes of two old escapees from the Clover Grove crime syndicate.

"Ivy, leave it alone," Palmer said, proving out my belief. "Let the police figure out what happened to Verna. I imagine she was almost ready to go now, anyway."

"Almost, but not quite," I said. "She wanted to settle her estate but she hadn't found a home for Pommy, her dog. Or the Picasso, I presume."

"I doubt she'd have chosen to go down in a pile of pumpkin," Sterling said. "Blue or otherwise."

"Sterling!" Jilly gave him a severe look. "Palmer didn't need to hear that."

"It's okay," Palmer said. "In my mind's eye, Verna is forever eighteen. She had a radiant smile, a sharp sense of humor and looked wonderful in blue."

My uncle smiled. "That's how men think, girls. You get hung up on the wrong things."

"Was Verna blonde then?" I asked.

He shook his head. "Beautiful sleek dark hair. And so tiny that I called her my little brown wren."

"Ah, of course. From the letters. But where does Henny come from?"

"My middle name is Hendrick. I hated it so she liked to tease me." He rubbed the corner of one eye and then the other. "I miss her all over, and I'd never stopped."

We all got up and I held out my hand to Palmer. "May I visit again, Mr. Harlow?"

"No," he said. "But the cat is welcome. Jury's out on the dog. He's very odd."

I laughed. "Well, Percy will need a ride."

"Sterling can bring him. I've heard about your driving."

"Seriously? You people have nothing better to talk about than a stick shift problem?"

"Leave the bird," Palmer said.

I clapped my hand over my pendant. "I'm not giving this up. It's a talisman."

He laughed. "I meant the real one. It reminds me of the old days." The bird hopped to the back of my chair after I vacated it. "Picasso. Isn't that a strange coincidence?"

In a life full of strange coincidences, it wasn't the biggest, but it was the most colorful.

"Take the box," he called after me.

"I'm not giving your things away," I said.

Sterling turned and said, "Sell the ring yourself, Palmer. Buy yourself a sweater that fits."

"It's roomy for a reason," Palmer said, patting what was clearly a weapon.

"No one carries rifles anymore," Sterling said. "They're unwieldy."

"Gertie Rhodes does," Palmer said. "Fine-looking woman. For someone who's looking. I'm not, but you can. There's still time to have a family, Sterling."

I didn't think it was possible to shock my uncle, but Palmer Harlow managed it.

"Get some rest, Palmer," Sterling said. "You've lost your mind."

# CHAPTER TWENTY-THREE

J illy asked me to drop her in town at the Berry Good Café to meet Asher. Although she wanted to cook most of the food for the wedding herself, she saw the sense in hiring a little help so as not to be the most exhausted bride in the world. Starting tomorrow, we would have back-to-back guests till a few days before the wedding. She had convinced Asher to take a half day off to test salads at the café and then head over to Mandy's Country Store to land on the wedding cake and other sweets. As much as I liked eating, I was grateful to pass up that duty.

Besides, there was something less tasty on my menu that afternoon. Specifically, humble pie.

Keats gave me an encouraging mumble. Edna often annoyed him but she did back him up admirably in his self-imposed job of keeping me alive. If he was willing to forgive and forget, I could rise to the occasion, too. The sooner the better, if it was making Jilly feel even slightly uneasy about bridesmaid politics. She was an easygoing bride and deserved for her big day to be nothing but joyous.

"Let's get this over with," I said, pulling up outside Edna's house. "She's probably sulking in her recliner after Kellan shut down SurvivalDare for the second time. I didn't want to tell Kellan about what Mandy said, but there's got to be a safer way to run this program, and Edna will figure it out."

The Edna I met a year ago spent much of her time sulking in her recliner, and the rest spying on me with professional grade binoculars and night vision glasses. She'd cleared plenty of trees to have a better view of Runaway Farm. Lately, however, she wasn't often at home doing surveillance, and that was the case today.

"We'll stop in at Gertie's and then try Bunkertown," I said, as we got back in the truck. "If it takes the rest of the day, we'll find her and smooth things over."

I took the trail through the bush to the farm. It got so much use from Edna's ATV that it was nearly a comfortable ride.

Keats gave me a questioning look as I passed the barn and pulled right up to the inn.

"There's something I want to check before we go," I said. "Palmer Harlow got my mental wheels turning. I bet yours are turning, too."

He shot me an appraising look with his blue eye. Whatever he was thinking apparently wasn't ready for prime time. Percy, on the other hand, seemed a little skittish. His sideways dance across the porch made me nervous. Or maybe I was nervous and the cat picked up on it. We'd all become so interdependent that it was hard to know where ideas began anymore.

Daisy was upstairs getting ready for guests when we came in, so it was easy to slip downstairs unnoticed. The birdcage was locked in a storage room behind the furnace, and just to be doubly sure of its safety, I'd run a chain through it and padlocked that to a hook in the wall. Anyone who wanted this cage badly enough would have to take the house with it.

I released the padlock so that I could examine the birdcage from every angle.

"Finch said his grandmother got the cage from a friend," I said. "And that might very well have been Mrs. Cobbler, since Vernie had set her bird free. I know people used to keep painted buntings captive because they're so beautiful."

Keats pawed at my leg until I unhooked the cage from the stand and set it on its side on the storage room floor. His sniff turned into a snort and then one white paw came up.

"Aha," I said, pulling out my utility knife. There was a small slot in the bottom about the size of a dime. A couple of minutes and a broken nail later, I pried open a recess and a bit of fabric dropped out. I unraveled it and found a key.

"Here's my theory," I told the boys as I slipped the chain through the cage and locked the storage room again. "That key is all that stands between the Langman sisters and the original Picasso piece their father sold Palmer Harlow. Vernie probably locked the painting away and put the key in the birdcage to keep her parents from seeing it. But then her mom was angry about losing the bird and gave the cage away. Vernie may never have seen the cage—or the Picasso—again. But at some point, the Langmans probably found a record of the transaction and have been putting the pieces together ever since."

Keats led the way up the stairs, mumbling.

"Exactly. That's why they stole the birdcage last year, but they didn't have a chance to find the key before we got it back. Same thing again recently. So all we need to do now is find out where the key fits and reclaim the painting for Palmer Harlow."

Jumping into the passenger seat, Keats got into position and grumbled.

"I know. It still doesn't prove the Langmans killed Vernie, but it's one step closer. Maybe we can find evidence. They tend to be a little slapdash in their technique. They're too busy snooping around town to watch crime shows for research."

I had intended to go straight to Vernie's on the highway but Keats urged me to turn off and take the trails.

"I agree we need to master the ins and outs of navigation back here, but is today the day, Keats?"

He confirmed that today really was the day, and steered me down to where Edna's shipping containers had been set up. They were gone now, likely confiscated by Kellan.

"Now what?" I said. "It would have been good to get the apology behind us, and maybe even enlist Edna's help, but she's not here, either."

Keats' white paws bounced off the dashboard and onto the passenger window.

"All right, buddy. I hope this isn't a wild goose chase because we'll lose the light in an hour. Vernie's house is creepy enough in the daytime."

It wasn't a wild goose chase. I should have known Edna wouldn't give up on her commitment so easily. The bunkers were gone but less than five miles away, Keats had me pull into the bushes and then led me to a series of five camouflage army tents. What should have been a moment of triumph quickly turned spooky, however, when his ruff came up. Percy puffed at the same moment and the headache I'd been fighting all day jangled a warning.

"No daring stunts, boys," I said. "They're probably fully armed and simulating zombie defense maneuvers. We're the zombies."

"Edna?" I called. "Edna! It's me, Ivy, And Keats and Percy. Don't shoot!"

A sharp crack of a rifle lifted my boots right off the soil, although Percy and Keats didn't flinch.

"Hey! Stop that!" I yelled. "I'm calling the cops if you fire again."

There was a movement in the bushes and Annamae Muir stepped out in full-on camo, from her helmet to her boots.

"Are you nuts, Annamae? You could kill someone. This training is about simulation, not the real thing." I stomped over to her. "Where's Edna?"

The bushes rustled again, but it wasn't Edna who emerged but the Agnew sisters from Crow's Landing.

"Edna is fishing for dinner, down at the creek," Annamae said. "With your sisters. Sorry for the misfire, Ivy. You startled me. This is all so new."

"Trigger happy," Beatie Agnew said. "I told you she'd be useless in combat, Alfie."

"Oh Beatie, be nice," Alfreda said. "Combat is new to most of us. Me, included."

"Well, you didn't kneejerk a bullet into the sky," Beatie said. "Edna will string us up when she gets back." She lifted her protective eye shield and stared at me. "Not literally."

"Edna's been very kind to all of us," Annamae said. "She's changed, Ivy. Now I can see why my cat preferred her to me. And Gertie, too. I was too mousey for Fleecy then. Too mousey for a cat. Silly me."

She giggled and I wondered if she was studying under Mom as well. "It's okay, Annamae. No harm done. I'll head down to the creek and have a word with Edna."

"I wouldn't," Beatie said. "She's set a few snares and maybe worse. This place is off limits to enemy invaders."

"I'm not the enemy, Beatie," I said. "Edna and I are good friends."

"Didn't sound like it when you were down here last. You tossed her apology aside and made her feel awful. Didn't even visit her in jail."

"She was never in jail. None of you were." I glanced around at the new Bunkertown. "The chief might not be too thrilled when he learns you've relocated."

"He won't learn about it, though," Beatie said. She lowered her eye shield and then raised her rifle. "Will he?"

"Are you seriously threatening me, Beatie?" I asked, pulling out my phone. "Because it's not the end times. I've got great cell connection."

Alfie Agnew reached over and pushed her sister's rifle down. "Beatie. We can't take all this too seriously. Edna is very fond of Ivy. In her own way."

She pushed up her eye shield and gave her sister a look, which succeeded in deflating Beatie. Keats and Percy kept their flags up, however, so I decided to leave my apologies till tomorrow. The Agnews didn't deserve to see me eat humble pie anyway.

"Good luck, soldiers," I said. "We'll check in with Edna another day. It's nothing urgent."

"Bye now," Annamae called after me. "I'd love to stay at your inn again someday, Ivy. Sleeping on rocks wasn't something I enjoyed at twenty, let alone eighty."

"It sure does build character," Alfie said. "And callouses where you never knew you needed them."

We all laughed and I thought that might be enough to calm my pets, but as we walked back to the truck, it remained a full hackles situation for all concerned. I didn't give the women the satisfaction of turning around. Besides, knowing snares had been set unnerved me.

I picked up both the dog and the cat and staggered over the rough terrain with two squirming animals.

"Careful! Bear trap!" Beatie called after me.

There was a strange feeling of weightlessness and then a whooshing sound in my ears.

# CHAPTER TWENTY-FOUR

"I can't believe I fell for that," I said, as we drove back through the trails. The so-called bear trap had been nothing more than a mudslide down to the creek. I managed to release the animals before I skidded and rolled, and now I was the only one wet, dirty and uncomfortable.

Keats mumbled a question and I said, "No, we're not going home. We're completing our mission. A damp soldier is a fierce soldier."

A collision with a rock had stopped me from falling right into the water, which I considered a win. Having recently had a dip in that silty creek, I was more worried about leeches than bruises.

I patted the front pocket of my overalls. "It's all good. The keys are still there. The one for the back door and the new one. Let's get in and out before it's dark."

The dog's grunt pointed out the obvious. It was already dark, or at least it would be when we reached Vernie's house.

"We could wait till tomorrow, I suppose. It would be the sensible thing to do. Or we could go one better and surrender the key to Kellan and let him find the painting. Are we that sensible, boys?"

A yip and a mew confirmed we were not.

"The thing is, Kellan would probably have to call us out anyway. If there was something obvious to be found, his team of investigators would have done it already. This is a case for special agents Keats and Percy."

Percy jumped onto my headrest and purred. He liked the title.

"That said, we're smarter than we used to be," I continued. "I'll send Kellan a note to tell him what we're doing just as soon as we get there. That ought to give us about fifteen minutes to suss the place out. Tune up your sniffers because we won't have much time to lose."

Keats was excited, too. This was his favorite kind of treasure hunt. The stakes were high and the deadline tight.

I left the back country trails sooner than I would have liked. There were shorter ways to Vernie's house but if I got myself spun around, we'd lose the light before we even got there.

It was the right call even though I had to backtrack from the feed store. Traffic wasn't heavy so I geared up till it felt like we were flying. Keats yipped again to tell me to open the window, and the good vibes continued almost until we turned into Vernie's lane.

Almost.

A scent floating in on the breeze didn't agree with the boys.

Someone was there already. More like a pair of someones.

There was a vehicle parked in the bushes near the woodpile. It was a white van that very likely had a long scratch down the driver's side from one of my oak trees.

"The Langmans are here? Why?"

Percy hissed and Keats growled.

"I know. Why do the Langmans do anything? They know about the painting and they think they can find it before we do. So we need to get rid of them, got it?"

Keats' next growl basically said it would be a pleasure. That wasn't a sentiment I shared. Now we'd lose our lead time arguing with them because the only way to get rid of them safely was probably to summon the police for real. Not a casual call to my boyfriend. Sirens would scream and it would be five minutes instead of fifteen.

But first I'd try reasoning with them. Reasoning with the Langman sisters had never worked before but there was a first time for everything.

Before we got out of the truck, I texted Kellan and asked him to join me to find the painting. Then I dropped the phone in the front pocket of my overalls before he could answer and tell me not to move till he got there.

I figured Heddy and Kaye would already be inside, but instead I found Heddy wedged into the small cellar window while Kaye pushed. There was a fair bit of grunting and even some mild cursing, which is how they didn't notice us coming up behind them.

Signaling Keats, I let him do the honors. He crept up, belly low, and then unleashed his big, rarely heard, I-mean-business bark. Both women screamed and though I laughed, I did feel a little sorry for Heddy, stuck at the hips and unable to see her potential assailant.

"Hey ladies," I said, taking a photo and then hitting record on my phone. "Lovely evening for a break-in."

Kaye gave me a withering look. "We're not breaking in, Ivy. Heddy saw a stray cat go inside and we're trying to save it."

"Looks like Heddy ran into a bit of a snag. Someone else is going to have a rip in her khakis, I'm afraid. But the police are on their way and there will be enough officers to ease you right out of there, Heddy. Don't you worry."

Heddy started writhing and kicked Kaye right in the chin. They exchanged some unsisterly words and then Heddy yelled, "Pull me out of here right now, Kaye. You'd better help her, Ivy Galloway. I will not be manhandled by officers."

"Well, I won't be kicked in the head by a thief," I said. "Get yourself out."

Kaye grabbed her sister's legs and pulled as if she meant it. The house spit Heddy out like a breech birth and she scrambled to her feet.

"Let's get going, Kaye," Heddy said. "We can't afford another run-in with the chief. He said he was on his last nerve."

I couldn't imagine Kellan using that expression, but I was sure the sentiment was legit.

"Not buying the cat story," I said, following them around the house. "What were you really looking for?"

"Like we'd tell you," Kaye said. "But it's something that rightly belongs to us. Our father was bilked out of a priceless object years ago by a young man who saw something in Verna Rae Cobbler no one else ever did. Dad was a romantic and he let this collectible go for far less than it was worth. We've been trying to get it back for years but Vernie never admitted she even had it. Now it's at risk of getting swallowed up in legal hassles."

"If no one has found this collectible, maybe Vernie was telling the truth," I said. "She probably gave it back to the gentleman in question."

"No one gives back a Picasso, Ivy," Kaye said. "That piece is worth millions. And we intend to find it."

There was no time to beat around the bush, so I got right to the point. "Did you two kill Vernie by trying to part her from this potential Picasso?"

"Of course not," Heddy said. She looked neither shocked nor guilty at the accusation—just impatient and frustrated. "We were waiting for her to die, just like we do everyone else. We have a—"

"A code of ethics," Kaye finished for her.

I almost choked at that. "Are you kidding? You two are turkey vultures."

"Say what you will, but there's a place for vultures in the ecosystem, just like anything else." Kaye pushed Heddy ahead of her as they got closer to their van. "We redistribute valuable objects and foster the arts in our own way."

I would have liked to question them in a more leisurely fashion, but Kaye got behind the wheel and Heddy ran around to the passenger side.

"What does my birdcage have to do with any of this?" I asked, before Kaye closed the door.

"Nothing at all," she said, starting the engine. "It's just a pretty bauble that deserves to be appreciated, not left sitting in your basement."

"A bauble that once belonged to Vernie's mother, apparently," I said.

She closed the door and rolled down the window. "You've been hit in the head once too often, Ivy. You're imagining connections where none exist."

"Okay. Well, I'm not imagining sirens, so if you're going you'd better get a move on. I'll share the photo of Heddy's awkward moment with Kellan and see if *he* buys the missing cat story."

"You do that," Kaye said, deliberately cutting too close to me as she pulled the van around.

"Don't hit my animals, Kaye. And don't get any big ideas about looking for the birdcage tonight, because Asher will be at the inn by now. It's so handy to have a cop at home."

Heddy stuck her head out the passenger window as the van's wheels spun in the moist soil. "Good luck poking around. You wouldn't know a Picasso if it bit you, Ivy Galloway."

"Don't be so sure," I called after her. "I've got my own library card now."

I didn't *want* Kaye to hit the stone fawn on the way out but I'd be lying if I said the crunch of the van's fender when it connected wasn't highly satisfying.

# CHAPTER TWENTY-FIVE

I n retrospect, I shouldn't have wasted time setting the fawn back on its feet, but it seemed disrespectful for an animal lover like me to leave it lying there. In the end, the delay worked out to my advantage because I was still watching when Kaye switched on the lights in her van and turned right to head toward town. Only when I was sure they were really gone did it feel safe to go into Vernie's house.

Keats wasn't so sure it was safe even then. He was puffy and prickly over the whole situation. This wasn't the treasure hunt he'd signed on for earlier.

"Let's make the best of it, buddy," I said, pulling the key out of my pocket and opening the back door. "I was lying about the sirens, but we've probably only got a few minutes till Kellan gets here, so do your thing. Maybe we'll still get the satisfaction of finding the painting first. We've got to take the wins where we can. Even the small ones."

Keats accepted the challenge, dropping his nose to the floor and moving so fast that I could barely keep up with him. He didn't waste a moment in the kitchen but did a full circuit of the dining room before moving on.

"Are you sure?" I said.

He paused long enough to shoot me a blue-eyed look that said I was ridiculous for even asking.

In the living room, he stopped in front of the portrait of Pommy, lifted his paw and looked at me again. He was sure about this, too.

"Interesting. So, Pommy is hiding something."

I grabbed a hoop-backed chair and set it in front of the fireplace. Percy jumped up on the mantel to add his support to the endeavor.

"I hope it's not as heavy as it looks," I said.

It was as heavy as it looked. I had to lift it high enough to free the wire from the hook on the wall and the awkward weight of the old ornate frame nearly knocked me off the chair.

Keats gave a mumble that sounded less like concern than alarm.

"I'm okay," I said. "Just surprised. And confused."

Where the painting had hung was a safe built into the wall.

The key from the birdcage would very likely fit in that lock, but I couldn't see how a painting would fit in the safe. Unless it was a miniature. Maybe it was. Why hadn't I asked Palmer Harlow for its dimensions? Or even the Langmans.

"I suppose it would make sense for it to be small. The painting, I mean." I tried to juggle Pommy's portrait and find a way to reach into my pocket for the key. "Otherwise, no one in hill country could afford it."

"Makes total sense," someone said.

"Absolutely," someone else agreed.

For a moment, my mental gears didn't engage and I actually thought the voices came from Keats and Percy. Or my overactive imagination, since both voices belonged to women. Had the concussion finally severed my hold on reality?

But heavy footsteps made me freeze on the chair. Clutching the dog portrait, I considered how to play this. I was outnumbered, that much was clear. I didn't want them to take the painting, search me for the key or open the safe. No matter who it was, that would be a tall order. But if I could just stall for time, Kellan would protect the Picasso.

My mind immediately went to the Langman vultures, who might well have circled around and come back. They weren't known for giving up easily.

Only the voices didn't sound like either Heddy or Kaye. They didn't sound familiar at all because they were muffled. Audible, but muted.

There was nothing to do but turn and find out.

Pivoting on the chair while juggling the portrait required more coordination than I had at the best of times, so I shuffled around slowly and carefully.

The two women were coming around beside me anyway. If it was the Langman sisters, they'd gone home and put on a full military-style uniform, including a hard helmet and shaded visor. It was similar to the gear the SurvivalDare participants wore, only this looked professional grade. Even Edna didn't have a helmet like that, although I bet it was on her wish list.

"Hey there," I said. "I don't believe we've met. I'm Ivy Galloway."

"We've met," one woman said. Her laugh sounded nasty even through the filter.

"Cool. But isn't it a little rude to block a friend with a visor?"

"We're not friends," the woman said. I noticed there was a small orange reflective sticker on her collar. The other woman's sticker was yellow. It was probably the way they labeled their clothes. Like kids.

"People keep telling me that, lately," I said.

"Why do you think we suited up?" Orange Sticker said. "You're just not friendly, Ivy. Anyone who has a difference of opinion with you ends up—"

"In jail," Yellow Sticker interrupted.

"That's a little extreme," I said. "I have four sisters and a brother. We rarely share the same opinion about anything. None of them are in jail." I waited a beat and grinned. "Yet. Sometimes it seems inevitable."

"That's a terrible thing to say," Orange Sticker said. "You don't deserve sisters."

"She puts her animals above family," Yellow Sticker said. "A traitor."

Okay, so I was dealing with dysfunctional sisters. Unfortunately, I knew three possible pairs. Four if you counted my own. Which I didn't.

"Let's talk face to face," I said. "I'll come down and—"

"Don't bother," said Orange Sticker. "Just stay where you are and hand us the painting."

"And the key," Yellow Sticker said. "We know you have it."

"What makes you think so?" I asked.

"We ran the Langmans off the road and they told us what you're doing."

"Ah. And where are Heddy and Kaye now?"

"We didn't kill them, if that's what you're wondering. Or hoping."

I shook my head. "They're a thorn in my side, no question, but I don't want them dead."

"Then you'll find them roped to a tree and gagged," she said. "They couldn't ID us."

"I can't either," I said, scanning them from head to foot. They were solid and capable. Built like they could move armoires. That had me leaning toward the Carnegies. But on the other hand, the apocalyptic gear certainly fit with the Agnews' interests.

"Stop stalling and hand over that painting," Orange said.

I started to do just that, but then realized I had an opportunity. Fumbling with the frame, I let the corner connect with the helmet of the closest woman and then lifted. The edge did exactly what I'd hoped and flipped her visor.

"Beatie Agnew," I said. "Is this some sort of SurvivalDare stunt?

Because I can't see how you'd have any connection to Verna Rae Cobbler."

Only I did. I saw the connection immediately. A little late, but I saw it.

"Don't spend another second speculating," Beatie said. "Just hand it over. Nicely, this time."

"And the key to the safe," Alfreda said, flipping up her visor, too.

"I don't have the key," I said.

"Sure, you do." It was a new voice. "Because you have the birdcage."

This time it *was* the Langmans and seeing them walk into the room startled both Agnews. Their identical green eyes widened.

"You Agnews need to study knots in your survival course," Kaye Langman said. "Our father made sure we knew the ropes. Pun intended."

"Survival training was just a routine part of our upbringing," Heddy said. "For collectors, it comes with the territory."

"Came in handy today, because the police never drove by," Kaye said. "Ivy must have been lying about calling them."

"They're coming," I said.

At least, I sure hoped so. I didn't know whether to be glad or terrified that the Langmans had joined us. For all I knew both pairs could team up against me. Even Kellan would have his hands full when he got here. Meanwhile, my goal remained the same: to stall until he did.

Glancing at Keats and Percy, I silently told them to stand down. The logistics were going to be tricky. The room was a decent size, but with the furniture it seemed smaller and five people took up a lot of space. There were too many moving pieces for an easy resolution.

Keats crouched behind a wingchair, waiting for my cue. I noticed his blue eye landed on Alfie time after time. She was the one to watch here.

"I wish I'd known it was family night at Vernie's," I said. "I'd have brought my sisters, too."

"Enough of your doubletalk, Ivy," Beatie said. She turned to Heddy and Kaye. "This is between the Langmans and us, now. And they were just leaving."

"We're not going anywhere. At least, not without the Picasso," Kaye said. "It belongs to our father."

Alfie crossed her camo arms. "Well, that's strange. Because it belongs to *our* father."

Heddy crossed her arms right back. "Since I know our father isn't your father, what you're saying is impossible. Explain yourselves."

"We don't need to explain anything," Alfie said, walking over and turning on the overhead light. "Because we're the ones with pepper spray."

Kaye patted her khaki jacket, which matched her pants. "Do you think we would have come after you unarmed?"

The Langmans could be concealing pepper spray or guns, but I suspected they were armed with nothing more than sharp tongues. In all our altercations, they'd never shown a weapon. They were professional bluffers.

"Maybe you ladies should talk things out," I said. "How could you both think the Picasso—if it even exists—belongs to your father? Kaye, you told me earlier that your dad sold it."

"He didn't sell it, so much as give it to a lovestruck young man," Kaye said. "No money changed hands."

"Maybe they bartered," I said. "Happens all the time."

"You know nothing about this, Ivy," Heddy said.

"I do, actually. Today I met the man who did just that. Heddy, your father was happy with what he got in return for the painting. Regardless, it was a gift from Palmer Harlow to Vernie, and now that she's passed, it belongs to her estate. Not to you or to Palmer's children."

The Langmans fell silent, trying to put the pieces together. Meanwhile the Agnew twins stared at me with the same translucent green eyes I'd seen in an old man's face earlier that day.

"You found him," Beatie said, at last.

"I did. Although he said he didn't have kids."

"He doesn't," Alfie said. "Not really."

"I'm getting confused," Heddy said. "Kaye, what's going on?"

"Let Ivy figure it out," Kaye said.

I thought about it for a moment. "I'm guessing the twins' mom left before Palmer knew she was pregnant."

"Bingo," Alfie said. "You win one lottery and lose another."

"I'm also guessing that your mom found the love letters between Palmer and Vernie. And knew about the Picasso, too."

"Correct again," Alfie said. "Yet still a loser."

"So you grew up angry, knowing Vernie was sitting on a fortune. And when your mom passed away, you finally started harassing Vernie. That's why she got thinner and even more miserable. When she wouldn't give it up, you came in person."

Beatie shrugged. "She was a tough nut to crack, that's for sure. We were ready to settle for some of her own works but she didn't think she owed us anything."

"Palmer Harlow should have given that Picasso to our mother," Alfie said. "I suppose she was just someone to keep him warm in hiding."

"He didn't think of it that way," I said. "He didn't want her to leave and I'm sure he would have loved to have been part of your lives."

Alfie looked down. "You have no idea what it's like to grow up scrambling for crumbs when there's a three-layer cake in reach."

"Our lives and our history may not be as different as you think," I said.

Her green eyes rose again and locked on mine. They were so like her father's, only Alfie's were filled with torment. She'd gotten the worst share of the Harlow genes and perhaps the circumstances had triggered the wrong synapses to fire.

"Then you know what a difference this would have made to us," she said.

"Vernie tried to return the Picasso painting to your father," I said. "He refused to accept it."

"That's not true," Beatie said. "Why would he do that?"

"To encourage her to pursue her art," I said. "That was his real gift to her—something he could leave her besides a broken heart. Those were cruel times."

"What was cruel was marrying our mother when he didn't love her," Alfie said.

"It wasn't that simple. He waited fifteen years for Vernie to change her mind and it sounded like he hoped it could work with your mom. I'm sure he would have wanted to help raise you. He's a decent man."

"You only met him today, Ivy," Beatie said. "What do you know?"

"Well, she knows where the safe is, for starters," Kaye said, trying to get things back on track. "And now we all do."

"Open it," Heddy said. "Then we can figure out who has the biggest claim on the painting."

"The painting can't be in here, unless it's pocket sized," I said. "Is it?"

"We're telling you nothing till we see what's in there," Kaye said. "We're talking about the only Picasso in all of hill country, to our knowledge. Our father had the sense to acquire it and he passed it off for less than a quarter of its value even at the time. So we plan to reclaim it. Vernie wouldn't give it up in life, so—"

"Someone had to make sure she'd give it up in death," Alfie said.

Kaye's single-minded focus shifted for a second. "Are you saying you killed Vernie Cobbler?"

Alfie stared at Kaye. "All I'm saying is that we had discussions with her about doing the right thing. And in the end, she did. By dying. Now we can claim what's ours."

"But it's not yours," Heddy said.

"Well, it's sure not yours," Alfie said. "And you really don't stand a chance against us. We're warriors."

Kaye shrugged. "And we're buzzards, according to Ivy."

"Vultures," Heddy corrected. "I think that's the bird she said."

"Neither gives up easily," Kaye said. "Sounds like we're all warriors here."

The energy shifted in the room and I knew I wasn't going to get out of this unscathed. Alfie Agnew had basically bragged about murdering Vernie and it hadn't fazed the Langmans one bit. There was no way of brokering a peaceful settlement. And Kellan still hadn't arrived. Now I was worried I hadn't hit send.

Very worried. I'd just assumed he would show up. That I wouldn't be on my own with four crazed women.

There was a simmering moment of tension before Beatie made the first move. She started walking toward Kaye, but turned at the last moment and lunged at me.

The chair tipped and I landed on my back under the painting. Even with the wind knocked out of me, it was good to see the orange missile launch from the mantel.

Percy couldn't land on Beatie's helmet, so he had to settle for delivering his signature 20-claw massage to her shoulder and neck.

Judging by the screaming, it did the trick.

Keats, meanwhile, was circling trying to figure out which of the remaining three to take down.

Another defender decided for him. I lifted my head just in time to see a burst of colorful feathers emerge from the fireplace and fly directly into Alfie's face. She screamed and swatted at the diving, pecking bird.

Heddy and Kaye could have seized that moment to be heroes. Instead, they came at me stooping, with arms outstretched like zombies, their eyes glazed with the mindless hunger of the treasure hunter.

Beatie Agnew stepped between us just in time. She'd thrown off Percy and armed herself with the black iron fireplace poker. "Heads up, Alfie," she called, before throwing her sister the tongs.

My dog dodged back and forth, trying to find the right angle in the small space to attack someone.

Anyone.

It was too dangerous now.

"Keats, stop," I said. "We need to give up."

"Never give up, dagnabit! On your feet, Ivy Galloway."

# CHAPTER TWENTY-SIX

The room suddenly filled with smoke and the clanging of metal against metal. It sounded like more than fireplace implements and as the air cleared, I saw the flashing gleam of a longer, silver blade.

Edna Evans expertly used her sword to parry with both Beatie and Alfie, who were making wild jabs and stabs with the iron poker and tongs.

Behind Edna were three other women in camouflage. The one with the long braid and poncho I expected. The two who looked just like me, only even more frightened, I didn't.

My sisters.

Poppy and Violet jumped into the fray valiantly, despite being armed only with what came readily to hand in Vernie's kitchen: a wooden spoon and a spatula.

Gertie had fared better with the carving knife, and judging by her stance, she knew how to use it.

Basically, the room was now far too crowded for battle.

It was too crowded for more than a tea party or book club meeting.

And yet there was a fight to finish.

Heddy stood holding the fireplace shovel and Kaye the broom. Once again they had a chance to do the right thing. Instead, their eyes met for a moment. Then they dropped the tools and turned as one to come at me.

I had been assaulted any number of times, but having my front pocket frisked by four Langman hands was perhaps the ultimate indignity.

"Get off me," I said, lifting my knee and shoving it into Heddy's midriff.

"Not till we get that key," Kaye said, reaching into my pocket again and trying to find a better angle to reach the bottom.

The rapacious hunger in her eyes hadn't dimmed one bit. Fortunately, that hunger kept her focused on the wrong things and she missed what counted.

Specifically, my furred warriors. Percy was back on the mantel and Keats had coiled right in the fireplace, among the cold ashes of Vernie's last fire. Picasso had wisely relocated to the curtain rod.

Heddy recovered from my shove and charged at me again. Kaye continued to grapple with me and I managed to get my leg up to knee her, too. They were unstoppable.

"Ivy, I've got this," Edna called.

"Wait, Edna," I said.

It was Keats' turn. He'd wanted to put the Langmans in their place for a long time and deserved this moment. With Edna and Gertie slashing madly at the Agnews, he could handle the Langmans.

On my signal, Percy took the first leap, smacking Heddy right in the face. I hoped he wouldn't blind her with his claws, but it was out of my hands.

Kaye didn't stop to help her sister. She probably knew Heddy would want her to continue when the treasure was still for the taking.

That's when Keats catapulted out of the fireplace, hit Kaye square in the chest and knocked her onto her back.

"Don't fight him. You'll lose," I warned Kaye.

In typical Langman fashion, she was deaf to good advice. Keats gave her a fair chance to calm down but when she continued to thrash and snarl, the dog clamped down on her earlobe until she let out a shriek.

"Music to my ears, if not hers," Edna said, bringing her sword down in a dramatic arc that knocked the poker out of Beatie's hand. It rolled to land at my feet and I grabbed it.

Running over, I delivered a full-on kick to Alfie's backside and knocked her onto her face. Edna rushed toward Beatie, her boots moving as lightly as an Irish dancer's. While Alfie got her bearings, I swung with the poker and knocked the tongs out of her hand.

Now, the Agnews were unarmed but they were still dangerous.

"Langmans, get up and fight on the side of the righteous," Edna bellowed. "Otherwise, prepare to meet my sword and Gertie's."

"You've got this," Heddy said, shaking off Percy, who climbed up the heavy velvet curtains to prepare for another launch. Picasso flew back to the mantel, sitting right below the exposed safe. "You said so."

"We have got this," Edna said, puffing from exertion. "But I spent three weeks training these two zombies in combat and they don't tire easily."

"Heddy, it's a chance to redeem yourself," Violet called, poking prostrate Alfie with her spatula.

"A chance you don't deserve," Poppy added, swinging her wooden spoon. "But take it anyway."

Heddy picked up the shovel she'd dropped earlier and joined their ranks with what appeared to be grim resolve.

Only then did Keats release Kaye's earlobe. He swiftly repeated his maneuver on Alfie, which left the rest of us to vanquish Beatie.

Many hands made light work, and by the time Kellan charged into the room, followed by Asher and more police than the room could possibly hold, both Agnews were face down and trussed up with Edna's rope.

My brother cased out the situation and then used his old line-backer moves to split the crowd and cross the room. Kaye Langman was standing on the hoop-backed chair trying to open the lock with the key she'd apparently managed to pilfer from my pocket.

Blood from her fanged earlobe covered her right hand and made it too slippery. The key fell to the hearth just as Asher applied his shoulder to her midriff and carried her out of the room.

Picasso shot down from the mantel and snatched the key in his beak. Then he flew over to me, hovered briefly and dropped it into my waiting hands.

There was a moment of silence as everyone stared at the beautiful bird in awe.

Relative silence, that is. Kaye was still wailing from a distance. I expected Heddy to follow, but her sister's welfare apparently came second to the safe. I guess they had an understanding about family priorities.

Kellan held out his hand and I surrendered the key. It might have felt anticlimactic, if he hadn't grabbed my hand with it and squeezed. For a moment, we laced fingers with the key in between our palms.

I expected Keats to ruin the moment, but Edna beat him to it.

"Honestly, Chief," she said, sheathing her sword. "It took you long enough. Did you stop for donuts? Typical cop cliché?"

"Our police resources were decoyed by your students down to Bunkertown, Miss Evans." he said. "There were reports of explosions. That meant we had more ground to cover getting back here."

"So, you're saying it's my fault," Edna said.

"Mine too," I said, quick to take some of the heat. "I told Kellan it wasn't an emergency."

"I told him it was," Violet said. "Once Edna figured out what was happening."

Poppy wanted a piece of the action. "Annamae had overheard the Agnews scheming, but she was crying so hard it took time to get the facts out of her."

"She'll never make a warrior," Edna said. Then she gestured from my sisters to me. "You three just might."

Kellan signaled for his officers to escort the cuffed Agnew sisters out of the house. "Miss Evans, you took monsters and trained them to be *skilled* monsters. Was that in your master plan?"

Edna pulled off her helmet and patted her perm. "Not exactly, Chief, no. I will be revisiting my program after these unexpected outcomes."

Kellan shook his head grimly, and flicked his fingers at Edna when Asher came back in.

My brother cuffed Edna swiftly. As she squirmed, he pushed her helmet back on her head and over her eyes.

"Kellan, is that really necessary?" I asked.

"I did save her life, Chief Tomfoolery," Edna said, stumbling as Asher led her out.

"She did help Keats and Percy save my life," I corrected.

"And me," Heddy added. "I helped, too."

My throat clenched for a second and then released. "Please do take Heddy away. The best punishment for scavengers is not to see the treasure revealed."

Another officer cuffed Heddy, but Kellan let Violet and Poppy go along freely.

"It's going to be crowded at the station tonight," he said, releasing my hand and keeping the key. "A regular slumber party."

Keats was the first to give a ha-ha-ha. Then the dog took a little dive at Kellan's uniformed pant leg just to confirm it was time to lighten the mood.

## CHAPTER TWENTY-SEVEN

The next morning, Kellan and I drove down to Port Perry with Percy and Keats to visit Palmer Harlow.

We took my truck and Kellan came in plain clothes, as Palmer had requested.

Insisted, actually. He didn't want to be seen mixing with police, and it took a fair bit of wheedling on my part to get him to welcome Kellan into his small apartment as my date. I thought it might annoy Kellan but my boyfriend looked too weary from dealing with the dueling sisters to fuss over anything.

Palmer put the kettle on and listened to the story as he made tea in his bright kitchen.

"I don't know whether to laugh or cry," he said, setting a mug in front of me. The china rattled on the table, and he waited a minute or two before delivering Kellan's cup. "I find out I have twin daughters in one breath and lose them in the next."

"I'm sorry, sir," Kellan said. "They've only been on American soil for a month or so. From what I could tell, your ex-wife moved around a lot and ultimately ended up in Australia."

"I suppose she wanted to keep them safe," he said. "From her family and mine. But she couldn't protect them from their genes. They came into the world wired to be criminals."

Keats moved under my fingertips and I sighed. "They had a choice, sir. I have genes like that from my Galloway ancestors. Maybe they could drive me to crime. Instead, I try to fight crime."

"Perhaps you've got enough good genes on the right side of the scale," he said. "Beatie and Alfreda apparently got dealt a heavy load." He brought over the last mug and sunk heavily into a chair. "Not that I'm excusing them in any way. I'd prefer to avoid meeting them, actually. If that's all right, Chief."

"Entirely your choice," Kellan said. "It was my duty to tell you and I wanted to do it in person."

We sat in silence for a while, staring out the kitchen window over the courtyard. The painted bunting sat on the top branch of the pear tree. His beak was open and his wings fluttered. I assumed he was singing a song of triumph.

"Do you mind if I open the window, sir?" I asked. "I think Picasso wants to sing for you."

The old man found a smile and I got up to slide the glass open a few inches. Sure enough, a merry warble greeted us. A few moments later, the bird lit on the windowsill and delivered his tune from close range.

"How nice," Palmer said. "A spot of cheer on a bleak day."

"There's more," I said, handing him an old brown envelope that had come out of the safe. "We didn't open it. For obvious reasons."

That reason was that his name was written on it, in the same elegant handwriting as the letters from the tin box. Vernie was probably still a young woman when she locked that letter away.

Opening it, Palmer took out several documents. He looked over the top one and then slid it toward us. It was a statement of authenticity for the Picasso piece, with a request that it be returned to him if Vernie predeceased him, or sold for fair market value with the proceeds going to benefit animals if she did not.

"I'd like to see it again," he said, glancing at the heavy frame I'd wrapped in burlap I found in Vernie's garage.

I cut the string to reveal the portrait of Pommy. Palmer Harlow laughed, and Kellan and I joined in. Keats gave a happy pant beside me, and Percy jumped into Palmer's lap, purring.

"That's not the Picasso I remember," Palmer said. "Please tell me she didn't paint over it."

"In a manner of speaking, yes," I said. "Before the fight began last night, I realized there were two canvasses in this frame. The portrait of Pommy wasn't her best work, nor was it meant to be. I suspect the dog was supposed to repel interest rather than attract it."

"I see," he said. "And where is this Pommy now?"

"I returned her to the rescue where Vernie got her. She's in good hands." I used my utility knife on the clasps to release the paintings from the frame. "Unless you'd like to give her a good home."

He shook his head. "It would attract too much attention. The bird's bad enough, but him I'll keep." The bunting stopped singing and Palmer added, "Not in a cage. You're just welcome at my window anytime. Birdseed for life."

Slipping on a pair of gloves, I carefully separated the two paintings and beheld my first original Picasso. There had been exhibits in Boston galleries over the years, but art wasn't something that had attracted me as the grim reaper of HR. Seeing this startlingly vivid painting now made me interested in learning more. Perhaps I would read the library book after finishing the farming resources Dottie Bridges had reserved for me. I still had priorities.

"That's it," Palmer said, with a relieved smile. "I confess it didn't do much for me. Never fancied art. Only one particular artist. And Verna loved this."

"Yet it didn't seem to influence her work, from what I've seen," I said. "But what do I know?"

"I don't know much, either," Kellan said. "But what she might have painted with a happy heart probably changed with a broken one."

Palmer sighed. "Mine became very dark, too. It's always been a struggle to find the color in life, but I did my best." He gestured to the bird. "Now, look."

"I know someone who's done a series of paintings of that bird," I said. "Would you like to hang his portrait here?"

Palmer thought about it for a moment and then shook his head. "Perhaps, but not yet. Knowing about my daughters gives me more darkness to clear out before I can allow myself to see so much color every day."

I sat down again and touched his arm gently. "Verna Rae would want you to give yourself color. I'm sure of it. She may have grieved but remember, she made the decision for both of you."

"She wanted me to be safe. It wasn't really possible in our time," he said. "Being in the crosshairs of Vernie's dad was bad enough, but then my brother went and pulled me into a harebrained stunt."

"Lewis?" I asked.

"Lewis," he confirmed. "He wanted out. *I* wanted out. But I didn't want to go so far from Vernie, either. In case she came around, you know."

"And where is Lewis now?" I asked.

Palmer shook his head. If I read him right, it was less of an "I don't know" than "I won't say." Either way, the door had closed.

"It's safe now," Kellan told the old man. "The police departments are working together across jurisdictions to make that true."

Keats mumbled something from under the table and Palmer nodded. "The dog's right. It's less safe now than it was a year ago."

Did he have to say a year? The exact amount of time since I got home?

Kellan smiled and took my hand. "Things were bubbling up even before that, Mr. Harlow. That's why I came back when I did."

"He said it was because of me," I told Palmer, grinning.

"That too," Kellan said. "I had my pick of several posts and chose Clover Grove because of you. But I wanted to be in hill country for other reasons, and it wasn't to raise chickens."

"The chickens are just a bonus," I said. "Kellan named my emu after his aunt, sir. And he helped me deliver baby goats."

"A good life," Palmer said. "Enjoy it to the fullest. While you can."

Picasso tapped on the glass with his beak to get our attention and then twittered what may have been a warning.

"Things sound a bit ominous," Kellan said. "Is there more you'd care to say, sir?"

"Not today." Palmer Harlow's tone was weary and resolute. "When your lady brings my bird portrait, you can come along and we'll talk about the rumors."

"A little bird told you something?" I asked.

He nodded. "In the meantime, you go sell that Picasso to benefit the rescue Verna liked. Get top dollar for it, but under no condition can it go to the four scavengers."

"Understood," I said. "We'll make sure it finds a good home."

"And make sure Verna's dog wants for nothing," Palmer added.

After flipping through the other documents, he slid them back inside the envelope and passed it to Kellan. "Consider that a wedding present."

"My friend Jilly is the one getting married," I said, feeling heat rise in my cheeks.

Kellan didn't seem to register the comment because he was peering into the envelope. His eyebrows came together and then rose.

"I don't want to be rude," Palmer said, rubbing a hand over his flyaway gray hair. "But don't leave it too long before you're delivering more than baby goats together. Life is shorter than you think. And twice as violent."

Keats mumbled something again.

"Even more violent than that," Palmer said. "I agree with the dog. He's odd but very astute."

"That he is," I said, as the feathered Picasso warbled loudly. "Let's agree to seize the moments of music and color while we can."

We all raised our mugs and clinked them together with a cheer.

Picasso shot away across the courtyard and we took that as our cue to leave, too.

# CHAPTER TWENTY-EIGHT

"I seriously dread to think about what your militant friends can do with the money they raised today," Kellan said. "They could run a small country off those donations."

"Cori for president," I said, looping my arm through his as we walked to the edge of the cliff at Garnet Point. I had navigated the way here using my father's markers, and Kellan was suitably impressed. "Vernie would be so pleased at the outcome."

"More pleased than she was with your manure?" he asked.

"Well, not that pleased," I said. "But there's a time for blue pumpkins, and a time to rescue animals with a helicopter on charitable donations. Both are important."

He laughed and led me to a large flat rock that had provided seating for countless lovers over the last hundred years. "Seems like you went a little rogue on me this time, Ivy. One minute you're trying to rehome love letters, the next you're dueling for your life with a fire poker. There was too much going on in one room for Keats and Percy to protect you fully."

"It crept up on me before I realized," I said. "It's a good thing Edna showed up when she did. And of course we've buried the hatchet."

"Not in anyone else, fortunately. I've tried to impress on Edna the stupidity of training potential enemies in combat."

"She saw the error of her ways," I said. "And hopefully Mom will think twice about her class, too. Think of the good they could do if they harnessed their energy for the right purpose."

"I only wish I could find more evidence to put the Langmans away," he said. "Fines don't deter them at all. They consider it the cost of doing business."

"I wish I could say the scar Keats left will serve as a reminder, but they're incapable of being rational. At least you detained them through the fundraiser. That is probably the only punishment they understand."

"I'll be keeping a closer eye on them," he said. "They grow more reckless by the day."

His lips pressed into a grim line as he stared out at the gorgeous sunset. It wasn't the time to ask, but I couldn't resist.

"Are you going to tell me what was in the envelope Palmer gave you?"

Kellan shook his head. "Not yet."

"He said it was a wedding present."

"And he gave it to me for safekeeping." He shook his head. "It's not related to weddings at all, trust me. When I've done my due diligence, you'll be the first to hear about it."

"Fine," I said. "I can be patient. It's a quality I fertilize every day."

He pulled a velvet box out of his pocket and handed it to me. My heart started to speed up but then I realized it was too big and flat for an engagement ring.

Probably.

I opened it, hoping I might be wrong. Instead of being disappointed at the contents, I smiled. It was a gold brooch nearly as big as a saucer, featuring a complex replica of the solar system. The planets took the form of dozens of garnets that no doubt came from the rocks nearby.

"It's—it's so interesting," I said. "So large. And ornate."

"My grandmother loved it," Kellan said. "Though perhaps it's not to the modern woman's taste."

"I appreciate it so much," I said, kissing his cheek. "I would be nervous about wearing such a precious piece often. Imagine what could happen around the farm."

"My grandmother always said jewelry is meant to be worn, not kept in a drawer," he said. "I remember her using that brooch to pin her sweaters together. And later her shawls. She said it was her shield against the slings and arrows of Clover Grove."

"That is so sweet. Of course, I'm more of an overalls kind of girl. And I like to fly under the radar. A brooch like this would get noticed."

He slung his arm around my shoulders and pulled me closer. "That's what I like about it. You'll have trouble flying under anyone's radar wearing that. May I?"

"Please." I handed him the box and swallowed hard as he pinned the huge piece to my coat. The lapel wouldn't hold the weight so he attached it right in the center of my chest. "Oh my. It looks a bit like a... like a target."

"I was thinking a stop sign, with all that red. Like the ones your mom ran over. So maybe people would stop seeing you as a target, you know?" He waggled his eyebrows. "I'm not always the most romantic guy but this time I pulled out all the stops. Get it?"

I had tried hard to hold back a guffaw and now I could let it go. The peals of laughter came back in echoes as strange sounds that could have been children. Or coyotes. Percy climbed onto Kellan's shoulder and blocked my boyfriend's face so I couldn't read his expression. "Are you making fun of my gift?" he asked. "This treasured family heirloom?"

"Not at all. It's very romantic that you want me to wear it."

"All the time. To remind you to slow down and stay alive."

"And to hold my shawls," I said. "It's a very practical gift, with so much sentimental value. I just hope it doesn't fall off and injure any of the animals."

He lifted Percy and set him on the other shoulder and we grinned at each other. "I'll get that catch reinforced for you. To be extra cautious. Wouldn't want to knock out either of the boys."

Keats mumbled something cheeky and gave each of us a nip. There was too much hilarity going on for his liking.

"Oh, let us enjoy the aftermath," I told the dog. "It's romantic sitting out here at Garnet Point with my best guy. No matter what he pins on me."

"Just to put you out of your misery, I thought we could get some of those garnets reset into something you actually *want* to wear. Until you're old enough to wear cardigans and shawls with a shield attached. The brooch will be there for you when you actually want to slow down."

I reached for his hand and laced my fingers through his. "I would love that."

Maybe he meant a ring, or maybe not. It would be rude to press.

Keats disagreed. He put his paws on Kellan's knees and mumbled something right into my boyfriend's face. It sounded like "make an honest woman out of her." Or something fatherly that my own dad would never say.

"I don't take orders from you, dog," Kellan said. "But there may be a few garnets left over for your collar. And Percy's. For formal events."

Like weddings, I hoped.

"Ivy," he said. "Let's put the jokes aside for a moment. There's something I want to ask you."

"Sure, go ahead." My voice had caught a case of the wobbles. I sounded breathy and girlish. Like someone who'd wear precious jewelry every day, and not get into duels or kick people. Maybe I could be that bejeweled girl for Kellan.

"I don't want you to change," he said, as if reading my mind. "What I really want is for us to..." His voice trailed off as something caught his eye. "Look at that."

Over the valley, at least a hundred dark birds spiraled, tipping and turning on eddies.

"Are they crows?" I asked.

"Hawks," he said. "Gathering to migrate."

"I've never seen so many together before. It feels a little ominous."

I shivered and Keats didn't help matters by shooting me a look with his eerie blue eye.

"It's a good thing you have your breastplate then," Kellan said, hugging me closer. "Every hobby farmer who sleuths needs armor."

Maybe the moment for a proposal had passed, if it had been that moment at all. But before I could feel too disappointed about it, a colorful speck flew away from the hawks in our direction.

The painted bunting did an aerial show that would have stolen the hawks' thunder, if they cared.

"Picasso is saying goodbye," I said. "Going south with the hawks."

Kellan watched the bird as he dipped over the edge of the cliff right at our feet and then shot up again like winged fireworks. "He's chosen good company for the journey. I'm sure he'll be fine."

Keats walked over too close to the edge and barked at the bird.

"Come back," I said. To Keats *and* the bird.

Only one of them obeyed.

Soon Picasso was just a tiny speck again among the bigger birds. I touched the pendant around my neck and smiled.

This talisman I could wear until Kellan provided me with something more tailored to my current lifestyle.

Meanwhile, I had no doubt that Vernie and Imogen Pigeon and

maybe even Ima's husband Carl would watch over us as we did our best to protect Clover Grove.

Keats rested his muzzle on my knee and filled me up with warmth from his brown eye. Kellan worked from the top down with a kiss that felt like a promise. And Percy delivered a rolling purr that was full of sheer optimism.

It was a perfect moment in a perfect place with my perfect companions. I wouldn't waste it worrying about what was to come. My heart took wing and soared into the sunset with Picasso.

When a mysterious rascal raises a ruckus, Ivy plans an overnight stakeout... in Edna's bunker! Join my newsletter to read *Things that Go Grunt in the Night*—an exclusive free short story.

# RUNAWAY FARM & INN RECIPES

**Apocalyptic Strata**

## Ingredients

- 3 packages frozen spinach, thawed, squeezed dry, and chopped
- 2 cups finely chopped onion
- 3 tablespoons unsalted butter
- 1 teaspoon salt
- 1/2 teaspoon black pepper
- 1/2 teaspoon freshly grated nutmeg
- 10 cups cubed French bread
- 8 ounces coarsely grated Gruyère cheese
- 4 ounces finely grated parmesan cheese
- 3 cups milk
- 10 large eggs
- 2 tablespoons Dijon mustard

## Instructions

Sauté onion in butter until soft, about 5 minutes. Add 1/2 teaspoon salt, 1/4 teaspoon pepper and nutmeg and continue cooking for another minute or two. Stir in chopped spinach and remove from heat.

Spread one third of the bread cubes in a well-buttered 3-quart ceramic baking dish. Top with one-third of spinach mixture, and one-third of each cheese. Repeat layering twice.

Whisk eggs, milk, mustard and remaining 1/2 teaspoon salt and 1/4 teaspoon pepper together in a large bowl. Pour evenly over bread mixture. Cover with plastic wrap and chill for up to a day.

Let the strata sit at room temperature for 30 minutes while preheating the oven to 350°F. Bake, uncovered, until puffed, golden brown, and cooked through, about 45 to 55 minutes. Let stand 5 minutes before serving.

**Chef's note:** This hearty make-ahead breakfast is ready when you are! Serves 8 people in your bunker of choice.

More Books by Ellen Riggs

---

*Bought-the-Farm* Cozy Mystery Series

---

- *A Dog with Two Tales (prequel)*
- *Dogcatcher in the Rye*
- *Dark Side of the Moo*
- *A Streak of Bad Cluck*
- *Till the Cat Lady Sings*
- *Alpaca Lies*
- *Twas the Bite Before Christmas*
- *Swine and Punishment*
- *The Cat and the Riddle*
- *Don't Rock the Goat*
- *Swan with the Wind*
- *How to Get a Neigh with Murder*
- *Tweet Revenge*
- *For Love Or Bunny*
- *Between a Squawk and a Hard Place*
- *Double Dog Dare*
- *Deerly Departed*
- *Think Outside the Fox*

*Bought-the-Farm Mysteries* - Boxed Sets

- *Bought the Farm Mysteries - Books 1-3*
- *Bought the Farm Mysteries - Books 4-6*
- *Bought the Farm Mysteries - Books 7-9*
- *Bought the Farm Mysteries - Books 1-10*

"Mystic Mutt Mysteries" Paranormal Cozy

- *I Want You to Haunt Me*
- *You Can't Always Get What You Haunt*
- *Any Way You Haunt It*
- *I Only Haunt to be with You*

Books by Ellen Riggs and Sandy Rideout

*Dog Town* Series

- *Ready or Not in Dog Town* (The Beginning)
- *Bitter and Sweet in Dog Town* (Labor Day)
- *A Match Made in Dog Town* (Thanksgiving)
- *Lost and Found in Dog Town* (Christmas)
- *Calm and Bright in Dog Town* (Christmas)
- *Tried and True in Dog Town* (New Year's)
- *Yours and Mine in Dog Town* (Valentine's Day)
- *Nine Lives in Dog Town* (Easter)

- *Great and Small in Dog Town* (Memorial Day)
- *Bold and Blue in Dog Town* (Independence Day)
- *Better or Worse in Dog Town* (Labor Day)

---

*Dog Town* Boxed Sets

---

- *Mischief in Dog Town - Books 1-3*
- *Mischief in Dog Town - Books 4-7*
- *Mischief in Dog Town - Books 8-10*
- *Mischief in Dog Town - The Complete Series*

---

Subhead

---

Block Quote

---

*Verse here*

Alignment Block

End

WHAT'S NEXT